More Praise for *The Silent Conspiracy*

"*The Silent Conspiracy* has got such a delicious conceit at the heart of it that I wish I'd thought of it. You'll wonder how on earth the author is going to pull all the threads and characters together, then marvel as they manage it, page after page-turning page."

—Simon Toyne, *Sunday Times*
bestselling author of the Sanctus trilogy

"Foreboding, timely and necessary, *The Silent Conspiracy* is a gripping page-turner, rife with corruption, intrigue, and haunting suspense. Totally engrossing!"

—A. F. Brady, author of
The Blind and *Once A Liar*

Praise for *The Network*

"Revel in L. C. Shaw's thriller, *The Network*. . . . Part Dan Brown, part Ira Levin, part Ian Fleming, part Steve Berry—and wholly terrifying—*The Network* displays Shaw's talents, skills that enable her to produce nearly unbearable tension and multiple shocks as she seizes the reader and never lets go, not even on the final page."

—*Free-Lance Star* (Fredericksburg, Virginia)

"Exhilarating. . . . From the opening pages to the thrilling conclusion, *The Network* is an intense and action-packed roller-coaster ride of emotions. . . . The suspense and intrigue are relentless from beginning to end."

—*New York Journal of Books*

D0067940

"The merciless Crosse makes a timely villain in this thriller from Lynne Constantine, who with her sister, Valerie, writes under the name Liv Constantine."
—BBC, "Ten Books to Read in December"

"Readers with a taste for action thrillers will best appreciate this one."
—*Publishers Weekly*

"A staccato-paced series opener that will appeal to readers seeking conspiracy-laced thrillers."
—*Booklist*

"Once you start reading, you'll be hooked."
—*Suspense*

"This is mandatory reading for any thriller aficionado."
—Steve Berry, *New York Times* bestselling author

"Washington power plays, Supreme Court intrigue, religious relics, and a chase for the ages. Fans of Brad Meltzer and James Rollins will love L. C. Shaw's *The Network*."
—Anthony Franze, author of *The Outsider*

"Sophisticated, suspenseful, and unpredictable, Shaw's deft plotting and breakneck pacing set the standard for the modern political thriller. Once I started reading, I couldn't stop."
—Jennifer Hillier, *USA Today* bestselling author of *Jar of Hearts*

"Blistering pacing, compelling drama, and tight prose. . . . Breathtaking."
—K. J. Howe, international bestselling author of *Skyjack*

"A superb blend of a political, speculative, and action-thriller. . . . a throwback to Robert Ludlum and a testament to Dan Brown. The kind of tale Alfred Hitchcock would have loved to adapt and thriller lovers are certain to devour."

—Jon Land, *USA Today* bestselling author

"With a decades-old cabal, ancient relic, conspiracy, action, and twists, *The Network* delivers on the goods. The result: an addicting read that keeps you up long past bedtime."

—Tosca Lee, *New York Times* bestselling author

"Thriller-writing at its best. . . . Jack Reacher and Jack Ryan, watch out!"

—Allison Leotta, author of *The Last Good Girl*

"Political intrigue, religious artifacts, great characters, and plot twists galore. You will not be able to put *The Network* down."

—D. P. Lyle, award-winning author of the Jake Longly and Cain/Harper thriller series

"Unfailingly entertaining, riveting, and breathtakingly timely— you will absolutely devour this thrilling and cautionary tale. Attention, Hollywood: this one has blockbuster written all over it."

—Hank Phillippi Ryan, nationally bestselling author of *The Murder List*

"With Shaw's breakneck pacing, intricate twists, and constant cliffhangers, thriller fans will blaze though this book in one sitting."

—Carter Wilson, *USA Today* bestselling author

THE SILENT CONSPIRACY

ALSO BY L. C. SHAW

THE NETWORK

THE
SILENT
CONSPIRACY

A NOVEL

L. C. SHAW

HARPER

NEW YORK · LONDON · TORONTO · SYDNEY

HARPER

THE SILENT CONSPIRACY. Copyright © 2020 by Lynne Constantine. All rights reserved. Printed in the United States of America. No part of this book may be used or reproduced in any manner whatsoever without written permission except in the case of brief quotations embodied in critical articles and reviews. For information, address HarperCollins Publishers, 195 Broadway, New York, NY 10007.

HarperCollins books may be purchased for educational, business, or sales promotional use. For information, please email the Special Markets Department at SPsales@harpercollins.com.

FIRST EDITION

Title spread art © Siamyimpics/Shutterstock.com
Chapter opener art © Mia Stendal/Shutterstock.com

Library of Congress Cataloging-in-Publication Data has been applied for.

ISBN 978-0-06-295094-9 (pbk.)

20 21 22 23 24   LSC   10 9 8 7 6 5 4 3 2 1

*For my father, Gus Constantine, gone
far too soon from this world but never
from my heart.*

THE SILENT CONSPIRACY

THE DARKNESS WAS THERE BEFORE MAGGIE RUSSELL WAS aware of it—the gentle May breeze whispering evil in her ear. When she arrived at the field, she was still in a good mood, eager to cheer on her son and his team during the last Little League game of the season, and she took a seat next to a friend at the top of the bleachers where she had a good view of the entire field. It was cool for a spring day in Baltimore, and she slipped her arms into her pink cardigan and pulled it tightly around her. Maggie generally found baseball boring, but she got a kick out of watching her nine-year-old son, Lucas, his face scrunched up in concentration as he tried to make the bat connect with the ball, and she faithfully attended all his games. But today he hadn't been played yet, and her mind started to drift to the long list of things she still needed to accomplish over the weekend. There was the Sunday school lesson to prepare, dry cleaning to pick up, and a meal she'd promised to make for her neighbor who was down with the flu. And she still had to finish her notes from her nursing rounds last night. At least she'd managed to get her roast in the oven so dinner would be ready when they got home from the game. Her husband liked for the three of them to have dinner together every night. She turned to her friend Agatha, whose son Phillip was pitching, watching as she carefully quartered apples and oranges on a cutting board resting on her legs.

"Run out of time?" Maggie asked. Agatha was always late, forgetting appointments, or misplacing things—one of those perpetually out-of-breath people. But she was funny, and her charm made it easy to overlook her scatterbrained tendencies.

Agatha rolled her eyes. "We were walking out the door when Phillip reminded me it was my turn to bring snacks." She shrugged. "Oh well, at least this fruit will get eaten. I don't know why I bother trying to feed my family healthy food. All they want is junk."

Maggie didn't understand why Agatha allowed a child to dictate what she bought at the grocery store. Her friend's son's eating habits were appalling. She was getting restless now and glanced at the scoreboard again. Only one more inning to go, and they were still tied up. She caught sight of Lucas sitting on the bench and felt a slow burn begin. The new coach hadn't played him at all. Her son was looking at the ground, his shoulders slouched, looking as if he might cry, and Maggie began to get angry. Okay, maybe he wasn't as good as the other kids. But how was he supposed to improve if he didn't get enough playing time? She and her husband didn't have the extra money to hire private coaches like some of these families did, and these kids were only nine years old, for goodness' sake. Wasn't this supposed to be a team-building exercise—a bit of fun for kids and a way to get them off their phones? Getting more annoyed by the moment, she turned back to her friend.

"What's up with this guy? Isn't he supposed to play all the kids?"

Agatha gave Maggie a sympathetic look. "I think so, honey. But this game will determine if they go on to the playoffs. Try not to get upset."

That was easy for Agatha to say—Phillip was always put in first.

She couldn't just sit here and do nothing. Almost without being conscious of it, she sprang up and yelled out to the coach, "Everyone's supposed to get a turn!" The coach ignored her, but she received plenty of dirty looks from the other parents. Agatha put her hand on Maggie's arm and whispered, "Honey, try to calm down." Maggie pulled free and was about to answer her when a dad sitting in front of her turned around and shook his head.

"It's tied up. If we want to win, we have to play our best." He looked disgusted as he turned his gaze back to the field.

Three big fat red words rose from his head. *You stupid bitch.* Maggie could see his thoughts as clear as day.

Her temples began to throb and she suppressed the desire to grab him and tell him to shut up. How dare he use that kind of language with her? Suddenly she had the urge to push him off the bleachers and watch his head crack open on the cement below. She wanted to put her hands around his neck and squeeze until he couldn't speak and watch the breath drain from him so he could never talk to anyone like that ever again. But instead, she rose from her seat again.

Agatha tried to get her to sit down. "Maggie, it's just a game. Sweetie, you're making a scene."

She pushed Agatha hard. "Leave me alone!"

"Coach! Coach!" she yelled again, louder this time.

The coach looked up at her and threw his arms up in exasperation.

"Put Lucas in the game. Now! I didn't come here to watch him warm a bench."

The coach strode over and whispered something to the umpire who was now walking toward the stands. Maggie wasn't going to let the coach ignore her or send his lackey to placate her. She began to march down the bleachers toward the field, then stopped, as both her arms began to itch with an intensity she couldn't ignore. She glanced down to see a swarm of angry bugs biting her. She tried to push them off her skin but they wouldn't budge. "Get off me!" she shrieked. A dull roar in her ears began to grow, like the sound of crashing waves getting closer. Heat worked its way up her chest again until she felt like she was on fire. She turned back to Agatha, grabbed the knife out of her friend's hands, and started stabbing at the bugs, though she kept missing and piercing her skin instead. She ran straight down the bleachers, as the other onlookers moved out of her way. Once she reached the field, she stood in front of the coach, who was looking at her with hatred. It was obvious that he was out to get her and her son and had been from day one. Maggie felt as though she'd been infused with a super strength as she plunged the knife deep into his chest over and over, and the blood began to pour out of him. That would show him. She felt hands pulling at her but they weren't strong enough to stop her. When he slid down to the ground, his body still, she suddenly felt cold. What had just happened? The roar was gone and, in its place, she heard the screams of people around her. Lucas was yelling, trying to get to her as a sea of arms held him back.

"Mom! Mom!"

"I'm sorry!" she called to him, tears streaming down her face. What had she done? She looked down again at the man on the ground. A loud voice boomed from the sky. *Look what you've done. The only remedy for this evil is to turn the knife on yourself.*

Yes, she realized, that was only fair. Maggie looked at the bloody knife still clutched in her hand. One swift slice to the jugular was all it would take. Before she could change her mind, she raised her hand to her neck and cut. The last thing she saw before she lost consciousness was her son's heartbroken face.

CHAPTER TWO

JACK LOGAN'S HAND FROZE ON THE REMOTE. HE WATCHED the six o'clock news with growing dismay, as the anchor relayed the gruesome details of a doctor's killing spree at a hospital in Pennsylvania last week. During his rounds, he'd stabbed three patients to death with a scalpel. By the time their screams brought help, he'd also taken down two nurses and a nurse's aide before slicing his own throat.

Jack sat transfixed as he listened to the story, bloody images filling his mind. He called over his shoulder to Taylor, who was making tea in the kitchen. "It happened again."

She carried her mug into the living room and sat down next to him on the sofa, Beau padding closely behind her. "I just heard. A doctor. What in the world is going on? How many does that make now?"

Jack exhaled. "It's the seventeenth case since the beginning of April. I did some online research last night." He'd found that in the past month, there had been sixteen instances, all on the

East Coast, in which a previously model citizen had suddenly committed a violent crime. This latest was in Maryland; the rest were spread out between Massachusetts and Florida. "Something very strange is going on." He looked at Taylor, brows raised. "My editor's good with my chasing this. I just want to make sure you're really okay with my being gone so much now that you're working on the Supreme Court story and going into New York more often."

She nodded. "Of course. You've been so supportive of both Evan and me. And since we're not much further with our investigation into the Institute than when we started, I think it's time to get out of limbo and back to work."

It had been two years since Damon Crosse, the head of the immense training facility in upstate New York known to insiders as the Institute, had taken his own life. In the forty years that the facility had been operating, Crosse had placed its graduates in top positions in government, entertainment, and business. He had recruited them from top universities, but some came from the orphanage he ran, and he'd been able to mold them from early childhood. Like a puppet master, he had controlled his network of people and coordinated their efforts to further his corrupt agenda in the United States and around the world. After Taylor found out that her late husband, US Senator Malcolm Phillips, had been part of it, she and Jack had worked with Crosse's son, Jeremy, to bring Crosse down. After weeks on the run, untangling the web of corruption, they'd found a way to infiltrate his headquarters and gather enough evidence to put him in prison for life. But Crosse had cheated them all, destroying all the evidence from his computer system before poisoning himself, leaving them no way to identify and ferret out all the men and women he'd indoctrinated over the years.

After Taylor's interview on *Newsline* had aired, exposing the Institute and the fact that it had been established by a Nazi, droves of people had come forward claiming to have been trained at the Institute or to know someone who had been. Over the past two years, Taylor, Jack, and Jeremy had methodically interviewed each one and had come up with nothing. Most had been cranks, but even the promising leads had turned out to be dead ends. Crosse's real people were either too entrenched in whatever positions he'd placed them in to jeopardize them, or they were too afraid to come forward. The fact that Taylor and Jack had made so little progress was more than frustrating.

The only solid lead they were still working on was a handwritten list of twenty-one names that Jeremy had found in Crosse's journal. They had recognized two names on the list—one a member of Congress and the other a federal judge—but they were both dead. The other nineteen had led them down a dead end, and they now believed that the list had been code names or the like, though they had yet to make any headway on that theory.

In the letter that Taylor's first husband, Malcolm, had left for her in the event of his death, he'd told her that Brody Hamilton, his Senate colleague, was involved with Crosse, but they had no proof beyond that. And to make things more complicated, when the vice president stepped down due to health issues six months ago, Hamilton had been tapped to replace him. He was virtually untouchable now.

Jack and Taylor had hoped that they would be able to trace some of the orphans who had grown up at the Institute, but unfortunately, those records were also wiped out when Crosse erased the network. They did, however, have one advantage. Jonas, Crosse's longtime valet, had come over to their side after a crisis of conscience and supplied them with the names of churches and organizations Crosse had used to find orphans. Crosse had sent Jonas and his wife to pose as a couple looking to adopt a number of times, and they'd always told the churches the same story:

they'd lost a baby in childbirth and his wife had almost died herself and could no longer bear children. They'd had luck with the story and the fact that they were open to an older child. Of course, what looked like altruism was more nefarious: children had to be at least three years old for preliminary testing to determine if they were good candidates for the Institute.

Jack, Taylor, and Jeremy had been getting in touch with anyone who had past ties to those organizations to try to track down any records. But this line of inquiry had yielded very little, as back in the sixties and seventies, record keeping was sketchy at best. Many of the children had been left on doorsteps or given false names. But they did have one lead that Jack thought might be worthwhile.

He clicked the remote, turning off the television, and nodded at Taylor. "If you're sure. I was planning on heading to Baltimore to talk to the husband of the woman who killed her son's coach. Which means I can also stop by St. Katherine's High School, where the nun from the orphanage we're interested in works now. Jonas believes she might remember something about the child he pretended to adopt."

Taylor smiled. "We'll be fine while you're gone."

"I'll head out in the morning then." He leaned over and kissed her, and Beau, their golden retriever, jumped up and nudged himself between them, not wanting to miss out. Taylor laughed and rubbed the dog's head.

"Now that we're both knee-deep in these stories, it might be too hard to coordinate our schedules so we're not gone at the same time," Jack said.

Taylor nodded. "I'm glad you convinced me to try the day-care at the network. Evan's always happy when I pick him up from there."

She had been reluctant to leave Evan with sitters, but the truth was, Jack felt better not leaving either Evan or Taylor.

Despite Crosse's death, he couldn't shake the feeling that there were still people after them. That first year, he had constantly looked over his shoulder and hardly ever let them out of his sight. But after another year had passed uneventfully, they were both trying to get back to a normal life. He didn't want Evan growing up in a bubble. They couldn't let what had happened to them turn them into parents who suffocated their child.

"Yes, it's good for him to have other caregivers," Jack said. "Eventually, he's going to go to school. We can't be with him twenty-four hours a day."

She rolled her eyes at him good-naturedly. "I get it."

He watched Taylor as she walked away, thinking again how grateful he was to have finally made a life with her. He had lost her once, and even though the breakup had been his fault, he'd been devastated when he learned she had married Malcolm Phillips. As he'd followed her life from afar, reading about them in the Washington papers and magazines, it looked like she'd found her happily ever after.

Until the night Malcolm had showed up at Jack's apartment, telling him that he would soon be a dead man and that he needed Jack to look after Taylor. Jack had thought he was nuts—but then Malcolm *had* ended up dying a few weeks later, and Jack had raced to her side. After Taylor and Jack had come out of hiding, Taylor had finally held a funeral for Malcolm. Eight months later, she and Jack had married quietly at the Greek Orthodox church Taylor's mother had loved so much, with only close family members in attendance.

Less than a year later, they'd been out for a Sunday drive and come across the house they were living in now. It was a Greek Revival they'd both fallen in love with immediately. Located on the Hudson River, the views were magnificent and the house was bright and airy, with a casual elegance that suited them both.

Taylor was thrilled to be back on Karen Printz's team, an anchor she had been a producer for years ago. So far, Taylor had been mainly on the ground here in New York; she hadn't taken any assignments requiring travel. But at Jack's urging, she'd accepted Karen's recent offer to produce a story on a class action suit against an insurance company that had made it all the way to the Supreme Court. Evan was eighteen months old now and thriving. It was time they all got used to their new normal.

Jack leaned back and closed his eyes, planning his next steps. He needed to confirm his two meetings. If he left early, he should be in Maryland before noon. He also wanted to talk to a few people who he'd left messages for who had witnessed the incident, so he might end up having to spend the night if the interviews spilled into the next day. In the meantime, he had some more research to do before he took off. He pulled up one of the latest news stories online and read over it again. Just two days ago, a local teacher had shot up his own school. Then, in another incident a few days later, a man had driven his truck through the glass window of a restaurant, killing eight people. What was the possible connection among all these events? They couldn't be random. Jack was reminded of one of his father's favorite expressions—Where there's smoke, there's fire. *Well, Pop, you might have liked clichés but that doesn't make you wrong.* He thought about Damon Crosse again, and a shiver went up his spine. If he didn't know that Crosse was dead, he'd swear this was his handiwork. But that was impossible. And why was he assuming there was some mastermind behind it? More likely there was a simpler explanation. But still, he couldn't shake the feeling that things were going to get much worse before he found any answers.

CHAPTER THREE

TAYLOR HEARD THE VOICE CALLING TO HER FROM THE WOODS. She was outside in the dark, the wind blowing the cold rain so hard it felt like pinpricks on her face. The sodden leaves at her feet made little noise as she ran toward the siren's song, despite the warning in her head that it wasn't safe. She ran deeper and deeper, turning left and right toward the voice until, when she turned to look behind her, she couldn't see where she'd come from. But she had to reach it. The more she listened, the more familiar it became. And then it came to her: it was her mother's voice, one she hadn't heard in over twenty years.

"Mom!" she yelled back, running faster now.

"Taylor, hurry!" Her mother sounded more urgent.

Tree branches scraped her as she ran past. Her feet slid over a patch of mud and she slipped and slammed into a tree trunk. Wincing as pain shot through her head, she brought her hand to her scalp and felt something wet. She looked at her hand. Blood.

"Taylor, there's no time!" Her mother was louder now.

Taylor ran toward the voice again and then stopped short. The woman standing in front of her was young, maybe her own age, and looked like her mother, but she couldn't be sure. She had on a flowing white dress, and a smile so beatific that Taylor felt a warmth spread through her entire body. The woman's arms opened and Taylor ran into them. They enveloped her in a hug that filled her with a profound sense of peace and contentment. She wanted to stay in this embrace forever. But the woman pulled back and gave her a look of such despair that Taylor felt shaken. When she saw her up close, she realized it wasn't her mother, but someone who looked a lot like her.

"What is it?" Taylor asked.

"He's in danger. You must be on guard."

"Who? What are you talking about?"

The woman began walking backward, fading.

"Wait. Who?"

She shook her head sadly. "Evan. His life is at risk."

Before Taylor could ask her anything else, the woman vanished into the mist. Taylor began to yell when she felt hands on her shoulders, gently shaking her, then heard her name being called again. This time by Jack.

"Taylor, wake up."

Her eyes flew open. The room was dark, but she could see Jack's outline, standing over her. She turned on the lamp next to the bed and soft light illuminated the room. She was out of breath, and her hair was wet with sweat. "What time is it?"

"Almost five. I was just about to get in the shower when I heard you yelling. You okay?" His face showed his concern.

She looked over at Evan, whom she'd brought to their bed last night when he'd awakened crying. He was fast asleep. Sitting up gingerly, careful not to disturb him, she sat on the edge of the bed, her feet on the floor, and put her head in her hands. She took a few deep breaths, then stood. "Let's go downstairs so we don't wake him."

Jack followed her into the kitchen and made coffee while she told him about the dream. When she had almost gotten to the end, she swallowed. "She told me that Evan was in danger."

Jack put his arms around her. "T, it's okay. He's safe. It's just nerves. We're on all on edge with the news lately and all these crazy things happening."

She sighed. "I know. It just seemed so real. She looked so much like my mother. I wonder if it was my Aunt Maya. Maybe she's paying me a visit from beyond, trying to warn me."

He gave her a skeptical look. "More likely it's your subconscious at play. Evan is fine. No one is going to hurt him. They'd have to go through me first."

She knew he was probably right, but she still had a hard time shaking the dream. A thought occurred to her. "What if it's a warning about Warwick? We have no idea where he is." Saying her father's name brought a lump to Taylor's throat. She'd grown up believing he was her biological father. Even now, though she understood that he'd never loved her or her mother, that he'd been another of Crosse's puppets, it was impossible for her to completely grasp his bitter betrayal. She would never be able to erase from her mind the image of him aiming a gun at her, gleefully delivering the news that he'd been the one to kill her mother and that Taylor was next.

Jack looked at her a long moment. "Well, I don't know why he'd want to take Evan. Besides, if he returned, Evelyn could implicate him in your mother's death, so I don't think he'd just come waltzing back into the country."

"What if he's still looking for the coins? He killed my mother over those religious relics and was willing to kill me, too. He could think we have them."

Jack seemed to consider this. "But why would he wait all this time?"

"I guess you're right . . . besides, he wouldn't be able to get back in the country without getting arrested, unless he has a new identity," she reluctantly agreed. "No, it's probably nothing to do with him."

He brought her a cup of coffee and sat down with his.

"Let's just think about this a little. If your gut's telling you something, we don't want to dismiss it out of hand."

That was one of the many things she loved about Jack. He never treated her like she was hysterical or invalidated her feelings. Ever since they were kids, he had been the one she told all her secrets to, the one she could be completely at ease with. He continued, "Have you noticed anything unusual that maybe your subconscious picked up? A car around a lot? Anyone who seemed to be watching you, or I don't know, just a feeling of unease when you've been out?"

She thought about his question, then said, "No. Nothing like that." She ran a hand through her hair. "We looked over our shoulders for so long, but I'm actually finally feeling safe again. I'm happy to be back at work, and Evan's right there in a great daycare. Maybe it's just jitters about the travel I have coming up. I'm probably more nervous about leaving him than I realized."

He nodded. "Probably. It was just one of those crazy dreams. We've all had them." He drummed his fingers on the table. "Still. Maybe I should postpone my trip to Maryland."

"Absolutely not." Beau ambled over and nudged her with his nose. She ruffled the fur on the dog's head, looking at him as she spoke. "We have Beau watching out for us, and the house alarm, and I haven't been busting my ass doing martial arts for nothing. I can take care of myself, and Evan. We'll be fine."

He raised his eyebrows. "Okay, killer. I'm going to go take that shower now."

Alone in the kitchen, Taylor decided to distract herself by going over her notes before her meeting that afternoon with Karen and her production team. For her latest piece, Taylor had been interviewing families who were suing Jefferson Health Care for discrimination. Jefferson had recently rolled out a low-cost health insurance policy but hadn't made customers aware that by opting into the low-cost policy, many previously covered procedures were now excluded. The lawsuit claimed that Jefferson was targeting protected classes—women, the elderly, and the disabled—and discriminating against them with the reduced coverage. The families of individuals who had been refused treatment and had consequently died or suffered damages began to sue the insurance giant, and there had been enough lawsuits that it had turned into a major class action suit.

Ultimately, the plaintiffs had lost in federal court and continued appealing until the case reached the Supreme Court, which had certified it. The closing arguments had been heard last month, and the court was expected to render a decision in the next sixty days. In the meantime, Taylor was trying to narrow down the families who would represent the plaintiffs on Karen's news show.

She thought about her dream again. She hadn't told Jack about the dreams she used to have as a kid—nightmares that would have her crying out until her mother came to her room to comfort her. Most of the time they were vague, without a clear sense of what the danger was. But on two occasions, they had been very specific. The first had been when she was fourteen. She saw her mother in a dark room with a large man looming over her. Her mother's screams had been terrifying as the man held a cigarette to her hand and her flesh began to burn. When she awoke, she didn't tell her mother about it, not wanting to worry her. Two days later, her mother was murdered.

In the second dream, they were all at Jack's father's funeral. The next day, his dad had a heart attack and died a few hours later. She'd never told Jack about that dream, not wanting to upset him further, and from that moment until last night, she hadn't been burdened by any more prophetic ones.

Why now? The other two times, there was nothing she could do to prevent the outcome. But this time, the dream seemed more like a warning than a premonition. A sense of foreboding filled her, and she took a deep breath. She had to keep a clear head. Before she went back upstairs to get dressed and check on Evan, she walked to the front door and peeked out the side window. Was there someone out there watching? Waiting? Someone who wanted to hurt her, or worse, hurt Evan?

CHAPTER FOUR

Jack thought about Taylor's dream while the shower water beat down on him. He wasn't superstitious, but maybe Taylor's subconscious had registered some kind of threat she wasn't fully aware of. Crosse was dead, and for the life of him, Jack couldn't think of a reason his followers would come after Evan or Taylor. Still, he was feeling a little bit leery about leaving her today.

He decided he would give Jeremy a call and see if he could check in on her later. Despite Jeremy's upbringing at the hands of Crosse, he was a warm and gentle soul, filled with goodness and integrity. And even though he and Taylor had only found each other two years ago, their bond was unshakable. When Taylor had discovered that her real father was Damon Crosse, the only thing that had mitigated her horror was the fact that she found her brother. His mother, Maya, and her mother were sisters. Unfortunately, Taylor had never met Maya as she'd died in childbirth with Jeremy. Jeremy was only a forty-minute drive away in Stamford, Connecticut, where Alpha Pharmaceuticals, the company he'd inherited from his father, was now located. Perhaps he'd be able to drive down and have dinner with Taylor and Evan while Jack was out of town.

As Jack was getting out of the shower, he heard Taylor return to the bedroom, so he quickly dried off and wrapped the towel around his waist. When he came out of the bathroom, he found Evan in her arms. She leaned over and kissed Jack, her hand resting a moment on his chest.

He gazed at her as a wave of affection overcame him, then he reached out to tousle Evan's dark curls. "Hey, buddy. Good morning." He looked at Taylor. "What time is your meeting again?"

"Not till this afternoon. We're going to go over the research and decide where we want to focus the story. But I have two interviews later this morning, so I'm going to drop Evan off at the company daycare first then drive to see my sources."

"Do you have a definitive angle yet? I mean besides the fact that the insurance company tricked people into exclusions?"

"Still working on it."

Evan started fussing, and Jack reached out to him. "Come here, big guy." He gave him a gentle kiss on the head. "I'll feed him while you get dressed."

Jack took Evan to the kitchen and put him in his highchair while he made him some eggs. He laughed as he watched Evan pick up the television remote next to him and point it to the TV. His chubby fingers pressed the buttons, and he looked perplexedly at Jack when nothing happened. The kid was a fast learner.

"How about a book instead?" Jack grabbed a few board books from a basket on the floor and put them on the highchair tray while he finished getting breakfast ready.

When Taylor came in the kitchen, he inclined his head toward the dog. "I fed Beau, too, but it looks like he's still hungry."

The golden retriever was sitting at Evan's feet, his attention laser focused on the toddler, and was soon rewarded when Evan threw a fistful of eggs on the floor.

Jack laughed. "You're no dummy," he told the dog. He turned back to Evan. "You're supposed to eat them, not throw them."

Evan gave him a somber look and put some eggs in his mouth.

Taylor smiled at Evan. "Yummy yum, you look like you enjoyed your eggs."

He smiled and held his arms up. "Mama. Up."

She took a wet cloth and cleaned his hands and face, then pulled out his tray and raised him out of his seat.

"I'm gonna take off," Jack said, kissing the top of Evan's head and then Taylor's lips. He held her a moment longer, reluctant to let go. Finally he pulled back and walked to the door.

"Think fast," Taylor said as she grabbed a protein bar from the counter and tossed it to him. "I don't want you going all day with nothing to eat."

"I'm a big boy. I can get my own breakfast."

She laughed. "You *can*, but you won't. Just take it. Otherwise you'll end up eating a Snickers." She shook her head. "Your eating habits are still appalling. We're not kids anymore, you know."

He walked back over to her and put his arms around her. "But you, my love, still make me feel like one."

"And that"—she kissed him again—"is why I love you."

○ ○ ○

As he drove toward the highway, Jack prepared himself for the meeting with Maggie Russell's husband, Kent. The man would still be in shock—the murder-suicide had taken place only a week ago. Jack couldn't imagine the horror he must have been feeling or how he'd explained to his nine-year-old son—who'd actually witnessed it—why his mother had done what she'd done. Jack had read a few more articles about it last night. Maggie had been a pillar of the community—a nurse who taught Sunday school. It made no sense, but then again, there was a lot in the news these days that made no sense.

Jack cranked the volume on the car stereo as AC/DC's "Back in Black" blared through the speakers, then unwrapped the bar Taylor had given him and took a bite. It tasted like cardboard. Making a face, he threw it on the passenger seat and pulled a candy bar from the center console. *Sorry, T,* he thought as he took a bite. Some habits die hard.

CHAPTER FIVE

AFTER ONLY A FEW MINUTES IN THE CAR, TAYLOR HEARD THE sound of Evan's steady breathing and glanced in the rearview mirror to confirm that he'd fallen asleep. All her years of infertility treatments and her prayers for a child still hadn't prepared her for the crushing love she felt the first time she'd held him. She'd suffered three miscarriages before getting pregnant with him, and then, when she and Jack had been on the run, she'd worried almost constantly about losing him, too. After he'd been born, she hadn't wanted him out of her sight at the hospital, and it was only exhaustion that finally allowed her to hand him back to the nurse. Most mothers probably felt that same way, but most mothers didn't also have an insane biological father like Damon Crosse going after their children.

Even after Damon was dead, part of her was still terrified of someone trying to take her son. For the first six months of his life, she'd never left Evan. In the beginning, she and Jack had moved a bassinet into their bedroom and she slept with one hand on it—only half asleep, ever vigilant. Beau must have picked up on her anxiety because he started sitting at the foot of the bassinet anytime Evan was in it and stayed there, a loyal sentinel, always keeping watch.

When Evan was six months old, Jack gently encouraged her to transition him to his crib in the nursery. She knew it was because he was worried about her and her lack of sleep, but still, she would wake up in the middle of the night to creep down the hall and make sure he was still breathing. She worried about SIDS. She worried about someone breaking in and taking him. She worried about everything. Soon her joy in her son was eclipsed by the constant and nagging fear that something bad was going to happen to him.

Jack tried everything to reassure her that it would all be fine. He had a top-notch security system installed, but still, she couldn't relax. Finally she'd agreed to see a therapist, who explained that a lot of what she was feeling was natural—new mother jitters. Her therapist had helped her understand that, while it was natural to overcompensate for past traumas by trying to control everything in her environment, it was unhealthy to do so. She started with small steps, leaving Evan with Jack for an hour or two while she ran an errand or went to the gym. Eventually she agreed to leave him with Jeremy so she and Jack could go out alone together. As time went on, her anxiety lessened and she was proud of the fact that, while still a protective mom, she was by no means a neurotic one. And when her worries started to get the best of her, Jack was there to calm her, in the same way that, when he started going off the rails, she grounded him. The fact that they'd been best friends long before they became lovers was something she never took for granted. No one knew her history like Jack, and no one understood all the demons from his past like she did. She also knew that if anyone could help her keep Evan safe, it was Jack.

When she had decided to join up with Karen Printz six months ago, Taylor had started looking for a nanny, but then UBC had opened a daycare. Though at first she'd been reluctant to leave Evan, getting to know the staff had made her feel much more comfortable—as did the fact that he was just a few floors away from her office. No one made her feel silly for dropping in to check on him—even every half hour, those first few times, as long as she abided by their rule not to enter during nap time. She now took him there without a second thought.

It was a little after eleven when Taylor arrived at UBC and dropped Evan off. Giving him a kiss, she left. When she got back into her car, she entered the Stamford address for her interview into her GPS. It took her a little less than forty minutes to get there. She'd already done some preliminary work with the couple so they'd be recording some of the interview now to save time. The camera crew was parked and waiting, and she walked over to the van.

"Let me just go in first and make sure they're ready."

"No problem," Matt, the lead camera guy, told her.

As she walked up the sidewalk, she thought to herself that the house had seen better days. The dull yellow paint was peeling and the shutters looked as though a gentle breeze would dislodge them. She walked up the cracked cement walkway and rang the doorbell.

A fresh-faced young woman greeted her and smiled shyly. "Ms. Parks?" Even though she'd taken Jack's name when she married him, Taylor still used her maiden name professionally.

Taylor put a hand out. "Please, call me Taylor."

"I'm Molly Edwards." She motioned Taylor inside and led her toward a worn sofa. "Have a seat. I'll call my husband."

"The camera crew is here, is it okay for them to come in and set up? As I mentioned, Karen will come back and finish the interview later, but we can get some sound bites now."

Molly nodded. "Sure thing."

Taylor waved in Matt, his two assistants, and the audio technician and took a seat while they set up. She looked around the room. It was bright and cheerful, the walls adorned with stunning photographs of trees that looked like they were professionally framed. Molly returned with a stocky man who gave Taylor a sour look, mumbled a hello, and took a seat in the armchair next to the sofa. Molly sat next to him. "This is Clyde."

Taylor stood and held a hand out. "Nice to meet you."

He merely nodded.

"It's going to take them a few minutes to set up." She called over to Matt. "Where do you want us?"

As soon as Matt got set up and gave her the thumbs-up, Taylor cleared her throat. "Okay, we can get started," she said. "I understand that you are being pressured to terminate your pregnancy."

Molly's hand went automatically to her stomach. Tears filled her eyes, and she swallowed.

Her husband reached over and grabbed her hand. "I would never have chosen that policy if I had known this. They never told me what would happen if I chose the cheaper one," he said.

Taylor waited, giving Molly time to gather her thoughts.

Molly picked up the thread. "I had my checkup last week. The doctor got the results of some blood work." She dabbed at her eyes with a tissue. "He said there are unusual levels of some type of protein that could indicate chromosomal abnormalities. Here, I wrote down the name." She passed her notebook to Taylor.

The blood test showed an incredibly high level of pregnancy-related plasma protein. Taylor had had a similar result with Evan. There was no way she would have terminated the pregnancy, whatever the case, but they were blessed since Evan had been born perfectly healthy. She remembered how upset she had been when presented with the same results and felt a kinship with Molly.

"There's only a *possibility* of chromosomal abnormalities, and they're insisting you terminate?" Taylor clarified.

Clyde replied, "Yes. And you know what that doctor told me?" He took a breath. "He said it's so early, not a big deal, and we can try again. Why have a child that's sick?' That's exactly how he said it, as casually as if I was picking out a new suit." He shook his head. "What kind of world are we living in when an insurance company has the right to try to force a decision like that on you?"

Taylor asked, "When did you sign up for the new policy?"

"During our open enrollment period. They were taking $300 a month out of my paycheck for my premiums. If I opted in to the new policy, that went down to $25. We thought the policy was a great deal. Saved us lots of money. They never told me I was signing over life-and-death decisions. I thought I just had to, you know, use the doctors they said, that kind of thing."

"Did your company hold meetings to go over the policy?"

Clyde replied, "Nope. Everything was sent through our email and we had to read up on the benefits on our own."

That in and of itself should have been illegal. Taylor made a note to look into it. She looked again at Molly. "What did you tell the doctor?"

She pursed her lips. "I told him there was no way I was aborting my baby. We're Catholic." She looked up. "He apologized but said he wouldn't be able to bill my insurance company for any future visits if I violated the policy."

"And now you have no coverage for the pregnancy?"

"That's right," Clyde answered. "The great money-saving policy is now going to bankrupt us."

"Well, there's hope, isn't there?" Molly said. "Once this case is decided, they can make them reverse these exclusions."

"While in the meantime, we get more broke every day," Clyde said.

Taylor felt deeply for this couple. "It's so important for the public to hear your story."

They both nodded.

"I'm hoping we can get the show aired before the court decision is made, get public opinion on your side. Maybe it will get the insurance company to rethink their policies," she said.

Clyde snorted. "Like they give a damn about public opinion. Those vipers will do anything for a quick buck. There's no justice in this world."

Taylor could understand his bitterness. One of the things that bothered her most about this case was the fact that the majority of people suffering were lower-income families. Taylor suspected that Jefferson Health Care had targeted those who needed to save money to test their new policy exclusions. Molly and Clyde were just two in a sea of voices.

Taylor wrapped up the interview, thanked them both, and left. Her thoughts were troubled as she made her way to the next interview, at Greenwich Hospital. She'd gotten a call just a few days ago from Mrs. Sampson telling her that their insurance company had stalled on approving a heart transplant for her daughter. She and her husband had appealed the decision and were supposed to hear back today.

After she parked and went into the hospital's main entrance, Taylor waited for the elevator, then slid into the crowded space. When it opened at her floor, she headed down the hall toward the room number they'd given her and found the door ajar. The couple sat in silence, the mother on the edge of the hospital bed holding the hand of a frail-looking young girl. The child's blond hair was fanned out on the hard pillow. Her eyes were shut, her breathing shallow. The hissing and beeping of machines joined together in a discordant symphony.

Taylor approached the bed quietly and held out her hand. "Mrs. Sampson?"

She gave Taylor a tired smile as she took it. "Please call me Darlene. This is my husband, Bill. And you must be Ms. Parks."

"Taylor."

"Let's go in the lounge. She's asleep, but . . ." Darlene trailed off. They stopped at the nurses' station to tell the one on duty where they'd be, then Taylor followed them down the hall to a room with two sofas and a chair.

Compassion filled her as she took in the Sampsons' pain-filled expressions. "I'm sorry that we're meeting under these circumstances, and I so appreciate your taking the time to talk to me. I understand your daughter has been on the transplant list for over a year now, is that right?"

Color flushed Bill's face. "They finally found a heart and we thought this nightmare was over. And then . . ." His voice broke and he turned away.

"The insurance company said that due to our exclusions, she might not qualify for it. They had to send our case to their committee for consideration, so UNOS gave it to the next person on the list," Darlene explained. "It took so long for us to have her. She's our little miracle. I was told I'd never conceive."

Taylor couldn't imagine what exclusion would preclude allowing a necessary heart transplant, but she'd wait until Darlene finished before asking any questions.

"We adored her from the moment we saw her and couldn't wait for our family and friends to meet her. Didn't think there was anything, really, to warn them about, but some of them made very unkind comments about how difficult our lives were going to be with a special needs child."

Bill stood up and began to pace. "Everybody wants perfection . . . whatever the hell that is."

Taylor remained silent, her full attention on Darlene.

The woman wiped a tear from her cheek. "We're not stupid.

We know that Down syndrome comes with challenges. But what doesn't? How could anyone look at our beautiful child and not love her?"

A doctor walked into the room. His expression was grim. "I have news." He looked at Taylor. "Who is this?"

Bill spoke before either of them could answer. "My sister."

The doctor shifted from one foot to the other, then cleared his throat.

"You've heard back from them?" Darlene asked.

He nodded. "I wish I were giving you different news, but your insurance company has decided that Cora is not a good candidate."

Both parents jumped out of their chairs.

"What do you mean? She's young, strong, and with a new heart will live a long, healthy life," Darlene said.

The doctor looked at the floor, unable to meet their eyes. "It's not that simple. They claim they have to look at optimizing the selection by giving organs to those who have the potential for a 'normal' life span."

Taylor's mouth fell open but she quickly composed herself.

"No." It came out as a whisper as Darlene sank back into the sofa.

A vein throbbed in Bill's temple. "Are you telling me that because our daughter has Down syndrome, she doesn't deserve a chance to live?" He was yelling.

"I share your outrage," the doctor said in a voice clearly meant to soothe. "I'll appeal, of course. But I have to be honest—we're running out of time."

Bill sighed. "What are we supposed to do until then?"

"Be with her as much as you can, and if you pray, now would be the time."

Taylor was speechless. To have the ability to save your child snatched out from under you because some faceless executive had deemed her unworthy was more than outrageous—it was inhuman. After the doctor had left the room, Taylor spoke.

"I'm so sorry." She shook her head. "This is—"

"All that damn insurance company's fault," Bill interrupted.

Taylor tried to think of something, anything, that might give them hope. "The Supreme Court decision should be coming in the next month or so. Hopefully this will be overturned and they'll have to give her a heart."

Bill said, "By then, it will be too late. Cora is getting weaker, and besides, hearts don't just come along every day."

Taylor couldn't accept that. If this had been happening to Evan, she'd move heaven and earth to save him. "We can't give up. If we tell your story, get public outrage—"

Darlene gave Taylor a weary look. "It'll be too late by then. They've already won." Then she took a deep breath and said, "But we'll come on the show. We'll do whatever we can to stop them from doing this to someone else. For Cora. The world needs to know."

Taylor stood and Darlene walked her to the elevator. "I wish I could do more," Taylor said.

Darlene reached out a hand and touched Taylor's shoulder. "I appreciate it. Just let us know when you're ready for us. We'll be there." Her bottom lip began to tremble and tears spilled down her cheeks. "By then, Cora will most likely be gone."

CHAPTER SIX

DAMON CROSSE REGRETTED HIS DECISION TO END HIS LIFE. At the time, faking his suicide seemed like the best course of action. But now, having to live in his Crosby Wheeler alter ego full-time, he wished he had thought of another way. At the time of his "death," the assets in his name had gone to Jeremy, as his only legal living heir. He'd had the foresight to set up his media conglomerate under Crosby so he had access to all his money, and no one suspected anything, since as Crosby he wore his hair much longer, sported shaded glasses, and looked like a man some twenty years younger, thanks to the magic of the coins. But it irked him that he'd had to lose the Institute. Jeremy had closed down all the programs and it was just sitting there, impotent. He thought of all the great work that had been done there and that could still be done. He sighed. No point in wallowing in regrets. He had a new plan now.

He checked the time on his new Patrimony watch. The red alligator band was a departure for him—Crosby rarely wore anything but black—but today was a special occasion. He was going to meet his daughter, Taylor, for the very first time. Of course, she wouldn't know it was him. He knew from the security log that Taylor had dropped Evan off earlier and just now had come back for her meeting with Karen and the production team. He'd also known that she would want to stop in to see her son before going to her meeting, but the daycare center had very strict rules. From one o'clock to three o'clock, it was nap time and no one was allowed in. When he established the daycare center, he had made sure to limit the number of children under two to only four, so he had to hire only one caretaker. The older children were in a separate area with different staff, a system he'd set up so he'd have unfettered access to Evan. Today, he entered the nursery from the back, making sure no one saw him, and Delilah, the daycare worker, looked up.

He needed to speak just one word.

"Imagine."

She closed her eyes, and he led her to a rocking chair and eased her into it. Delilah had seen the staff hypnotherapist to help her quit smoking, and after a few sessions, Damon had joined Dr. Halder so she would respond to Damon's voice as well. It had turned out to be quite fascinating to watch Halder hypnotize people. Damon used to think hypnotism was nothing more than a magician's parlor trick, but the man actually knew what he was doing. The doctor had been successful in helping his patients lose weight, quit smoking, and even cut back on their drinking. It was a win/win.

Damon went over to Evan's crib, where the boy held his arms up to him. He picked him up and carried him over to the small sofa, where he handed Evan the sippy cup full of apple juice he'd brought. Damon spoke soothingly to his grandson while he sipped. He'd been visiting him over the past several months and even though the child wasn't yet speaking in complete sentences, he seemed to understand quite a lot.

"Grandfather is so happy to see you today, Evan."

"Gee Gee," Evan said, smiling.

Just as well that Evan couldn't say anything close to *grandfather* yet, otherwise Taylor would get suspicious. The child looked at him, his eyes wide, and slid from the sofa to the floor. Damon brought over a box of blocks and set them next to Evan, pulling a few out and beginning to build a tower. Evan watched silently, and when Damon handed a block to him, he tentatively stacked it on top of Damon's tower.

"Can you hand me the red one?" Damon asked.

Evan picked up the red block closest to him and handed it to him.

"Good, my boy. Very good."

They played with the blocks for a few minutes, until Evan wandered away to the other toys and plopped down in front of a dump truck. Damon found a knob puzzle and placed it in front of himself, waiting. After a few minutes, Evan toddled over to Damon and watched as Damon placed the first piece, a yellow duck, into its space. He held out the beach ball to the child, who took it and, after only a moment, put it in the proper spot. Damon pushed the puzzle in front of Evan, and without any further prompting, the boy picked up the bear, then the car, and finally the balloon and finished the puzzle.

Damon clapped for him awkwardly, then got on his feet and put the puzzle back on the shelf.

"How about a story?"

The child walked over to the bookcase and picked up *Grimm's Fairy Tales* and handed it to Damon, then climbed up next to him on the sofa. Damon held the book out for him to see, but when he began, instead of reading the words on the page, he made up his own story.

"Once upon a time, there was a young prince named Evan. Evan's mommy and daddy didn't want him to be a prince because they didn't want to share him. They wanted him to be an ordinary boy. So they told him ordinary stories and took him ordinary places, but Evan knew deep in his heart that he was born to do great things. Evan's mommy tried to hide him from his grandfather, the king. But Evan's grandfather found him and told him that he would one day rescue him from his ordinary life. He spent time with Evan, and Evan grew to love the king even more than he loved his mommy and daddy. Evan understood that he had a duty that was more important than staying home and being ordinary. Evan had to be extraordinary. He was born to be a great leader. Everyone would serve him and he would own all the toys in the kingdom. The young prince asked if he could live with his grandfather, the king, so he could learn how to be a good prince. His grandfather said yes and took him, and they lived happily ever after."

Evan's eyes were closing, and Damon lifted him, taking the now-empty cup from his hand and returning him to the crib. The sedative in the juice would last for the next hour or so. Before leaving, he pushed up Evan's sleeve, pulled out a butterfly needle, and inserted it in a vein on the inside of the child's elbow. He waited until he had a full vial of blood, then extracted the needle and rubbed an alcohol swab on Evan's skin. He pressed a cotton ball to the site for a few minutes and was pleased when he removed it and there was no bruising or bleeding. He pulled the sleeve back down and left.

Once back in his office, he opened his laptop and looked at the nursey via a camera feed. Pressing the intercom button to the speaker installed in the nursery, he spoke the words that would break Delilah's hypnotic state.

"With each count, you become more awake and alert. One, two, coming back gradually, three, take a deep breath, four, coming back to your body, and five, open your eyes. You're wide awake." And just like that, Delilah stood up and resumed her duties.

CHAPTER SEVEN

Jack arrived in Baltimore in the early afternoon and followed his GPS's directions to the house in Lutherville, Maryland, stopping on a residential street in front of a well-maintained split-level. His phone rang before he got out of the car.

"Hey, sorry for not getting back to you sooner," Jeremy said by way of greeting. "I didn't have my phone in the lab. Everything okay?"

"Yeah, I just . . . I'm feeling a little uneasy about leaving Taylor. It's probably nothing but these stories in the news have me nervous, and I'm in Maryland and won't be back till tomorrow. Maybe you could go over tonight, spend some time with her?"

"No problem. I'll invite myself over for dinner and then stay the night."

"Great. Thanks, man."

His mind somewhat settled, Jack ended the call and opened the car door. The humidity enveloped him as soon as he was outside, and he was surprised at the difference in temperature just a couple hundred miles south of New York. The front door to the house opened as Jack approached, and a man in his early forties came out. He looked as though he hadn't slept for days, and a five o'clock shadow covered his jawline.

"You must be Jack Logan," he said with no change in expression as he moved aside to let him in.

"Thank you for seeing me, Dr. Russell." Jack knew that Kent Russell had had his own dental practice for the past eleven years. He followed him into the kitchen, noticing the pile of dirty dishes in the sink and the carton of milk sitting forgotten on the counter.

He held out a hand to Jack. "Have a seat."

Jack sat across from him at the square table. "Do you mind if I record the interview?"

Russell shook his head. "It's fine."

Jack pulled out his cell phone and put it on the table, then hit record. "First, let me offer my condolences. I'm very sorry for your loss."

Russell nodded, a faraway expression in his eyes. "I don't even know what to feel. This is a nightmare. I keep expecting to wake up and discover it's all just a bad dream." He looked back at Jack. "It doesn't make any sense. She actually killed him . . . Maggie's a nurse, a caretaker—not a killer. I don't understand." He began to cry softly, and Jack waited for him to compose himself. Eventually, Russell cleared his throat and sat up straighter.

"Had she been acting any differently recently?" Jack asked.

Dr. Russell thought for a moment. "Not at all. That weekend was a typical one. I would have been at the game, too, that day but I had an emergency at the office." He looked up, muttering to himself, "If only I'd been there, maybe I could have stopped her."

Guilt was a natural reaction, Jack knew. He also knew there

was nothing he could say to this man that would make him feel better about not being at that game. He cleared his throat and continued, "According to several witnesses, it happened very suddenly. Was there any prior animosity between the coach and your wife?"

Russel gave Jack a look of incredulity. "You don't understand. She had no animosity toward *anyone*. There wasn't a mean bone in my wife's body. Everyone loved her. Just ask around the neighborhood and you'll see. It's like she was possessed or something. It doesn't add up."

Jack exhaled. "There have been several similar occurrences up and down the East Coast, people committing acts that are completely out of character. I'm wondering if there's something linking them all."

Russell looked slightly bewildered. "Like what?"

"Could be anything. Exposure to some sort of chemical. A medicine that's been tampered with."

Russell was adamant when he said, "Maggie didn't take anything. Maybe an aspirin now and then, but that's it."

Jack knew there would be a lot more than sixteen cases if someone had tainted a medicine supply, but he couldn't rule out anything yet. "Had she traveled out of the country recently or gone anywhere unusual?"

"No. The most exotic trip she'd taken lately was a weekend in Ocean City."

"Any complaint of headaches or feeling dizzy?" Jack prodded. "Any head trauma? Recent illnesses?"

Russell shook his head. "She was in perfect health. She got her physical every year. In fact, we'd both just been to our internist. She took good care of herself. She was a nurse. I can't think of anything that would have caused her to . . ." He choked up.

Jack knew he had to tread carefully. Maggie's suicide meant

there would be an autopsy, so he gently asked, "Dr. Russell, do you know when they'll be releasing your wife's autopsy report? It might shed some light on why this happened."

He replied, "I don't. I hope they can find a reason—I still haven't figured out what to tell my son." He broke down again, putting his head in his hands.

Jack had one more question to ask, but he wasn't sure how it would be received, so he waited a moment before speaking again. "Forgive me for asking . . . any history of drug or alcohol abuse?"

Russell's mouth set into a hard line. "Absolutely not! My wife and I are devout Baptists. She never touched a drop of alcohol, and she would never take drugs."

"I understand. I had to ask." Jack stood up, pulled out a card, and handed it to him. "Thank you so much for your time. I won't take up any more of it, but I'm not leaving town until tomorrow. If you think of anything, please call me."

Jack's next stop was St. Katherine's High School, where Sister Francis was now headmistress. She used to take care of the orphans at St. Mary's Church, which had closed years ago. When Jack and Taylor had scoured online message boards for adoptees to see if they could find anyone who'd worked there, Sister Francis had answered more than one post, and from there, Jack had struck up an online conversation with her. He pulled up the steep driveway and around the circular drive in front of the reception building, as she'd instructed him. After parking in a visitor spot, he pressed the bell at the front door, announced his name, and was buzzed in by a young woman who led him to a large wooden door. When he opened it, he found an older woman dressed simply in a plain navy dress behind a desk. Her hair was white, and her blue eyes lively. She smiled at Jack and rose, extending her hand.

"Hello, Mr. Logan. Please, have a seat."

He shook her hand and smiled as he sat down. "Thank you so much for making time to see me while I'm in town."

"Of course, of course. I'm happy to help in any way I can."

Jack hadn't disclosed the reason for his interest in the child who'd been adopted by Crosse; he had instead told Sister Francis he'd just discovered that his deceased father had been adopted as a child, and Jack was trying to find any living relatives. Lying to a nun didn't make him feel good, but he told himself that the ends justified the means. "You lived at St. Mary's in the early sixties, correct?"

She nodded.

He continued. "I contacted Associated Catholic Charities, but unfortunately all the records from that particular orphanage were destroyed in a fire. I was hoping you might remember a child that was adopted by a couple from New York. A Mr. and Mrs. Jonas Hayes?"

She looked up at the ceiling for a moment, then shook her head. "I'm afraid that doesn't ring a bell." She spread her hands, palms up. "There were quite a lot of children coming through there."

"This couple had lost a baby in childbirth. The woman couldn't have any more children. And they were open to an older child, not a baby."

"Hold on . . . yes . . . I remember now. He was a big bear of a man and she was wisp of a thing. Very sad story. They adopted a quiet little boy. Martin we called him. I remember he used to keep to himself a lot. Smart as a whip but didn't quite fit in with the other children."

That was something, Jack thought. "Do you remember who brought him to you?"

"He was left on our doorstep, so I'm pretty sure it was someone local. Possibly a young girl who didn't want to tell her parents she'd gotten into some trouble."

"There was no note, nothing?" Jack felt his earlier optimism fade. This whole process had been like searching for a needle in a haystack.

She said, "No, nothing like that. But . . ." Her eyes went to the ceiling again. "Actually, there was something left with him. I remember because it looked expensive and made me wonder if his mother was from a wealthy family. It was a gold chain with a St. Nicholas medal, also in gold."

"The patron saint of children," Jack said.

She looked pleased that he knew this. "Yes. When he was adopted, we gave it to his new parents."

Jack sighed. That was interesting, but not helpful in figuring out who this particular orphan was. He pushed his chair back. "Well, thank you."

"There *is* one more thing."

Jack stopped and waited for her to continue.

"It was a numbered medal. A limited lot, I think. The company who made them moved out of state, but I think they are still in business. You might be able to track down who bought it."

"How many of them were made?"

"I don't remember, I'm afraid. It's been too long."

"That's okay. This is really helpful. Do you remember the company's name?"

"I'm sorry, but I don't."

"Thank you, Sister, you've been a great help."

Jack left and drove ten minutes to the Sheraton in Towson. Tracking down every store that had sold that sort of medal would take time that he didn't have, and it still might not provide them with any useful information. Their Institute research would have to go on the back burner for now. He needed to continue with his research on his current story before heading to his next interview tomorrow morning with Agatha Moroni, the woman whose knife ended up becoming a murder weapon.

When he got to his room, he stretched out on the bed and closed his eyes, thinking about Maggie's husband again. How could you be living your very normal life one day and then, all of a sudden, lose your wife in a murder-suicide? Nothing that the dentist had told Jack set off any alarm bells. What would make someone suddenly go crazy like that? Sighing, he sat up and opened his laptop. He typed *What makes people go suddenly crazy?* into the search bar and clicked on an article about sudden personality changes. The usual suspects came up: mental illness, drug abuse, head trauma, stroke, tumor. None of them seemed to be the case with Maggie Russell. He could only hope that the autopsy would reveal something helpful.

CHAPTER EIGHT

WHEN TAYLOR RETURNED TO UBC SHE WENT BY THE DAY-care to check on Evan but a sign was on the door, NAP TIME—PLEASE DON'T DISTURB, so she headed straight to the conference room for the production meeting. She was a few minutes early, for which she was grateful because she needed some time to compose herself. The image of that frail young girl hooked up to machines, the life slowing leaving her body, was still fresh in her mind. She couldn't accept that there was nothing to be done, that a group of executives in their glass towers had the authority to decide who got to live and who had to die. She looked up as the door opened and Karen Printz walked in with two production assistants trailing behind her.

"Taylor. Good to see you," Karen said, taking a seat at the head of the table. "How's that darling boy of yours?"

"Which one?" Taylor teased. She and Karen went back a long way and had an easy camaraderie.

Karen chuckled. "I was referring to the baby, but I hope Jack's good too."

"They're both great. And I'm so grateful for the daycare center here. It makes it *so* much easier, and Evan really likes it."

"Glad it's all working out. So . . ." Karen opened her portfolio and pulled out her trademark Montblanc pen. "Where shall we start?"

Taylor slid her laptop from her briefcase and pulled up the documents she'd been working on. "I was thinking since we have an hour, we'd divide it into four segments. That way we can cover each discrimination class."

Two of the show's writers filed in and joined them at the table, and Karen cocked her head at them. "Let's recap for Chad and Mira. The Supreme Court case arguments closed a few weeks ago. The suit was heard on the basis that Jefferson discriminated against protected classes in its coverage details." She held up a hand and ticked off each finger as she spoke, and her first assistant transcribed her words onto an iPad. "Age, disability, religion, and pregnancy."

"I still have about ten more families to interview to narrow down the age and religion plaintiffs, although I think the couple I spoke with this morning qualify as protected under both pregnancy and religion," Taylor said.

Karen leaned forward. "How so?"

"They're Catholics who don't believe in abortion, but prenatal testing showed the possibility of chromosomal abnormalities, and the insurance company is telling them that if the child is born with any of the birth defects excluded in their policy, they won't cover the birth or allow the child to be added to their insurance."

Karen nodded. "That's a good possibility. What about disability?"

Taylor filled her in on Cora, passing around pictures of her and the family. "As you know, hearts don't come along every day. They were all ready to do the transplant when Jefferson stopped it." Taylor took a deep breath. "I don't think she has much time left."

Karen studied the photo, then handed it back. "A lovely young girl. What a shame. What are they basing the denial on?"

"They are essentially saying they don't want to waste a heart on someone with less than a full life expectancy."

"Because of the Down's?"

"Yes."

Karen nodded. "I agree she'd make a good addition to the story."

"Not so fast." A melodious voice from the doorway startled them, and Taylor looked over to see a bohemian-looking man, dressed in black trousers and a black turtleneck, standing in it. He was tall and thin, wearing sleek silver glasses and with dark eyes that bore right through her. She recognized him from pictures she'd seen on the Internet—Crosby Wheeler.

Karen jumped up from her seat. "Mr. Wheeler, I didn't . . . didn't . . ." she sputtered.

Taylor was surprised to see typically calm Karen so flustered. A talent of her caliber didn't usually kowtow to anyone. What was she so nervous about?

He walked to the head of the table, and Karen moved from her seat to an empty one next to it. He looked at Taylor.

"It's very nice to finally meet you, Ms. Parks." He extended a hand to her and she took it.

"You as well," she said, her eyes locking with his, though she felt a sudden urge to pull away.

He released her hand and took the seat Karen had vacated, then addressed the group.

"I'm concerned that this young woman's plight opens up a whole can of worms. Organ donation is fraught with difficult decisions anyway, and it's such an expensive procedure. We might be better served with something everyone can get behind."

Taylor took her time answering, wanting to weigh her words. "I'm a little confused. Are you saying that there are people who will agree that she shouldn't get the heart?"

Wheeler fixed her with a steely gaze. "There are those who might agree that the heart would be better utilized by someone with a full life expectancy. People with Down syndrome don't usually live much past sixty."

It took everything Taylor had not to let her jaw drop. "Cora is only *twelve*. Even if what you say is true, that's still forty-eight years. Are you saying that we don't give a new heart to anyone over forty? Because I'm pretty sure that's not the case."

Karen shot her a warning look. "Taylor, no one is arguing with you, but Mr. Wheeler has a good point. Even though your logic is correct, I'm afraid the public won't see it that way."

"Is our job to report the facts or to please the public?" Taylor asked.

"I would venture to say it's both," Wheeler said, standing up. He looked at Karen. "I trust you'll find a more suitable candidate." He withdrew from the room without giving Taylor a second glance.

It seemed to take a few seconds for everyone to regain their equilibrium, especially Karen. Her voice cracked when she spoke, and she cleared her throat. "Well, let's get to work on finding a different plaintiff for the disability angle."

Taylor deflated. What was she supposed to tell Cora's parents? She was so upset she couldn't focus on what Karen was saying. And the more she thought about it, the angrier she got. She would have to find a way to convince Karen to try to change Wheeler's mind, but in the meantime, she played along. "Okay.

I'll go back to the drawing board on the disability and email you some options tomorrow."

Karen nodded but wouldn't meet Taylor's eyes. "Great."

"We're still good on the Edwards couple for the pregnancy?" Taylor asked.

Karen gave a distracted nod before looking at the group. "Okay, well, I guess that's a wrap for today."

They filed out of the conference room, and Taylor went to one of the cubicles that had been designated as a work area for the freelancers. She was unsettled. When Taylor had worked with her before, Karen never would have buckled under network pressure like that. What was it about Crosby Wheeler that could turn someone like Karen into a sycophant?

Taylor pulled her laptop from her bag and opened the file with the names and summaries of the families involved in the case. The truth was that all the families who had been affected by Jefferson's low-premiums program mattered, and they all deserved to be heard. But it was Taylor's job to make sure that whichever ones were chosen did a good job of representing the group. Sighing, she clicked on name after name, scanning the details, looking for a family that might be an acceptable substitute for Cora and her parents.

The parents of Dustin, a five-year-old nonverbal autistic boy, were trying to get him a communication assistance device that cost over ten thousand dollars. It had been used successfully with many children, allowing them to bridge the communication gap, but the insurance company denied the claim on the basis that there was not enough statistical data to prove its efficacy. Then there was a man who'd lost his leg in an accident whose insurance company refused to cover the artificial limb recommended by his doctor. The inferior, cheaper prosthetic irritated his skin, and despite numerous appeals from the doctor, Jefferson continued to deny authorization. He eventually got a skin infection that caused more of his leg to be amputated, and yet Jefferson still refused to cover the prosthetic and offered him a wheelchair instead. Taylor became more enraged as she read each story, but she feared that none of these were going to strike enough of a chord with the American public. These sorts of injustices had been going on for a long time, and sadly, the public was becoming inured to them. She needed something more shocking, more akin to Cora's situation.

She glanced at her watch to see that an hour had passed, so she gathered her things to go pick up Evan. When the elevator doors opened, she felt her heart skip a beat as her eyes met Crosby Wheeler's. She stepped in, and he didn't move aside to make room, so she quickly sidestepped toward the wall, leaning against it.

"Hello," she offered.

He simply nodded, not speaking.

The ride up to the fifteenth floor seemed interminable, and she looked down at her feet, her heart beating furiously until the doors finally opened. She didn't know whether she should say good-bye or not, but based on his silence, she decided to exit quietly. As she did so, she could swear she felt his eyes boring into her back. It wasn't until the doors closed again that she expelled a pent-up breath. Why was she so unnerved? It certainly had nothing to do with his position as CEO. She'd been married to a senator, had attended affairs with heads of state, and had grown up as the daughter of a prominent Washington newspaper editor; she was used to dealing with VIPs. No, it had nothing to do with his position at the network. It was something else. An intangible quality about him that made her blood run cold. Something in his eyes—a look she'd seen before but couldn't quite place.

Before Taylor had signed her contract with UBC, she'd done her research. Crosby Wheeler was a bit of an enigma, known for his standoffishness. There was never anything about his social life or his family in the news—he was extraordinarily private, which wasn't so strange. There were other public figures who were more eccentric. But the more she had investigated him, the less she'd been able to find out. Even his background was sketchy. There was a mention of his having grown up in the Midwest and coming to New York in his twenties, where he worked his way up in television, but that was it. Karen seemed to think highly of him, though, and Taylor had trusted her opinion. But now, something gnawed at her.

Evan was playing with some trains when she walked into the daycare. She smiled at Delilah and went over to where he was sitting. He looked up and broke into a wide grin.

"Mama!" He stood up and held a train in one fist out to her. "Choo choo."

She leaned down and hugged him. "Time to go home, sweetie." She kissed a chubby cheek and tousled his dark curls. "Did you have fun?"

He nodded. "Fun." He pointed to another little boy. "Josh."

Delilah walked over. "He made a new friend today."

"Thank you for taking such good care of him."

She smiled at Taylor. "It's my pleasure. He's such a doll."

As Taylor was gathering his belongings, Evan walked over to the bookcase, grabbed one of the books, and brought it over to her.

"Mine."

Taylor gently took the book of fairy tales from his hand. "The book stays here, sweetie. You can read it next time."

"No. Mine!" His voice grew louder.

She crouched, so she was eye level with him. "Evan, sweetie, calm down. This book doesn't belong to us. If you like it so much, I can buy one for home. But we can't take this one."

His face crumpled as he began to cry and he hugged the book closer to his chest. "No, no, no, no."

Delilah came over and whispered to Taylor. "You can take it and bring it back next time."

Taylor shook her head. "Thank you, but he has to learn."

She sat down on the floor, pulled Evan to her, and let him cry, rubbing his back and trying to soothe him. After a few minutes, he began to calm down. "It's okay to be sad, sweetie. I know you want that book, but we can't always have what we want."

He sniffed and nodded, handing the book back to her.

"Thank you, love."

He clung to her as they left, his head on her shoulder all the way to the car. She buckled him in, handing him a cup of water. "Hungry?"

He shook his head.

Evan's tantrum seemed to have worn him out, and he was asleep shortly after she started driving. That was the first time he'd thrown a fit like that. Normally he was so easygoing and good-natured. Were the terrible twos rearing their ugly head early?

When Taylor pulled up to the house, she saw that Jeremy's car was parked in the driveway. He'd called her a few hours ago and said he had a meeting in the area and wanted to stop by to see her and Evan. She had a sneaking suspicion that Jack had orchestrated the visit, and despite not wanting to be coddled, she was happy nonetheless that her brother had come.

Evan seemed to be back to his pleasant self as she unclipped him from his seat and picked him up.

"Uncle Jeremy's here," she told him.

"Jay Jay," he said, pointed at the dark green sedan.

Jeremy had a key, so he was already inside, but before she could give her brother a hug, Beau darted in front of him, tail wagging furiously. She stroked the dog's head. "Hi, boy. Did you have a good day?"

"We just finished half an hour of ball playing. He could go forever," Jeremy said, laughing.

She dropped her purse on the console in the hallway and put Evan down.

"Hey there!" Jeremy opened his arms and Evan flew into them.

"Jay Jay."

"I brought you something." He handed Evan a box wrapped in bright red paper.

Taylor gave Jeremy an amused look. "I keep telling you that you do not have to bring him a present every time you come over," she said, chiding him.

Jeremy shrugged. "I love doing it."

"Let's go in the kitchen and you can open it there, sweetie." When they got there, Evan plopped down on the floor and began to tear at the paper to reveal a box of periodic table blocks in bright pink, green, orange, and purple.

Jeremy helped him open the packaging and Evan began playing, stacking them into a tower.

Taylor chuckled. "You're determined to turn him into a scientist." She went to the refrigerator and took out a container with chicken and potatoes she'd pulled from the freezer that morning. "Hungry?"

Her brother nodded. "Starved actually. I don't think I ate anything today."

"You and Jack and your atrocious eating habits." She turned the oven on, then the kettle for some tea. "I'll just warm everything up and we'll eat soon. Tea?"

"Yeah, thanks."

Bringing two cups with her, she sat down at the kitchen table and looked at her brother, letting Evan stay absorbed in stacking his blocks and humming to himself. "So, to what do I owe this unexpected visit?"

"Maybe a little birdie thought you could use some company."

She pursed her lips. "No kidding. How long did it take for Jack to call you?"

"He left me a message around ten, I think. I didn't get it till later. He worries about you, that's all."

She marveled at how easily she and Jeremy had fallen into an easy sibling relationship. It was like people who go through a disaster together—they become bonded for life. Both she and Jeremy shared the genes of the same monster on their paternal side, but the genes of two loving and upright women on their maternal side. She liked to think that they'd both inherited the qualities of their mothers.

Of course, she'd been spared a life growing up with Damon Crosse, but Jeremy had suffered under him from birth. Taylor couldn't begin to imagine what it must have been like for him, motherless, alone, and with a father who saw him only as an extension of himself, born to carry out his heinous plan to corrupt humanity. It still astounded her that Jeremy was such a kind and gentle soul. She knew that it was in part due to his conversion and deep faith, but it went beyond that. She'd met plenty of people of faith who weren't as nice. There was an inherent goodness about him, and she was so grateful that he'd escaped Damon and that they had found each other.

She didn't like to ask him too much about his childhood—she knew it was painful for him to talk about it—but she wanted to understand more about Damon, to try to find a reason that he'd turned out the way he had. But she let Jeremy talk about his upbringing on his own terms. She desperately wanted to believe that it had been nurture, not nature, that was responsible for what Damon had become. It terrified her to think that encoded in her genes was the same recipe for evil.

"Yeah, well, I'm fine. But I *am* glad you're here. I was going to call you myself." Taylor lowered her voice. "I wanted to tell you about my dream." She recounted the details, which were still as fresh as when she'd woken from it, while Jeremy listened without comment. "It just seemed so real, not like a dream at all." She hesitated, wanting to mention her theory about his mother, but not wanting to upset him. "I thought the woman calling me was my mother, but when I got a better look, it wasn't. Do you think it was yours?"

He took a sip of his tea and tilted his head. "I don't really know if the departed are capable of visiting us from beyond. I do think sometimes dreams can be visions, but it's hard to know which dreams are messages and which are products of our imaginations. It's very possible that it was your fear manifesting in a dream. Especially since there really wasn't a specific thing she told you."

Taylor nodded. "I guess you're right. Jack's been tracking a story about all these crazy things happening—people killing people with no provocation. I could be in the grocery store with Evan and something could happen to us. I don't even want to read the paper or turn on the news anymore. It's one horrible thing or another, and I feel so powerless."

"Try to put it out of your mind. Trust God."

"Jeremy, I was thinking: Do you ever wonder if you could be wrong? What if there is no God and this is all there is?"

"No, I don't wonder if I'm wrong. I've felt His presence and seen His power." He looked at her intensely. "What brings this up? Did something happen?"

"Not really. I mean I *do* believe. But sometimes it's hard to see all the bad things that happen and continue to have faith that God is working all things for the good. You know?"

He gave her a warm smile. "I do know. And I really don't have an answer other than He's God and we're not. I look at it like this. If you and Evan were walking down the street and you could see a car coming around the corner because of your height but he couldn't, you would stop him, tell him to stay out of the street, right?"

"Right."

"Well, what if he chose not to listen? He'd be putting himself in danger. And maybe you'd still get to him in time, but maybe not. Or maybe he'd be injured. It's like that with God. If we choose to let him lead us, he can keep us safe."

She wasn't really following his logic. "I understand what you're saying about being in His will. But there are many instances where people *are* listening and bad things still happen."

"Yes, but this life is not all there is. I'm more concerned with eternity. I look forward to meeting my mother one day and your mother, our grandparents. My life was so empty and dark that finding God was a literal lifeline, so I try not to love this world too much and to think more of the hereafter—especially as I was so close to spending it in a very bad place."

Evan came running into the kitchen, meowing like a cat and with black magic marker all over his face.

"Oh no! Where did he find that?" Taylor asked.

"Uh-oh. I may have left a Sharpie on the sofa. I meant to put it back in my briefcase," Jeremy said.

Her mouth dropped open. "A Sharpie? As in permanent maker?"

He gave her a sheepish smile. "I'm sure it's not *really* permanent."

She picked Evan up and twirled him around, kissing his cheek. "Come here, you little kitty cat. Let's see if we can turn you back into a little boy."

CHAPTER NINE

AMON HAD VIEWED THE PRODUCTION MEETING FROM HIS office via a video feed on his laptop. He'd watched with interest as Taylor spoke, noticing how similar her facial expressions were to Jeremy's. It pleased him to see that his genetic influence was strong. That boded well for Evan.

He'd frowned, though, when she began detailing the story of the girl needing the heart transplant. On the one hand, it might be a good way to take the nation's temperature on disabilities and the social utility of those unfortunate enough to have them. But the problem with the case Taylor wanted to use was that the child was attractive and sympathetic. People might be inclined to believe that she had something to offer society. That was no good.

These policy exclusions were his end run after his failure to get the Healthy Children Act bill through Congress. The bill required genetic testing for all pregnancies and the termination of those fetuses that showed evidence of any birth defects on the included list. Brody Hamilton had tried to sneak it through as a rider to a less controversial bill two years ago, but Malcolm Phillips had changed his vote at the last minute. That decision had cost Damon his bill, and Phillips his life.

But human nature being what it is, most people would do almost anything to avoid potentially bankrupting themselves, which is where his genius idea had come in—offering an affordable health insurance policy in exchange for a few exclusions. It accomplished the same thing as the bill would have, enforcing the termination of less than perfect children, but this way, people could retain the illusion of a clear conscience. After all, if the insurance company denied covering the pregnancy and the child, it was much easier to justify the decision to end the life and try again for a more perfect baby.

But now these damn ambulance-chasing attorneys with their lawsuits were putting everything in jeopardy. The Supreme Court case could go either way. The arguments from the plaintiffs had been compelling, but it would all come down to the law. The justices wouldn't be swayed by an emotional argument. If Jefferson Health Care could prove that their policy exclusions had everything to do with economic decisions and nothing to do with discrimination, the court would have to side with them. Not all the claims denials involved patients in protected categories. Still, it was probably best to keep the story of the pretty little blond girl with a weak heart off Karen's show. There had to be a better example, someone much less appealing.

He had watched Taylor closely to see how she'd react when he killed the story. She hadn't buckled like many of his underlings would have. She had fire. That was his genetic influence, he was sure. He'd felt a grudging admiration for her, but of course he didn't let her know that. He had to keep her in her place. This was his story, after all; she was just another cog in the wheel. But he'd speak to Karen about it later, have her smooth things over. He didn't want to be too heavy-handed with Taylor, since he knew that Phillips had left her very well off, and the network didn't have anything to hold over her to make her stay if they made her angry by interfering with her creative vision. He wanted her handled with kid gloves, to ensure she continued to come to this office with Evan for the time being. Once he had the boy, it wouldn't matter anymore. Her usefulness would have run its course. Evan already knew his grandfather's face and the sound of his voice. By the time he was ready to execute his plan, Evan would be so used to him, he wouldn't think anything about the fact that Damon was his sole caregiver.

CHAPTER TEN

T HE NEXT MORNING, JACK GRABBED A CUP OF COFFEE ON HIS way out of the hotel. He'd finally reached Taylor around nine last night and had been relieved to hear that Jeremy was staying overnight.

Agatha Moroni lived in a brick colonial on a picturesque street in Towson, Maryland. The magnolia was in bloom and the breeze blew the sweet scent in the air. Spring was Jack's favorite season—everything coming back to life after the desolation of winter. When he rang the doorbell, he heard the high-pitched barking of what he thought had to be a little dog.

Sure enough, when the inner door opened, a white poodle jumped between a woman and the screen door. The woman, who was wearing a lavender sweater set and tan pants, her hair and makeup perfect, shooed the dog away as she opened the door for Jack.

"Hester, go good place," she said in a southern accent. The dog gave a final bark and trotted over to a dog bed in the living room, plopping down. Agatha rolled her eyes at Jack. "Sorry about that. He thinks he's a German shepherd."

Jack smiled at her. "No worries. I'm a dog lover." He didn't mention that he didn't consider any animal under fifty pounds a real dog. "Thanks again for agreeing to talk to me."

"Of course. Why don't we go sit in the kitchen? I've just made some coffee."

He followed her though the marble hallway into a large, bright kitchen with a cozy built-in table by the window.

She poured them each a cup, and Jack took a seat where she had put his saucer.

"Oh goodness, I forgot spoons! Hold on." Before she'd gotten very far, she turned to look at Jack again. "Would you like cream or sugar?"

"Just black. Thanks."

She sat across from him but shot up from her seat almost immediately. "The muffins! I swear, if my head weren't attached . . ." She brought a plate of what looked like homemade muffins over from the counter and placed it on the table. "Oh shoot, no plates." She started to get up again but Jack put a hand up.

"It's okay, thanks. The coffee's all I need."

She gave him a sheepish smile and sat down, brushing a stray hair from her forehead. "Maggie always used to tell me to slow down. I get a little turned around sometimes." Her eyes filled with tears and she shook her head. "I still can't believe she's gone. It's unbelievable . . . just unbelievable."

"Had you known her a long time?" Jack asked.

"Since our sons were in kindergarten. We became best friends." She shook her head again. "It just doesn't make any sense. Maggie was the sweetest, most unselfish person I ever met. When I moved here from Atlanta, I didn't know a soul. She took me right under her wing that first day, when I stood there looking just as lost as last year's Easter egg." Agatha sighed and took another sip of her coffee. "I don't know what I'm gonna do without her. And her poor boy. He saw the whole thing. He's going to be needing help for a long time." She looked up at the ceiling for a minute then back at Jack. "I've never seen such rage. It was like someone took over her body. And it happened so fast. Sometimes I still think I imagined it."

Jack gave her a sympathetic nod but his mind was moving a mile a minute. "It must have been horrible."

"It was the worst thing I've ever witnessed. And that poor coach. She kept stabbing him over and over. Like she was possessed."

Jack was reminded of Dr. Russell's words describing his wife's actions.

"Do you know if she ever drank or maybe experimented with any drugs?"

She shrugged. "An occasional glass of wine, but don't tell Kent that. She had to sneak it from him. He's a bit of a Goody Two-shoes, if you ask me. Kept a tight rein on that household. But Maggie doing drugs? No way."

So much for her husband's assertion that she never touched a drop of alcohol. Jack suddenly wondered if there were marital troubles Dr. Russell had neglected to mention and if Maggie was keeping secrets. She was a nurse, after all; she could easily have had access to drugs. Maybe it was something that had been tampered with that was not widely distributed. Again, Jack thought of the autopsy results he hoped Russell would share.

"Was Maggie happy in her marriage?"

Agatha shrugged. "As happy as anyone. You know, we're all just trying to do our best, raising the kids, keeping the house. She also had a demanding career. She needed our girls' nights once in a while. But Kent's basically a good egg."

"Is there anything else you can think of? Anything at all that was off or different about her in recent days?" Jack asked.

"No. Nothing."

"To your knowledge, she wasn't taking any new medication—prescription or over the counter?"

"Not that I know of."

He handed her a card. "If you think of anything else, please call me."

"I will."

Even though Jack left without any more pertinent information, he was still glad he'd made the visit. It was always good to make a personal connection if possible and made people more likely to reach out if they thought of something else. As he drove away, something bothered him. He was going on the assumption that he'd find a common thread among the incidents, but he wondered if something more sinister was at play. Intentional almost, and his mind drifted back to his thoughts of a mastermind.

He'd go over the files again tomorrow and see if anything stood out, if he'd missed anything. If he got a move on, he might be able to avoid rush hour and get home by three. Tomorrow, he'd set up some more interviews. But tonight, he was looking forward to a quiet family evening.

As he was about to drive off, his phone buzzed and he looked down to see *private number*. Swiping the screen, he spoke into the phone. "Jack Logan."

The voice on the other end was breathless. "Jack. Don't hang up, please."

He froze, his mind taking a moment to register that it was actually her. "What the hell do you want?"

"I need your help. You're the only person I can trust."

He should hang up, tell her to lose his number. While his mind battled, she rushed on.

"Crosse tried to kill me. I've been in hiding, but I need my passport. I need to come back. Sybil's dying. I need to be there for her."

Her words were like a gut punch. His ex-wife Dakota's wonderful aunt Sybil was still young, only in her sixties. "What? She's sick? What is it?"

"Cancer."

He drew a deep breath. "I'm really sorry to hear that, but you have a lot of nerve asking for my help," he growled.

"I'm not asking for me. But for Sybil. She's all alone. I just need you to get my passport from her and get it to me so I can get back into the country."

"Have someone else get it for you. You can't seriously expect me to help you."

"There's no one else I can trust. Please, Jack. Do you really think I'd come to you if I had any other choice?"

"Where are you?" he asked against his better judgment.

"Mexico."

He sighed. "Let me think about it. Text me a number where I can reach you."

"Thank you."

"Don't thank me yet." He hung up, shaken. Why had he told her he'd think about it? He didn't owe her a damn thing. But Sybil was a different story. She'd been good to Jack. And Dakota, damn her, knew it would be hard for him to turn his back on Sybil. What would he tell Taylor? There's no way she'd understand. He put the car in drive and headed back to the hotel. What the hell was he getting himself into now?

CHAPTER ELEVEN

AMON CROSSE LOOKED IN HIS BATHROOM MIRROR AND WAS dismayed to see that the deep lines around his eyes were back. Just a few weeks ago, he had been able to stop using makeup because his wrinkles had faded, making it that much easier to masquerade as Crosby Wheeler, a man in his late sixties. But lately he'd noticed that the power of the coins was diminishing. The first time he'd been told about the coins and their power, he'd had a hard time believing it. But his adoptive father, Fred Crosse, whose real name was Friedrich Dunst, had convinced him. He told Damon all about them, how they had traveled to many different lands throughout history after Judas first received them for betraying Christ. After being used in the sale of the potter's field, the thirty silver pieces had been safeguarded by the church, protected by its trusted patriarchs for over a thousand years.

When the Great Schism occurred in 1054 and the Catholic and Greek Orthodox Churches split, legend had it that they each took ten coins to keep watch over and hid the remaining ten with someone outside the church as a precaution. Eventually, though, some of them made their way into Caligula's court. History doesn't highlight the fact that Caligula began as a benevolent ruler who freed citizens who had been imprisoned and eased their tax burden. What history recalls is an evil despot who raped his own sisters, killed his rivals while their parents watched, and even named himself a god. Legend warned of the power of the coins to turn men evil. Apparently, Caligula was too weak to fight against the power of the coins, and they became his undoing.

Over the centuries the coins had been lost and found, the battle between the power hungry and the church waging on. The coins' power to corrupt had made even some men of the cloth vulnerable, and they'd sold them for profit. Over the decades, it was believed that among the many who held the coins were Attila the Hun, Ivan the Terrible, Queen Bloody Mary, and Benito Mussolini. Hitler had searched for them in vain, and Damon wondered if history would be different had he gotten his hands on them. Friedrich had been stationed on the Greek island of Patmos during World War II, when the Nazis occupied the island. He'd had teams searching for relics on behalf of the Ahnenerbe—Heinrich Himmler's secret society tasked with finding evidence that German ancestry was linked to the Aryan master race he believed were the Nordic gods. The war ended before Friedrich could find them, and he was forced to leave.

Years later, his disease made it impossible for him to travel, so he had sent Damon back to the island of Patmos, in Greece, to continue the search. When Damon returned empty-handed, the look of disappointment in Friedrich's eyes had nearly broken him. Damon had exhausted every lead, knowing that if they didn't find them soon, Friedrich would be dead. His last lead was a cardinal claiming to know where the coins were hidden.

Damon flew to Rome and met with him, lining the man's

pockets with a hefty seven-figure sum, and he had led Damon to a cathedral where they were allegedly buried under the altar. They weren't there, and Damon found the cardinal the next day, killed him, and took back the briefcase of money. He was not going to go home without them this time. He flew to Turkey and eventually to Ephesus, where he was led to believe they were buried. He had asked around in the marketplace, mentioning a generous finder's fee to the person who could even arrange a meeting with someone who could find them. It took over three months, but he finally had left with them in hand.

When he returned home, he had walked into Friedrich's bedroom victorious but Friedrich could barely open his hands to touch them. As soon as Damon placed the coins in Friedrich's palms, his eyes flew open, and he looked at Damon with hope for the first time in months. Damon stood, watching in awe, as the color began to return to Friedrich's face and he was able to push himself into a sitting position. Within the hour, his voice no longer shook.

Over the next several weeks, he slowly improved but was still not able to walk. It was then that Friedrich told him what he required next.

"The blood of the innocent amplifies their power—even more so if it is from the bloodline of the family that was entrusted to watch over the coins."

"These were hidden in a church. There is no family associated with them."

Friedrich had shifted in his wheelchair. "I want to get out of this damn chair. You know what you must do."

That's when they'd started the orphanage at the Institute. Their first orphan was a young girl of two. Damon still remembered the gleam in Friedrich's eyes when they dripped her blood onto the coins. The coins began to smoke and Friedrich had grasped them in both hands, seemingly impervious to the fact that they were burning his flesh. Within minutes, he told Damon that he'd gotten the feeling back in his legs.

They took blood from that child every day, and every day, Friedrich got better . . . but it wasn't quite enough. The child had to be sacrificed if Friedrich was to be fully restored. Damon willingly did it; after all, the child was close to death anyway, with the blood they kept taking daily and the sedatives he had been administering. Once they had performed the ceremony, Friedrich pulled himself up to standing and took a tentative step, smiling at Damon.

"I can walk. I can walk again!" And he'd been well for decades . . . until more was required. This time, a sacrifice wouldn't do it—they needed more coins, but Friedrich died before Damon could find them.

He had taken possession of another set of ten two years ago, when his fool son Jeremy had thought he'd outwitted him and brought them to the Institute. They'd been locked away safely in a vault in his panic room until now. When he had first tried to use them and had put them next to his original ten, nothing had happened. He was not a man who panicked though, so he went back and methodically read Friedrich's extensive notes on the relics and realized that he had to pay a price for desecrating them, because he'd had Peritas swallow them and then retrieved them from the dog's feces. He needed blood for atonement, and because of the desecration, it had to be from the bloodline of those in charge of the coins.

Evan had solved that problem for him, and Damon now had enough to complete the ceremony of the blood cleansing to reactivate the coins' power. Trembling with excitement, he pulled the velvet pouch from his pocket and fingered the silver pieces. He took the handkerchief from his desk and opened it, placing the coins in the cloth, then rested the cloth in his left hand. Next, he took the vial of Evan's blood and poured a few drops on the first coin, rubbing it with his finger. He did the same with the rest of them. He waited but nothing happened. Something was wrong. The coins were supposed to heat up, make smoke.

This didn't make any sense. He picked them up to examine them more carefully. The blood should have worked. He pulled out the original ten and dabbed a bit of the blood on one. Smoke poured from it.

A horrible thought occurred to him—what if the ten he'd gotten from Jeremy weren't the real silver pieces? He picked one up again. It looked exactly the same as the others, but if they were the real Judas coins, Evan's blood would have affected them. Damon's own blood boiled and he cursed. Had Jeremy tricked him? Or hadn't Jeremy known they weren't authentic? Maybe something more than Evan's blood alone was required.

Damon sighed deeply. Maybe his blood was required as well. His own sacrifice for what he had done. Perhaps the coins would not work unless he proved his worth.

He walked over to the wall and took down one of the short swords hanging there, and before he could allow himself time to think, he brought it down swiftly above the knuckle on the ring finger of his left hand, cutting off the tip of his finger.

White-hot pain rippled up his hand, into his arm. It took all his strength to drip the blood from his finger onto the coins. He waited in anticipation, but still nothing happened. Blood was squirting from his finger at an alarming rate and he grabbed one of the original coins and held it to his finger. The coin became hot, and he finally lost his composure enough to scream as it cauterized the wound and the bleeding stopped. He was grateful the original coins still retained some of their healing power. He picked up his severed fingertip and pressed it to the nub. The skin throbbed and he watched in amazement as it reattached, the skin knitting back together.

He picked up the useless coins and threw them against the wall. This was unacceptable. It meant that Taylor's family still had their ten somewhere. He would find them—and after he did, he would kill Taylor *and* Jeremy. No one made a fool of Damon Crosse.

Scooping up the original ten, he pressed them between his hands, feeling the heat transfer from them to him. It began in his hands and rose all through his body, as though he were being painted with a brush of warm water. He closed his eyes and waited. After a few minutes, the feeling was gone. He looked down at his hand and saw the wound was completely healed. He walked over to mirror and noticed the wrinkles were gone, as was the silver around his temples, which was black once again. His skin was supple again . . . but it wouldn't last. He would need to get more blood. Any blood would do for the original coins and he fumed that he'd wasted Evan's precious blood on the fakes.

He went to the ancient book his adoptive father had given him and put the heavy black tome on his desk and began looking through it. There were spells and incantations, but he wasn't interested in those. He was looking for the chapter on regeneration. Friedrich had told him if he was able to unlock the secret, Damon might be able to live, if not forever, then close. He thought about the story of the coins and pulled up the Gospel of Matthew on his phone. In Matthew 26, Judas received the money before he betrayed Jesus. Once he'd actually gone through with it, though, he regretted it, gave the coins back, then hanged himself. Had the coins prompted him to kill himself? They were referred to as *blood money*. And Damon knew what the blood could do to the coins. He went to the black book and found the chapter. Sacrifices. Christ had sacrificed his life for the salvation of the world, and the coins had been used to secure his death. What if a blood sacrifice of more than a few drops was required to activate them to their full potential? He went between the black book and the Bible over the next several hours but came up with nothing.

He returned the coins to their hiding place in the panic room and, once back in his study, texted his housekeeper to bring him dinner. While he waited, he read various news sites online, interested to see the leading news stories. The image of a reporter standing outside a Catholic church drew his attention and when he clicked the link, the woman's voice filled the room.

"I'm here in Boston outside St. Luke's Church, where a local priest has been taken to the hospital by ambulance. He was counseling a couple when allegedly the wife pulled out a gun and shot him. She then turned the gun on herself pulled the trigger. Her husband was not injured."

He smiled. At least one thing was going as planned.

CHAPTER TWELVE

PPROVING NODS BOBBED AROUND THE TABLE. LEONARD Reed, CEO of Jefferson Health Care, leaned back into the supple leather chair and rested his head. He studied the faces of his board while gnawing at a hangnail on his pinkie. He dislodged it and spit it on the table. Leonard's lips parted in a smirk at the woman next to him; she had averted her eyes and was staring at the table where he'd spit his nail. She didn't dare allow her revulsion to show. He was amused by her lame attempt at nonchalance and moved so his thigh was touching hers under the table. She didn't react. He wondered how long it would take before she had the nerve to move her chair farther from his, only half listening as Marvin, his newest hire, droned on.

"Since adopting the policy changes last year, we've gotten an 85 percent acceptance rate from corporate clients. Within that base, 90 percent of employees in the low- and mid-income ranges opted in to the low-premium policy. That has resulted in a reduction of roughly 25 percent in premiums but is offset by 80 percent

lower claim payouts in just the first quarter." The board was getting restless, but Marvin didn't notice their waning attention and
continued to read statistics and performance results, all in his
mind-numbing monotone.

Leonard heaved a self-satisfied sigh. He had known when he
hired him that Marvin's genius would save them billions. How
ironic that the very changes he had proposed would have prevented his own birth had they been in effect when he was still
in his mother's womb. Oh, well, Leonard was glad that he had
Marvin on his team as he was brilliant at numbers. And after
all, it all boiled down to margins. It had been so easy to sell
cheaper premiums in exchange for intangible trade-offs. Half
the time, no one even read the damn explanations anyway. They
only cared about how much would be coming out of their pay-
checks. It had been a no-brainer for the board to adopt the policy
changes. After a few hitches with the insurance commission and
some greased palms, everything had fallen into place. Until the
damn class action suit.

Now, the repercussions of the new exclusions were increasing
and the Supreme Court had agreed to hear the case. Leonard
already knew how four justices would vote. He only needed one
more, so he was in the process of seeing what dirt he could find on
them. The decision would be made in the next month or so. He
was sure he'd find a way to make the decision go his way. Even if
someone didn't have any skeletons in their closet, he could always
place one there. He loved tricking people. It made him feel a little
like Rumpelstiltskin, a misunderstood hero if ever there was one.

The woman next to him cleared her throat. "What if the
court votes against us?"

"Unlikely," Leonard answered without bothering to look at
her. He didn't care to elaborate or explain himself. No one had
been able to stop them when they changed the rules and started

denying expensive treatments and diagnostic tests. They had the doctors jumping through hoops to get prior approval for costly tests like MRIs and other diagnostic tools that patients could live without. Maybe it made the doctor's job a little more difficult, having to navigate treatment in the dark, but in the long run, it saved a shit ton of money, which was all he cared about. No one did anything as the insurance companies grabbed more power from the doctors every day—it soon became accepted practice.

"There's still all the bad publicity. The Sanctity of Life Group is on the steps every day," she persisted.

He glared at her. "It's being handled. We don't spend millions of dollars on PR for nothing." He didn't mention the entertainment network that worked in concert with him to produce shows that supported his efforts. His eyes narrowed. "Isn't your department above the quota for claims? If I were you, I'd spend less time worrying about the company's future and more time worrying about my own."

She bit her lip and blinked.

Leonard sighed loudly and motioned for Marvin to continue. He wasn't worried about the protest groups. With one phone call, they would get the credit for an indefensible act of violence. In another week, their credibility would be in the toilet.

Bored now, he tapped his foot underneath the table and glanced at his watch. He had planned to spend the afternoon with Sissy, his mistress. He was eager to continue his carefully orchestrated campaign on her self-esteem. Maybe he'd leave a brochure for breast implants by the bedside today even though he didn't really want her to get them. After all, he'd be finished with her by the time the stitches were ready to come out. He just wanted her to remember her place, to know that she needed to be on her best behavior if she wanted him to stick around. He'd seen it enough times—good-looking women thinking the world owed them everything.

He reached out a fat hand to grab the last jelly donut and stuffed it in his mouth, not bothering to wipe away the red glob that ran down his chin. He stared at Michelle, his young secretary, and licked his lips. Perhaps he would call her in for some private dictation and make Sissy wait another day. He'd tell her that she had completely slipped his mind.

He grinned and winked at Michelle. The look of resignation and dread on her face only served to arouse him more.

CHAPTER THIRTEEN

IKARIA, GREECE

Rena swept the courtyard while her uncle Yiannis slept. He was sleeping more and more these days, and she worried that his time on earth was running out. The morning breeze was cool and she thought he might benefit from sitting on the upper deck and looking out at the blue Aegean Sea. That is, if he could muster the energy to walk the few feet from his bed to the deck. He'd had a visitor yesterday—a priest from America. The man had been in her uncle's room for over two hours earlier that day and now it was evident the toll the visit had taken on her uncle. He would be exhausted for weeks. She sighed.

When she finished her sweeping, she went to the small kitchen and boiled an egg for him. He probably wouldn't eat it, but she would try to get him to take a few bites.

The sound of his raspy coughing made her look up, and grabbing a cup of water, she walked to the door and knocked.

"*Eláte*," he answered.

She entered the simple room that contained only a small bed against the wall and a nightstand, the tile floor devoid of a rug, the walls painted a plain white, their only adornment a wooden cross.

"Uncle Yiannis, can you eat something?" she asked in Greek. He shook his head. "*Óxo, pethi mou.*"

Rena plumped the pillows behind his back and brought the cup of water over to him. Bending the straw, she placed it between his parched lips, and he took a small sip. He pointed a bony finger toward the chair in the corner of the room and she brought it next to the bed.

He spoke again, this time in English. "It is almost time. You have to go back. I don't have much longer."

She brushed a tear from her cheek. "No, don't say that. You're going to get better."

He shook his head resolutely. "Rena, let us not lie to each other. We both know that God is calling me home. I am ready. But you cannot stay here any longer. It will not be safe without my protection."

"I don't understand. No one knows I'm here."

"When I am gone, the spirits will know. People will find you. You must take the coins and go to America. You know what you need to do."

Her heart began to beat faster. "I can't go back. My life is here now."

Yiannis spoke haltingly. "I found out yesterday . . . there are . . . important reasons to get the coins back to America."

"What you're asking of me is impossible. I can't do it."

When she had come to live here with her uncle, she had cut herself off from all technology and committed to a life of quiet contemplation and service. The children on this small Greek island all knew her as *Teacher*. She taught them English and learned to love them as if they were her own. It had been hard, especially those first few years, but she'd been convinced that safeguarding the coins was her sacred duty and that superseded all else. And now he wanted her to leave the life she'd finally become accustomed to? It wasn't fair.

Her uncle began to cough again, and she gave him another sip of water. "The coins are always found. The only way it will ever be safe is to reunite all thirty and then have them destroyed by the unity of the two churches—Greek Orthodox and Catholic. The pope and the patriarch together can perform a ceremony to destroy them once and for all."

Her mouth fell open in astonishment. "But we only have ten. Who knows where the others are."

"I know where ten of the others are."

"What?"

"They've been hidden in Mount Athos for the past six months."

She was stung that he had kept this from her. It made her feel like he didn't trust her, and after everything she'd given up in service of the coins, that was unacceptable. "Why did you keep this from me?"

He reached out a hand to her. "I just found out, *pethi mou*. I'm telling you now."

"Why don't I take our ten there then? Surely they would be safer with the monks?"

"You know that women are not allowed on the mountain. And besides, their presence there is disturbing to the spiritual well-being of the monks. I've already made arrangements for those coins to be taken to America. You must take ours back as well."

"How?"

"You will have help—you know who you must go to. And

when the twenty we control are together, the coins will call to their lost ones. You will see. You can do this. It is your destiny. Wait for Father Basil to come."

Who was this Father Basil? She'd never heard her uncle speak of him before. Maybe he was hallucinating. He certainly wasn't making any sense to her. She was supposed to find coins that men had fought and killed for from the time of Christ and *then* casually get in touch with the pope and the patriarch? It was the most insane thing she'd ever heard.

His eyes were closed now, and he was moaning. She put a hand on his forehead—he was running a fever. She got a washcloth, wet it with cool water, and placed it on his head. She'd watch over him tonight and pray. Reaching out to take his hand in hers, she brushed the tears from her cheek with her other hand. He'd gotten so frail in the past six months. She wished she could give him some of her own strength. He had become more than an uncle over the years; she thought of him as a father, and she didn't know how she was going to go on without him. She wasn't ready for him to die. She loved him. She needed him. No matter how prepared he thought she was, she wasn't equipped to take on this impossible quest.

CHAPTER FOURTEEN

TAYLOR SPRINTED AROUND THE STUDIO AS FAST AS SHE COULD, the adrenaline pumping through her and her heartbeat racing. She needed this. For this one hour, four times a week, she could forget all her worries and focus instead on the art. Jack had encouraged her to take a self-defense class after Evan was born. She'd looked into all the martial arts and had settled on Krav Maga because its focus was on training people for real-life encounters. The philosophy, *go home by any means*, resonated with her. She had just tested for the advanced class last month, which meant she could participate in weapons training now. She and her fellow students fell in line and awaited direction from their instructor. She was paired with a well-muscled man in his forties as her sparring partner.

They stood facing each other, waiting for the signal to begin. She assessed him quickly, sizing him up. The material was tight over his left knee—maybe a knee brace? That could be an area of vulnerability. The whistle blew and he came at her, pulling out the knife he'd hidden in the waistband of his sweats. Taylor grabbed his wrist and jerked it backward, causing him to release the knife. A kick to the back of his knees felled him and she put a knee on his chest, holding the knife at his throat now.

"Excellent," her instructor called out to her.

She let the man up and this time, she went after him with the knife so that he could practice his moves. When the class ended, her muscles were already aching but she felt good. Powerful, even. She was determined to be ready for whatever or whomever tried to hurt her in the future.

○ ○ ○

Seated at the dining room table, Taylor read through the deposition once more, prepping herself for the video call in a few minutes. She would be speaking to the parents of a young woman who had died after treatment had been denied to her because it was considered experimental. Fawn had been born with spina bifida and had always had a host of health issues. She'd developed lupus at age sixteen, which had progressed aggressively, and despite trying many treatments, it continued to wreak havoc on her joints and organs. Her rheumatologist wanted her to try a new biologic combination that he'd had success with in other resistant patients. Jefferson Health claimed the drug regimen was experimental and denied the claim. Fawn's organs began to fail, and despite numerous appeals, Jefferson stonewalled the family.

When, in desperation, they'd finally hired an attorney, the firm had discovered that they had approved the drug for other patients with the same policy coverage. Fawn's family had joined the class action suit on the basis that Jefferson had denied the treatment for their daughter because of her disability. By the time they were able to obtain an override, she had died.

Taylor called them via Skype, and after several rings, she was face-to-face with a woman in her sixties. "Mrs. Brooks?"

"Please call me Rita. You must be Taylor."

Taylor smiled. "Nice to meet you. I'm sorry I couldn't be there in person."

Rita waved her hand. "It's fine. I'm just grateful for the chance to tell our story."

"Will your husband be joining us?" Taylor asked.

She lowered her voice. "No, he wasn't up to it. He sleeps a lot these days."

Taylor nodded sympathetically. "Of course. I know this must be difficult for both of you. I'm so sorry for your loss."

"Thank you. It's been almost a year and it still doesn't seem quite real." She dabbed at her eyes with a tissue. "Everyone expects us to just get on with it. We have three other children who are healthy, thank goodness, but it's almost as though some of our friends hint that we're better off." The woman stopped for a moment to take a deep breath, then continued. "Obviously, taking care of Fawn was a full-time job. She was never going to live on her own. But we all loved her. She was a person. Just because she had physical difficulties, that didn't make her less of one. And she never complained. She was like our sunshine." Rita shook her head. "She had a lot of medical issues. I think they just wanted to not have to cover her anymore."

"From what I've read, there were others on the same policy as you who had been green-lighted for the procedure, correct?"

"Yes, but the company is claiming that every case of lupus is different and because of the severity of her case, the drug had less of a chance to work."

They spoke for a few more minutes, but as they hung up,

Taylor quickly realized this wasn't the right case for the show. It would be difficult to convince the public that the company's intent was to discriminate based on Fawn's previous medical condition and not based on the advanced nature of her illness. She would talk to Karen about it tomorrow.

CHAPTER FIFTEEN

S HE ARRIVED BACK IN NEW YORK FROM MARYLAND, JACK called Taylor and told her he'd stop at Tarantella's on the way home and pick up a pizza for dinner. As he pulled in front of the restaurant, he saw an open spot right in front and parked the Jeep. He was about to get out when a commotion on the sidewalk got his attention. A man and woman were fighting—he was pushing her and screaming obscenities. A crowd had begun to gather, but no one was stepping into the fray. Jack flung his door open and jumped out, running toward them just as the man moved in closer to her and wrapped his hands around her neck. She fell backward to the ground, gasping for air. The man went down on his knees, his hands never leaving her neck.

"Get off her!" Jack yelled and grabbed the man's shoulders with both hands, trying in vain to pull him off the woman. With seemingly superhuman strength, he shrugged off Jack's grip, letting go of the woman's neck with one hand, backhanding Jack across the chest with it. Jack went flying backward onto the sidewalk. He jumped back to his feet. "Someone call 911," he yelled into the crowd as he ran back toward the two, trying again to get the man to let go of the woman, who was lying still. Jack couldn't tell if she was breathing or not. Two other men came up next to Jack and the three of them together managed to pull the man off her, even as he continued shouting obscenities; swinging wildly, he shook the other men off.

His eyes were wild and he stormed toward Jack, his hands clenched into tight fists. Jack didn't retreat, but waited until the man threw a punch, then ducked and knocked him off balance with a roundhouse kick. The man jumped back up and came at Jack again, narrowly missing Jack's jaw with his fist. He lunged at Jack and Jack winced when the man's fist connected with his abdomen, knocking the wind out of him. Another man from the crowd jumped in and pushed the man down and Jack caught his breath. As the man stood again and came toward him, the sound of sirens filled the air and two police cars raced up. Before the officers could reach him, the man sprinted down the sidewalk, then threw himself into the street into the path of an oncoming truck.

The truck's brakes screeched as the driver tried unsuccessfully to avoid hitting him. Jack watched as the police ran over to protect the scene and wait for the ambulance to arrive. His hand trembled as he pulled out his phone to text Taylor that he'd be late. *What in the hell had he just witnessed?* He ran back to where the woman lay, hoping she was still alive. His heart sank when his eyes met those of the police officer taking her pulse. The man gave a subtle shake of the head. The officer stood up and addressed the crowd.

"Everyone please stay put. We'll need to question everyone about what happened here."

"Of course," Jack said. The guy had clearly been out of his

mind. Jack felt a chill go through him. This had been way too close to home. What if Taylor and Evan had been here instead of him?

○ ○ ○

It was another hour before Jack finished giving his statement to the police. He learned that the man had died from the impact of the truck. He'd follow up tomorrow once the names of the couple made the news and see if he could talk to any relatives or friends. Still shaken, he got into his car and drove home.

Taylor's Volvo SUV was parked in the garage when he got there. He found her in Evan's room, getting him ready for his bath.

"If you're happy and you know it, clap your hands," she sang as she wrapped Evan in a towel.

Evan put his little hands together and giggled at his mother.

"Hey, guys," he said, leaning in to kiss her. "I didn't end up going to Tarantella's, but I'll just call and have a pizza delivered."

She gave him a puzzled look. "Why not?"

"I'll tell you after bedtime."

"Okay."

"Da Da." Evan started wiggling out of her arms, reaching for Jack, who happily took him.

"I already fed him. I was just getting ready to give him a bath and then put him down," she said.

He handed Evan back to her. "I'll go call for pizza." There was no way he could make small talk right now. He walked downstairs, his stomach still in knots, and poured himself a scotch. Throwing it back in one swallow, he poured another and took a few deep breaths. After ordering the pizza, he opened his laptop and did a search for recent news stories. Nothing yet on what had just happened. He reread his notes from his interview with Maggie's husband and her friend. He couldn't make sense of it. Something was happening to make people lose their minds. He was still thinking about it when Taylor came into the kitchen and touched his arm.

"I met Crosby Wheeler yesterday," she told him.

He raised his eyebrows at her in a *go on* gesture.

"He gave me the creeps. Something about him made me so uncomfortable."

"Well, he doesn't have a reputation for being the nicest guy. It *was* his network that ran *Teenage Wasted* and he kept it on even after the lawsuit and those kids getting hurt. What does Karen think of him?"

Taylor shook her head. "She seems to respect him, but to be honest, she also seems a bit scared of him. They all do. Maybe he's just austere, and I'm being paranoid."

"You know what they say: just because you're paranoid doesn't mean they're not after you."

Taylor gave him a sidelong look. "Not helping."

"Listen, I need to tell you something."

She gave him a concerned look. "What's wrong?"

Jack was trying to figure out the best way to relay what had happened without sending Taylor into a panic. "I did actually stop at Tarantella's but before I could go inside, something happened on the sidewalk. I saw a man choking a woman. I think they were a couple, but I'm not sure."

"What are you saying? A couple had a fight outside the restaurant?"

"It was more than a fight. The guy was nuts. He was ranting, cussing, and choking her. It was like he had superhuman strength." Jack took a breath and shook his head. "We tried to save her, but it was too late. He ran when the police showed up and a truck hit him. They're both dead."

Her mouth fell open. "Are you serious? It's like those other stories on the news . . ."

"Exactly."

"Jack, that's only five minutes from here! What is going on? This is terrifying."

"I know. But we can't panic. The only thing we can do is be vigilant. Don't open the door for anyone you don't know."

"I wouldn't do that anyway. But do you have any theories on what's going on?"

"There has to be something linking them all. I don't know what yet. I interviewed the husband of that woman, Maggie, who killed her son's Little League coach. He's still so raw, it was . . . brutal."

Taylor replied, sympathy in her voice, "I can imagine. Did he have any indication that she was capable of something like that?"

"No. Nothing. Neither did her best friend." He shrugged. "It makes no sense. I've got to talk to some more families to see if I can detect any sort of pattern besides all the incidents happening on the East Coast."

"That does seem to support your theory about some kind of contamination. What's your next move?"

"I'm going to drive up to Boston tomorrow to interview the husband of the woman who flipped out during their marriage counseling session and pulled a gun out and shot the priest."

Taylor shivered. "How is the priest doing?"

"Fortunately, he's going to make it; in fact, I'm scheduled to stop by the hospital and see him, too. But the woman succeeded in killing herself."

She looked at Jack. "You've got to talk to the police. Make them all talk to one another. There needs to be more eyes on this."

"I've been thinking the same thing. I'm going to swing by the police station in the morning before I head out." He took another sip of his drink. "Whether or not this is a part of a bigger plan versus some accidental toxin remains to be seen, but either way, it's not necessarily going to stop on its own. I'll talk to the priest in the morning, then the husband in the afternoon."

Taylor asked, "Will you stay over at your sister's tomorrow night? I'm sure she'd love to see you."

"I was going to, but not after what just happened. I want to be here. I'll be back as early as I can tomorrow night." He was suddenly overcome with the need to be close to her, to eradicate the dark images in his mind. He forced a light tone. "Let's go to bed," he said as he pulled her toward him and put his lips on hers. "I've been looking forward to getting you there all day." A small voice in the back of his mind warned him that the longer he put off telling her about the call from Dakota, the more upset she would be, but he wasn't about to let that spoil their evening. He'd tell her tomorrow.

She pressed herself against him and ran her hand through his hair. "That makes two of us."

○ ○ ○

When Jack woke up, the bed was empty. He heard Taylor's voice coming from Evan's room and, rubbing his eyes, he rolled out of bed and joined them.

"Good morning! We were just coming in to wake you up," Taylor said.

"Da Da." Evan reached out to him and Jack took him from Taylor's arms.

"How's my boy this morning?"

Evan reached out and patted Jack's face in response, then blew some raspberries. Jack looked at Taylor and laughed.

"Come with Mommy to feed Beau and let Daddy get dressed," she said to Evan, and Jack put him down.

He took a quick shower and got dressed. When he went downstairs, Evan was on the floor with Beau, and Taylor was making eggs.

She turned around at the sound of his footsteps. "Hungry?"

"Nah. I'll just grab a cup of coffee before I go." He poured himself a cup. "I forgot to tell you about my visit to the school, and my conversation with the nun. I meant to fill you in last night, but you distracted me."

She tilted her head. "Well, don't expect an apology."

He pulled her to him and kissed her on the lips. "Not a chance."

"So?" she asked after he pulled away.

"We might have a lead. Sister Francis remembered a little boy, around three, that was adopted by a couple with the story Jonas used."

"That's great. Did she know anything about the boy's real family?"

He shook his head. "Not really. A few things for me to follow up on." He paused a long moment. It was now or never.

"Listen, I got a phone call yesterday." He winced before continuing. "From Dakota."

She whirled around and stared at him. "What?"

"Yeah, she reached out to me for help."

Taylor glared at him. "Are you kidding me? What the . . ."

He put a hand up. "I know, I know. I almost hung up on her, but her Aunt Sybil is dying."

Taylor's eyes blazed. "What does that have to do with you?"

He conveyed their conversation to her.

"So, what? You're supposed to go flying off to Mexico to give her her passport? You can't believe a word that woman says. How do you even know Sybil is sick? This is ridiculous. With everything that's going on, you can't seriously be considering doing it?"

He hated seeing her so upset and he didn't blame her, but she had to understand how conflicted he was too. "Of course I'm not going to Mexico. I'm just going to call Sybil and see if it's true. Figure out a way to help somehow."

Taylor started to speak then closed her mouth, finally saying, "I can't even . . ." She picked Evan up, gave Jack a disgusted look, and stormed from the kitchen. He started to go after her, then thought better of it. *Let her cool down.*

"Guess it's just you and me, huh, furball?"

Beau gave him a measured look, then turned and left the kitchen, too.

"You're mad at me, too?" he asked, grabbing his keys and heading for the door. He needed to take a drive and think. He'd known Taylor would be angry, but he thought they'd be able to talk it out. Wasn't she always telling him to open up, that the two of them could work anything out as long as they were honest with each other? Then when he was up front with her, the first thing she did was bolt. So much for honesty.

CHAPTER SIXTEEN

Leonard Reed was irritated. He was supposed to be on his way to Sissy's apartment, but his wife had called and insisted he come home immediately. He'd had a long day and had been looking forward to one of Sissy's long massages that ended very happily. He pulled out his phone and sent a short text to Sissy. Can't make it. Something came up. He could have explained that he had a situation at home, but he preferred to be vague. It would keep her on her toes. Let her wonder if he was seeing someone else. He also could have refused his wife, Patrice, but the grief he would have to endure wasn't worth it. It was easier to go home and deal with whatever drama she had drummed up. He had to play the good husband; otherwise, she'd go into another one of her fits of depression, upsetting the whole household. And while he might not give a crap about her, he did dote on his eight-year-old twins who were, unfortunately, very close to their mother.

Before he left for the day, he unlocked his center desk drawer and pulled out his burner phone. He dialed the number, put in the code, and hung up. A minute later a second burner rang and he snapped it up.

"It's Reed."

"Well, this had better be important. I was just about ready to cut into a six-inch filet," Vice President Brody Hamilton boomed through the receiver.

"I just wanted to double-check that we're still on in two weeks for the event."

"Why wouldn't we be? I told you last week it's on. I swear, you're more nervous than a long-tailed cat in a room full of rocking chairs."

Leonard rolled his eyes. Hamilton and his stupid expressions. Did he really think anyone was still buying that corny southern crap? "I'm being thorough, that's all. Our boss wants to make sure that everything stays on course. You know as well as I that the president's schedule is volatile. We need to make sure this is nailed down, rock solid."

"Well, I ain't the president's chief of staff." Hamilton's laughter came over the line. "But lucky for us, she's under my thumb, among under things. Don't you worry. It'll go off without a hitch, and if some national emergency crops up and we have to reschedule, I'll let you know. Now, if there's nothing else, my steak's getting cold."

○ ○ ○

Leonard pulled up to the gated driveway of his Stamford, Connecticut, home and hit the button on the visor of his BMW 740e. The iron gates swung open and he made his way up the long driveway to the white plantation-style house. Pulling into the four-car garage, he killed the engine and got out of the car, steel-ing himself for the crisis du jour. The garage door entrance led into the kitchen, where the twins, Dolly and Darcy, were sitting at the enormous island, eating spaghetti, while Lena, their house-keeper, was doing dishes.

"Daddy!" They both jumped down from their stools and ran into his arms.

"How are my two princesses?" he asked, enveloping them both in a hug.

Before they could answer, his wife, Patrice, walked in and cut them off.

"Darlings, I need to talk to Daddy. You can tell him about your day later." She turned to Leonard. "I've got a drink waiting for you in the library."

He sighed and followed her. Despite his annoyance, he had to admit that the sight of her backside in those tight pants was arousing. But sex with Patrice always exacted a price, and he was in no mood to pay. It was easier to go elsewhere, and more fun anyway. He walked into the library, a room that never failed to impress guests with its shiny oak floor-to-ceiling bookcases filled with first editions. A wooden staircase led to a second-level bal-cony for reaching the books on top shelves. The furniture was Queen Anne style but the focal point of the room was the antique wooden desk that he took pleasure in telling guests had belonged to Thomas Jefferson. The Oriental rug covering the shiny hard-wood floor had cost him a fortune. He took a seat in one of the leather club chairs in front of the library table, where Patrice had placed a glass of port. He took a long swig, then wiped his mouth with the back of his hand.

Patrice rolled her eyes. "There's a napkin right there. Hon-estly, Leonard, a man with a bank account your size should have a little more couth."

He resisted the urge to tell her where she could put her couth and instead pressed his lips together. "Okay, I'm home. What's the big emergency?"

"It's my mother. Her doctor wants to do a scan to make sure her cancer hasn't come back. She wasn't due to have another scan for three more months, but she hasn't been feeling well lately and her symptoms are worrying the doctor. But they can't do it now because her health insurance company—*your* company—denied the procedure."

He narrowed his eyes. "How was her blood work? Did it come back normal?"

Patrice began to pace, wringing the napkin in her hands. "I guess it was normal. It didn't show any markers of cancer. But you know as well as I do that's not a guarantee that the cancer's not back. Obviously if blood work was the be-all and end-all, they wouldn't do scans and MRIs. Her doctor says if there's something brewing and they catch it early, she has a better prognosis. What is she supposed to do, wait three months to find out that it's back but that it's spread because they didn't treat it? It's ridiculous!" Her face was red, and her eyes were practically bulging out of her pretty little head.

He felt the heat spread to his face. "What are you bothering me with this for? Her doctor should just appeal the denial and explain why they need it sooner. I can't get involved at this level. I'm the frickin' CEO for crying out loud."

Her face turned redder. "Yeah, I know that. What I want to know is when your damn company changed from an insurance firm to a medical practice. What the hell do your claims people know about what's necessary and what's not? They should leave the doctoring to the doctors. It's disgusting."

"Disgusting?" He stood up and pointed around the room. "You like living here in this nice house? Driving that top-of-the-line Mercedes and having our children in the best school in the state?" She was just staring at him. "How about that expensive nanny, or the housekeeper, or the Pilates instructor that helps you keep your ass so tight? Well, you wouldn't have any of that if I didn't do my job and make my company money. So if a few people die a few months earlier than they night have otherwise, that's the cost of doing business."

"You can't be—"

He put a hand up to silence her. "Tell your mother to have the test. I'll pay for it. She can afford to pay for it herself, but never mind. Put it on my tab, just like everything else." He shook his head. "That's what's wrong with the country. People always looking for a handout. Blaming us. How about people take better care of themselves? Half the problems people face are of their own making. My company should pay for diabetes meds for people who won't lose weight? Or lung cancer treatment for smokers?"

"Are you saying that it's my mother's fault that she has cancer?"

"No. But what I *am* saying is that this is what happens when we have to pay the price for other people's poor choices—it ends up costing everyone. I have to look out for my stockholders. I have an obligation to them. And you certainly have benefited from my ability to do a good job. So get off your high horse."

"How dare you blame me for your soulless decisions about people's lives? I never asked for any of this."

He snorted. "Yeah, well, you never turned it down, either."

"I wish—"

"Save it. I know what you wish. That you could have a divorce. But I'll never let you have the kids. You can walk away, but they stay."

Patrice turned and strode from the room without another word. With his money and connections, Leonard knew that if she ever left, she'd be lucky to see the girls on the weekends. It was the only leverage he had to keep her from divorcing him. He really wouldn't have minded so much if she did, but he liked the appearance of the happy family she provided. He was the benevolent face of Jefferson Health Care and their Christmas cards wouldn't look as wholesome without a wife in the picture.

CHAPTER SEVENTEEN

STILL FURIOUS WITH JACK, TAYLOR PACKED UP EVAN AND GOT on the road after breakfast. Just hearing the name Dakota brought it all back to her. The memory of the only time Taylor had met her came rushing back. Wild red hair, icy blue eyes full of challenge, and those plump red lips giving Taylor a nasty smile then taunting her with her references to Jack as her husband. It had taken Taylor years to forgive him for his betrayal and despite knowing that Damon Crosse had been the one to place Dakota in Jack's path, it still cut her to the core every time she thought about them being together. And now Dakota was back and wanted Jack to help her? It was unthinkable. As soon as he had heard Dakota's voice he should have ended the call. Scenario after scenario filled her mind the entire drive and by the time she arrived at UBC her mood was dark. She drove into the underground parking lot and pulled into a space. Picking up her phone, she saw she had three missed calls from Jack and one text message. Please call me. I hate leaving like this. I'll try you again when I get to Boston if I don't hear from you before then. I love you!

She threw the phone into her purse.

When she freed Evan from his car seat, he started to fuss. "Walk, Mama."

"Okay, one minute, sweetie. After we get to the elevator, you can walk."

"No, walk! Now!"

There was no way she was letting him walk by himself in the parking garage. She tightened her hold as he tried to wiggle out of her arms.

"Evan, please. Just one minute." Her tone was sharper than she intended, and he started to cry.

Sighing, she hurried through the garage until they reached the elevator. Once inside, she put him down and reached for his hand, but he pulled away and stood in the corner. She let him be. At least he was safe in here, since the elevator opened into the actual office building. When the doors opened, he ran out ahead of her and she had to chase him down the hall before going through security. Not an auspicious start to her day. She reached him and scooped him up amid more squeals of protest.

When they got to the daycare center, he ran over to the bookcase and grabbed the same book of fairy tales from the day before and sat down on a beanbag chair.

Taylor rolled her eyes. "It's been quite the morning. He's a little out of sorts," she told Delilah.

The woman smiled and patted Taylor's arm. "It's hard being little. They can't communicate as well as they'd like. They get frustrated."

They're not the only ones, Taylor thought. She went over to her son and knelt next to him. "Evan, please look at Mommy."

He looked up, his big brown eyes earnest.

"Sweetie, it's not safe for you to run from Mommy. I know you wanted to walk, but I have to keep you safe. Okay?"

He gave her a solemn nod, then threw his arms around her. "Mama read."

She opened the book. "Which story?" She began to read from "The Frog Prince," but after a few words, he shook his head.

"No, no, no. Me." He pointed a finger at his chest.

She tried again but he grabbed the book from her and threw it on the floor.

Taylor stood up. "I think it's time for Mommy to go to work." She leaned down to kiss him. "Have fun. I love you."

Delilah gave her a sympathetic look. "He'll be fine."

Evan threw his arms around Taylor's neck and gave her a wet kiss on her cheek. Her heart melted. "See you soon. Be a good boy."

She left before any more theatrics could ensue and took the elevator to Karen's office on the twentieth floor. Karen was traveling for a story today so she'd offered her space to Taylor, who had scheduled two Skype interviews with families she'd identified as possible substitutes for Cora's.

"Morning, Krystal," she greeted Karen's admin.

"Hey, Taylor. Can I get you anything?"

"I'm good, thanks. I'll grab a coffee in a bit."

She flipped the light switch on and the lamp on the glass desk illuminated the room with soft light. Walking over to the large window, she gazed out at Central Park. The magnificent view from Karen's office never failed to lift her spirits. She forced Dakota from her mind, telling herself she'd deal with it when Jack got home from Boston. It was probably better that they had some time to cool off anyway. Opening her laptop, she went over her notes from her meeting with Molly and Clyde Edwards and emailed the camera team to get some available times to set up the recorded interview. Going through the rest of her emails took another hour, and feeling stiff, she got up and stretched,

then made her way to the kitchen, where she popped a pod into
the coffee maker and debated whether or not to stop in for a
quick check on Evan. After his rough morning, it might not be
wise, but she decided she needed to, for her own peace of mind.
When she got there, the nap time sign was up, but she turned
the doorknob anyway. It was locked. She stood there a moment,
paralyzed by indecision, but unable to walk away. Her stomach
suddenly in knots, she took a deep breath and rapped on the
door. It opened and Delilah, holding an infant in her arms, put
her finger to her lips.

"Sorry," Taylor whispered. "I just wanted to check on Evan."

Delilah pointed. Evan was asleep in one of the toddler beds.

Feeling suddenly foolish, she mouthed *thank you* and backed
out of the room. She returned to Karen's office and reviewed the
age discrimination cases. Georgia Lakos was an eighty-year-old
woman who had been active and vibrant until she began to ex-
perience shortness of breath and chest pains upon exertion. She
worked full-time as a professor at the University of Connecticut
and had been healthy and fit her entire life, so she'd been shocked
when her internist had referred her to a cardiologist. After an
echocardiogram, they discovered that her mitral valve needed replacing. She'd had scarlet fever as a child, which had apparently
weakened it.

The doctor's office submitted the paperwork for the surgery,
but the insurance company denied the claim, stating that her
age made it too dangerous and that, statistically, the outcome of
such a surgery for those eighty and over had a low percentage of
success. Since she was still working and had insurance, she hadn't
enrolled in Medicare Part B, which would have covered the procedure. If she'd wanted to proceed with no insurance, she'd have
been looking at close to fifty thousand dollars in medical bills. If
she hadn't had the surgery, she would have continued to decline.

Fortunately for Georgia, her son, a successful attorney, had had the money to pay for the surgery and did. He was the one who had initiated the class action lawsuit against Jefferson Health.

Georgia's surgery had been successful and within two months, she was back at work full-time, doing her gardening and taking her daily three-mile walk. Taylor clicked through the photos and was surprised to see how young Georgia looked. Even though she was now eighty-one, she could have easily passed for someone in her sixties. She had light brown hair, the gray most likely removed at the salon, and a pretty face, with warm, intelligent eyes. Reading about a woman in her eighties brought to mind someone frail and gray, and Taylor knew that stereotype existed in most people's minds. It would be good for the public to see the new face of eighty and to realize that people shouldn't have an expiration date forced on them. Georgia lived in Greenwich, and Taylor decided to take a chance and see if she might be available for a visit. Her home was only about 40 minutes north of the city.

○   ○   ○

After a quick phone call, Taylor was on the road, and less than an hour later, she arrived on Georgia's street and pulled up to a small blue Cape Cod in a quaint neighborhood. The outside was pristine, with vibrant pink and purple azalea bushes lining both sides of the front of the house. The front door was open, and not finding a doorbell, Taylor knocked on the screen door. She heard heels clicking and watched as a trim woman dressed neatly in a stylish navy skirt and cream silk blouse walked toward her. She looked even younger in person. She opened the door and extended her hand to Taylor.

"Ms. Parks, please come in."

"Please call me Taylor. Your azaleas are just gorgeous."

Georgia Lakos smiled at her, her brown eyes warm. "Thank you. Shall we go in the kitchen? I've put some coffee on."

Taylor followed her through the hallway to a cozy kitchen where a gentle breeze blew in from the open window over the sink. Taking a seat at the round wooden table, she noticed the *Times* crossword puzzle already three-quarters of the way finished, and in ink no less.

"How do you take your coffee, Taylor?"

"A little cream, please. Thank you, Dr. Lakos."

"Georgia, please."

"Thank you again for seeing me, especially on such short notice," Taylor said, then she asked, "Is Lakos Greek?"

Georgia smiled. "Yes. I'm first generation. My parents came over in their twenties."

"I'm half Greek. On my mother's side."

"*Milás Elliniká?*" Georgia asked.

"I speak a little Greek, but not well, I'm afraid. I'm out of practice."

Georgia put a hand on hers. "You must learn. One's heritage is very important. You've been to Greece, yes?"

"Many times. I haven't been in a few years but I'm planning to get there when my son's a little older. My family is from Patmos."

Georgia's eyes widened. "My family is as well! It's a beautiful island."

Taylor thought for a moment. "Lakos, Lakos . . . now I know why your name seemed familiar. Are you related to Panos Lakos? The doctor?"

Georgia smiled. "He's my cousin! Do you know him?"

Taylor nodded. "Yes, a few years ago when I was there with my late husband I sprained my ankle. After I saw Dr. Lakos at the clinic, he followed up a few times at my aunt's house. Such a kind man."

"What a small world," Georgia said.

"Well, I guess we should get started. I know you're a professor at UConn. You teach neuroscience, right?"

"Yes. The brain is a fascinating organ. So much of our behavior is influenced by chemicals. People tend to think their behavior is completely in their control. They don't realize how often other factors come into play."

Taylor was intrigued. "This is uncanny, actually—my husband is also a journalist and is working on a story right now where people seem to be acting out of character. There's been a string of violent crimes, all committed by previously model citizens. He's trying to see if there's something that connects them all."

The older woman tilted her head. "I saw something a few weeks ago on the news about that woman who killed her son's Little League coach. Are you saying there are more?"

Taylor nodded. "Eighteen, I think. All on the East Coast."

"That's very odd indeed."

Taylor cleared her throat. "So, back to the case with Jefferson Health. The angle we would take with your story would be that you were discriminated against based on age. I'd really love for our viewers to see you and to see that eighty is just a number and that—"

"I'm not washed up yet?" Georgia interrupted with a teasing tone.

"No. I didn't mean that." Taylor felt her cheeks grow warm.

Georgia patted Taylor's hand. "I know you didn't. Listen, I get it. My students almost fall off their chairs when I tell them my age. I want people to see that age *is* just a number. That you can be old at forty and young at ninety. There's no doubt in my mind that Jefferson thinks that their money is wasted trying to save the lives of anyone of advanced age. And, yes, I look young. But even if I didn't, it would still be wrong. Even if I were frail and wrinkled, who are they to dictate who gets to live and who gets to die?"

Taylor nodded. "I couldn't agree more. They've been playing God. I'm hoping we can stir the public up to say *enough*."

Georgia sighed. "I hope so, too, but I think everyone has become resigned to the fact that it's a losing battle. I was so lucky that my son had the means to pay for my surgery, but most people don't have that luxury. It's criminal."

"So you'll come on the show?" Taylor asked.

"Yes. I'd be honored to."

"Well, I need to get back and pick up my son from daycare. It was so nice talking to you. I'll get back to you after I speak with Ms. Printz and we're able to finalize the details. I'll likely come back with a camera crew and get the interview filmed next week."

"That sounds fine."

Taylor really liked this woman and acted on impulse when she said, "Any chance you're free tomorrow? I'd love to have you come over for dinner and meet Jack. Maybe you could shed some expert light onto his story."

"That sounds lovely."

Taylor wrote down her address on the back of her business card and handed it to her. "Shall we say five?"

"Perfect. I'll bring wine."

Taylor left feeling buoyed by the visit and her mood lifted even more as she thought about spending more time with Georgia. There was something so warm and genuine about her. Taylor hoped that when she was eighty, she'd have half the energy and verve that Georgia had, but more than that, she'd felt a connection to her interviewee. For a moment, she allowed herself to think of what her own mother would have been like if she'd lived. The familiar pain returned, and she took a deep breath.

* * *

It was just after four when Taylor pulled into the parking lot at UBC. She hurried to the elevator, suddenly anxious to see Evan. When she got to the daycare, he was lying on one of the sofas, hugging his stuffed dinosaur.

"Hi, pumpkin. You okay?"

He didn't move, but just looked at Taylor with sad eyes. She walked over and put a hand on his forehead. He didn't feel warm, but he did look a little pale.

"Has he been like this all day?" she asked Delilah, who was helping a little girl with her snack. She felt the fingers of fear grip her and she wondered if the warning about Evan had been about his health.

Delilah turned to Taylor. "No. Just in the past half hour. He had a good day, but he's a little tired. I think he's ready to go home."

Taylor leaned down and stroked his hair. "Come on, sweetie. Let's go."

He stood and held his arms up to Taylor, dropping the stuffed animal. "Up." She scooped him up as Delilah picked up the dinosaur and handed it to him. He put his head on her shoulder and his thumb in his mouth.

Delilah put a hand on Taylor's arm. "Taylor, about earlier . . ."

Taylor turned to her. "I'm sorry. I know I shouldn't have disturbed you during nap time. It won't happen again."

The woman smiled at her. "Thank you. I hope you know that

if there were anything of concern going on with Evan, I'd call you immediately."

Taylor nodded. "I do know. I'm sorry if I gave you the impression that I have anything but the fullest trust in you. It's just been a rough few days, and I needed to see him, but I'll respect the rules." Even as the words left her lips, she realized she only half meant it. She understood that they needed to have rules, but a part of her bristled at being told she couldn't see her own child whenever she wanted.

Delilah smiled at her. "Wonderful. Thanks for understanding."

"All right, sweet boy. Let's go."

Evan was quiet when Taylor put him in his car seat and asleep before they even pulled out of the parking lot. She hoped he wasn't coming down with something.

She wasn't looking forward to the inevitable confrontation with Jack tonight. She grudgingly admitted to herself that Jack's sense of loyalty—a trait she admired—could sometimes make him behave in ways she found hard to understand. Sybil had been the one who had comforted Jack during those times when Dakota was acting crazy and making his life miserable. But still, the thought of him even being in the same room with Dakota, much less coming to her rescue, made Taylor feel physically ill. Up until now, things had been so easy between Jack and her. After finding each other again, they'd been nearly inseparable these past couple of years. They'd easily fallen into their roles as husband and wife and parents to Evan. Jack had cared about Evan before he was even born and had done everything in his power to protect Taylor's pregnancy during their time running from Crosse. It didn't matter that Evan wasn't his blood; Jack was as much his father as Taylor was his mother. The voice of reason told her that she had nothing to fear from Dakota, that she wasn't a threat to their relationship and that Jack knew what a horrible person Dakota was. But the part of her that had been betrayed by those closest to her wouldn't stand down and made her wonder if the past few years with Jack had just been a pleasant illusion. An interlude of happiness that was about to end.

Her thoughts drifted to the other man who'd betrayed her, the one she'd always believed to be her real father, and she felt a tightness in her chest as a deep sadness overcame her. Even after all this time, she was unable to reconcile the memories of Warwick Parks with the man who had almost killed her. She didn't know what she was supposed to do with her memories—images of Warwick were intermingled with some of her happiest times with her mother. How could she discard him without losing the precious moments with the woman she'd loved so much? She'd grown up thinking he was a loving father only to find out he didn't care any more about her than he did an expensive piece of furniture or collectible bottle of wine. Was Jack going to break her heart, too? She wiped a tear from her cheek and took a deep breath, sitting up straighter. She wasn't about to be a victim again. Whatever was in Jack's heart and mind, she planned to lay it bare. She wasn't going to just sit back and let that woman poison their lives again.

CHAPTER EIGHTEEN

DAMON DEPLANED AT LUTON AIRPORT, WHERE A WAITING limousine drove him to the flat he'd just purchased in Kensington. Running the television network as Crosby Wheeler had helped him to further his plan to continue manipulating the public, but the tide was now turned so far in his favor that his leadership soon wouldn't be required. After he took control of the highest office in the land, he would appoint a new head of UBC in New York and fly to Washington, D.C., when necessary. But most things could be handled remotely these days, and he looked forward to being in London. Eventually he'd find a secluded country house outside the city as well, but for now, this would do.

Before he unpacked his suitcase, he peeked into the bedroom next to his. It was a little boy's dream, at least he hoped so. He'd asked the estate agent to put together the perfect bedroom for a boy. Model airplanes hung from the ceiling and bright green bookcases held stuffed animals, blocks, board books, and every toy imaginable. He'd never done anything remotely like this for Jeremy, and that may have been a mistake. He'd raised Jeremy at a distance, pushed him relentlessly to achieve, and look what had happened. This time he would make no such errors. He'd learned over the years how to affect emotion and pretend to care, and he would continue to do both until Evan believed he was a benevolent grandfather who could be loved and trusted. He would hire a nanny to do the lion's share of the childcare when Evan was small, but as the boy grew, he would teach and guide him, and their relationship would become more interesting. But those vital early years would require some coddling and giving him a sense of safety.

Damon thought back to his own upbringing, where filth and chaos reigned, and wondered again what would have happened to him if he'd never met Friedrich. When he was fourteen and his father had insisted he take the job as a companion to the invalid living in the house on the hill, he'd been furious. But refusing his father was not an option—at least not then. So he'd gone after school one day, trudging up the steep hill to the enormous colonial waiting at the top. He could still see himself in the moment that would mark the beginning of his rebirth: the gangly boy standing in the pouring rain, staring through the window at the man in the wheelchair. He hadn't flinched when the man's rheumy eyes met his through the glass, nor had he felt any sympathy for him. Instead, he had seethed with fury at the injustice of being made to come. Why did *he* have to look after some ancient war hero? War was for idiots, and he felt nothing but contempt for those who stupidly gave their lives for an abstract concept or propaganda handed down by corrupt politicians.

This was going to be a complete waste of his time—time that would be much better spent devouring his beloved books, the

only things in his life that gave him any pleasure. As he stood
staring, unmoving, he'd been startled to see a sardonic smile
spread over the man's face. It transformed his previously banal
expression, and the intelligence now evident in the man's watery
eyes beckoned to him on the doorstep. The door opened slowly,
and his elderly neighbor nodded, an acknowledgment of what
had passed between them.

"I have been waiting for you. Come in." The man's heavy
German accent was a surprise.

Damon had entered without another thought. His eyes
swept the imposing marble hallway and sweeping staircase and
the chair attached to it by metal bars. He took his time examining the oil paintings and sculptures around him, not yet knowing
that they were priceless works of art.

The man was patient and kept silent until he had taken it all
in. "Come with me into the study and we can begin." He pivoted
in his wheelchair and rolled down the hallway.

He had obediently followed the older man down the
dark, narrow passageway until they reached a large doorway on
the right. He'd felt a quiver of excitement when his eyes swept the
room. Books. Hundreds of them. Ceiling to floor, every square
inch festooned in books. The leather spines filled the shiny ma-
hogany shelves. They were beautiful, a bibliophile's nirvana—his
nirvana. He continued to take it all in, amazement and wonder
filling him like never before.

The man spoke. "I thought you would be pleased."

The boy's eyes darted to meet his. What did that mean?

The man laughed, a deep, satisfied chortle. "Ah, I see. You
thought you were here on a charity mission. No, my boy. I have
been watching you. You have more brains in your pinky than all
those nitwits put together. I have been waiting a long time for
someone with a mind like yours."

Damon had wondered what the crazy old man was talking about, if this was perhaps a twisted joke. He wouldn't put it past those cretins at his school to have set this up to humiliate him. And his parents would be just stupid enough to buy it. He wasn't going to hang around and see what this pervert really wanted from him—no matter how big his library was.

The man seemed to sense his discomfort. "It is not what you think. My tastes do not run to young boys." He sighed. "I am weary of all the imbeciles surrounding me. I long to discuss philosophy and science with someone worthy of my attention." He brought his hand down hard and slammed it on the armrest of his wheelchair. "But this damn thing limits me. For years I have waited and finally I found you, and you seem to have been gifted with intelligence. I believe we can accomplish great things together."

He took in the man's words. Damon, too, was sick of the inane conversations that surrounded him on an hourly basis, assaulting his senses. In all his fourteen years, he had yet to meet one—just one—person who could relate to him or appreciate his genius. The things they all thought about! Their pitiful worries and mediocre dreams disgusted him. How often had he lain in bed inventing escape scenarios where he would be rescued from the dreary, colorless existence he was chained to? His parents were the worst of all. How he came from two such ordinary, plodding nothings, he would never comprehend. They were weak. They smoked like chimneys, and what few brain cells they still possessed they set to destroying with their cheap booze. By nine o'clock every night they were both passed out, drooling and snoring on the worn and soiled sofa. What did they know of their son's gift? Was it possible that there was actually someone in this godforsaken town who recognized how special he was? Who wouldn't treat him like a freak and

invent new ways to taunt him? What did he have to lose? He
had looked at the man.

"Tell me more."

That had been the beginning of everything. And now Damon would be the same thing for Evan: a teacher, someone who
could set him free from Jack and Taylor, another set of parents
who were unworthy of raising their child.

CHAPTER NINETEEN

JACK SWORE AS HE HEARD TAYLOR'S OUTGOING VOICE-MAIL greeting come over his car's Bluetooth. He understood that she was upset, but she didn't have to act like a child and ignore him. He should have talked to Sybil and tried to find out if Dakota was on the level before even bringing it up with Taylor. No more secrets. No more lies. Yeah, look how well that turned out. He found the contact for Sybil in his phone and placed another call. He tapped his fingers on the steering wheel as the phone rang.

He was en route to Brigham and Women's Hospital to talk to the priest who had been shot. The priest had been lucky—the bullet had only grazed his shoulder—but he'd be in the hospital a few more days recovering from surgery.

"Hello?"

He recognized her voice right away. "Sybil. It's Jack."

"Hello, Jack. I've been expecting your call."

Her voice was flat. He'd thought at least she would have been happy to hear from him, but then again, she was sick and not herself. "I guess Dakota told you about her situation. I hope you can understand my hesitation to get involved."

"Yes, of course. It's kind of you to even consider helping her."

This was more awkward that he'd anticipated. "Okay, well. Listen, I'm very sorry to hear that you're not well. Dakota told me you were sick. That's the only reason . . . you know . . . if it helps you having her come back—"

"I'm not up to talking right now. But yes, I'm sick. Dying. Marcel's in a long-term facility so I have no one to take care of me besides Dakota. I still need to go to the bank where her passport is in a safe deposit box but have to wait until I have enough energy. Once I get her passport, I'll call you. Okay?"

"Um, sure. Okay."

"Bye, Jack." She ended the call, and he felt disconcerted by their conversation. She had sounded so robotic and unemotional. But at least he now knew that Dakota had been telling the truth about Sybil being sick. Dakota's aunt and uncle had no children and had treated Dakota like their daughter. They'd been heartbroken when she'd killed the unborn child she was carrying in an insane attempt to hurt Jack. The days following that horrendous act had been the darkest of Jack's life. Before that Dakota had made his life a living hell, but when she'd gotten pregnant he'd known he couldn't leave her and abandon his child. But despite his best efforts to protect their child, he ultimately failed when Dakota drove that knife into her stomach. It was Sybil who came over day after day, checking up on him, clearing away the empty bottles of vodka he'd consumed, making him eat, and refusing to allow him to wallow in regret. He didn't know if he'd have made it through if not for her. And now she was all alone, and there was no way he could turn his back on her. No matter how terrible a person Jack believed Dakota to be, Sybil loved her, and Sybil would want to have her with her. So that meant that Jack had to try to help her. He'd make Taylor understand somehow.

As he drove down the Mass Turnpike, he thought about the last time he'd been in Boston when he and Taylor were on the run from Damon Crosse and had to dump his Mustang into the Charles River. He still felt bad about that on more than one count, not the least of which was pollution. He put his signal on to change lanes, and the car in the left lane sped up. *Boston drivers.* He turned the indicator off, waiting for an opening, and darted over.

When he reached the hospital and made his way to the priest's room, Jack was surprised to realize that he was nervous. The last time he'd spent any time with a Catholic priest had been when he was a teenager, back when he was an altar boy. He'd always felt like priests read his mind, which more often than not was full of thoughts he preferred to keep to himself. Shaking off the jitters, he strode with purpose from the elevator into the hallway and toward Father Murphy's room. He heard voices as he approached and, when he reached the open doorway, saw two older women sitting by the hospital bed where the patient lay. Jack rapped on the doorframe, and they looked up.

"Sorry to interrupt. I'm Jack Logan. I'm here to talk to Father Murphy."

The priest looked over at him and smiled. "Come in." He nodded at his guests. "Thank you for the goodies. I'm sure I'll enjoy the brownies as well as the chicken soup."

They got up, looking a little put out at Jack's interruption.

"Okay, Father. You have our numbers if you need anything. We'll be back to check on you tomorrow."

"It's not necessary . . ."

One put her hand up. "Nonsense. You take care of us all the time. It's time for us to look after you."

Jack took one of the seats they had vacated and waited for the women to gather their things.

Once they had left, Father Murphy gave Jack a wry look. "They mean well, but I'm happy for the interruption. I couldn't listen to one more idea for the church bake sale."

Jack gave him a weak smile in return, still feeling uneasy. "How are you feeling, Father?"

"Good. Happy to be alive. The good Lord was looking out for me, I'll tell you that. Never seen anything like it in all my years in the church."

Jack nodded. "I'm sure. I know that you're bound to keep your counseling sessions confidential, but I'm hoping since Mrs. Doyle is deceased you might be willing to share a bit. Anything you can tell me may shed some light on this . . . recent phenomenon."

Father Murphy gave Jack a measured look. "Before we get started, can you explain what you mean by *phenomenon*?"

"There have been a few similar incidents lately, in which people with no criminal past have gone off the rails and killed others and themselves, with little or no warning or provocation."

The priest said, "I had no idea. I haven't seen anything like that on the news."

Jack thought about some of his other interviews. Everyone had said the same thing. But it was odd—normally, you could turn on the local news in Minnesota and hear the same feel-good story about a cat who found its way home that you would hear in California. Likewise, bad news traveled incredibly fast. So why were these stories being reported in isolation? "Well, I can assure you it's happening. One online search will show you that your case is the eighteenth just in the past month."

Father Murphy's eyebrows rose. "That's . . . crazy."

Jack nodded. "Yes. I just met with a man whose wife killed her son's Little League coach."

The priest's eyes widened, and he shook his head. "Evil is running rampant. It's getting worse every day."

"I think there may be more at play here than just evil. I'm trying to figure out if there's some sort of connection between the cases. A medication that the perpetrators have in common or somewhere they've all been recently."

The father shrugged. "I can't tell you about what medicine Shannon might have taken, but I'm sure Brian can. What I *can* tell you, though, is that I would have never in a million years thought she could be violent. She and Brian were devout Catholics who never missed a Sunday. She was a God-fearing woman who was trying to put their marriage back on track."

"Had they been coming to counseling for a long time?"

"About six months. She was—" He stopped, then said, "I'm sorry, Jack, but even with Shannon being deceased, I'm not comfortable divulging private information from our sessions. It's just not right."

Jack had thought the priest would feel that way. He tried a different approach. "I understand. I don't really need to know the specifics of their marital problems. What I'm more interested in is whether or not you saw a personality change in Shannon in recent days or weeks. Did she seem more agitated or angry? Did she exhibit poor impulse control? When she came to your office, was there anything about her that alarmed you?"

The priest was quiet, seeming to ponder the question. Then he shook his head. "I'm sorry, but no."

"Father, the reason they came for counseling—without disclosing what it was, did it surprise you? Whatever Shannon may have confessed . . . was it out of character?"

The priest smiled. "Quite a bit of fancy footwork, there, Mr. Logan. I suppose it doesn't violate any confidentiality to answer that. Honestly, all sins are in character, we're born into it. So, no, I wasn't surprised, only disappointed."

Jack felt frustration wash over him. Was this guy going to take every opportunity to preach to him? "Thank you, Father. If I think of anything else, I'll be in touch." He handed him a card. "And please call me if you think of anything further."

The priest took the card but held on to Jack's hand. "Before you go, I have a question for you, Jack Logan."

Jack wanted to pull his hand away but didn't. "Yes, Father?"

"How long has it been since your last confession?"

The familiar fingers of dread wound their way through Jack's gut. He blew out a breath and shrugged. "Many years ago."

The priest let go of his hand. "Don't you think it's been long enough?"

Jack felt like reminding him of what happened the last time someone spilled their guts to him. Instead, he gave him a neutral look. "Not sure I really see the point. I'm more of the mind to try not do anything that'll require a confession."

"Son, I'm sure your parents raised you to know better than that. All have sinned and fallen short of the glory of God."

Here we go again, Jack thought. "How did you know I'd been raised Catholic?"

"Logan's a common Irish name—Scottish, too—but you seemed familiar with the conventions of the church. But you're deflecting. It's true, you know, confession is good for the soul." He smiled at Jack. "I'm not going anywhere, and I'm a good listener."

Jack stood. "I appreciate the offer, but I'll pass."

"All right. But I hope you'll think about what I've said."

"Thanks again." Jack tapped the doorframe on his way out. He felt like a kid again, when he couldn't wait to grow up and get as far away as possible from his family and their guilt-inducing religious tradition.

His mood stayed glum as he pulled out of the hospital lot.

He wasn't meeting Brian Doyle, Shannon's widower, for another hour, so he drove to Jamaica Plain and parked the car. He walked into Same Old Place and ordered two slices of cheese pizza and a soda. After grabbing a table in the corner, he bit into the gooey pie, thinking it was just as good as he'd remembered.

Jack wasn't sure what kind of sin lying to a priest was, but he hadn't told the truth to Father Murphy about the last time he'd gone to confession. It had actually been almost fifteen years ago, the day after he'd cheated on Taylor with Dakota. He hadn't really been sure what he expected to gain, maybe a little counseling or some help in figuring out why he'd done what he'd done and how he could fix it. It had been years since he'd seen the inside of a church, so he'd just walked to the one closest to his apartment and gone straight to the confessional. After he'd poured his heart out, the priest had asked a series of canned questions and given him some prayers to recite. He'd left feeling worse and decided then and there it would be the last time he tried it. Confession might be good for some souls, but definitely not his.

His phone buzzed and he looked down at a new hit for his Google alert for Maggie Russell. He clicked on the article, which reported that Maggie Russell's autopsy indicated that she had methamphetamine in her system. *So much for her not touching drugs.*

If the other autopsies turned up the same result, the answer could be as simple as a tainted batch of meth. Jack did a search to see if meth was capable of causing violence, and sure enough, the drug overstimulated the amygdala and could cause aggressive behavior, and it also had the ability to alter serotonin levels in the brain and induce psychosis. He needed to find out if the others had been using drugs, but the only way he could do so was if the families would share the information. Cause of death was public record, but not the details of the coroner's report.

He finished his pizza and headed out. It took him only ten minutes to get to the Doyles' house in Brookline, so he was still a few minutes early and he parked and checked his email. He found a short message from Taylor telling him that she'd invited one of her sources over on Saturday for dinner. It was unlike her to invite a relative stranger to their home, and Jack wondered what had prompted it, but before he could give it any more thought, a car pulled into the driveway and a man he assumed was Doyle stepped out. He had a Red Sox baseball cap on and was wearing jeans and a T-shirt. Jack got of his car and walked over to him.

"Brian Doyle?"

"Yeah?"

Jack held his hand out. "Jack Logan. We spoke on the phone yesterday."

Recognition dawned. "Oh, right. Sorry, I've been in a fog. I'd totally forgotten."

"Is this still a good time?"

"Sure. Come on in."

Jack followed him to the front door of the duplex and waited while he found the right key and opened it. It was dark inside; the shades hadn't been opened, and all the lights were off. The whole vibe was bleak.

Brian flipped a switch and a lamp next to the sofa went on. Jack noticed a pillow and blanket at one end—looked like Brian was avoiding sleeping in his bedroom, not that Jack could blame him. He couldn't bear to even think of how he would react if he lost Taylor.

"Sorry for the mess. I just . . ."

Jack put a hand up. "Hey, no need to apologize to me. I'm so sorry for your loss. I can't imagine what you're going through."

"Thanks. Let's sit in the kitchen."

Jack sat at the kitchen table, and Brian opened the refrigerator. "I can offer you a soda or a beer. That's about all I've got."

"Thanks. I'm good."

Brian grabbed a bottle of Bass Ale and sat across from Jack. He opened it and took a long swig. "So what do you want to know?"

Jack didn't want to lead with a question about drug use, so he eased in. "As I mentioned on the phone, what happened with your wife is not an isolated incident. There have been cases popping up all along the Eastern Seaboard of people behaving in a . . . similar manner."

Brian said nothing, his eyes on Jack. "I'm not sure I'm following you. People do crazy things all the time. What does that have to do with Shannon?"

Jack sighed. "Your wife didn't have any criminal history, right?"

Brian shook his head. "Not unless you consider adultery a crime."

At least now Jack knew why they were going to counseling. He cleared his throat. "Were you aware that your wife was carrying a gun that night?"

Brian took another long swallow, then wiped his mouth with the back of his hand. "Yeah. I'd gotten her a gun for protection a few months ago. A woman was raped in the parking garage of the building where Shannon worked and I told her she should keep it with her."

Jack tried to hide his astonishment at Brian's carelessness. "Did she have a carry permit?"

"No." Brian threw his hands up. "I get it. It was stupid of me. I did take her to the gun range, so she knew how to use it, but . . . I don't know. I was just worried about her. You know? I know better now. Obviously."

Jack dropped it. There was no point in making the guy feel any worse. "Can you tell me a little bit about that day? Was there something that made her angry or escalate so quickly?"

Biting his lip, Brian took a minute to answer. "It was weird. I mean we weren't getting a whole lot out of the counseling, to be honest, and I think she was ready to call it quits. She said she'd stopped seeing Matt, but I didn't believe her. She was still texting someone all the time and going in the other room to take calls. During our session that day, I told her I was tired of the bullshit. She started yelling at me . . . and then she was speaking like she was answering me, but I hadn't said a word. She was having this whole conversation with me that I wasn't a part of. When Father Murphy tried to tell her to calm down, she freaked out. The last thing she yelled was 'I'll kill you first,' then she pulled out the gun. It all happened so fast, it took a few seconds for it to register. I still have a hard time believing it."

Jack saw his opening. "Did the autopsy report show methamphetamine in her system?"

His eyes widened. "How did you know?"

"Because the same thing was found when they did the autopsy of a woman who killed her son's Little League coach."

"She killed a Little League coach?"

Jack nodded. "Yes, and in front of her young son. Did you know that your wife was using?" he asked.

"No. She never did drugs. I mean, she'd just been to the doctor for her annual physical. Besides, I would have noticed if she'd been using hard drugs."

Jack tilted his head. "Maybe she wasn't a regular user, just a time or two?"

Brian took another sip from his beer, then looked up at the ceiling. "Maybe that jerk she was messing around with got her into it. I tried to find him, but he skipped town. Probably knew

I'd beat the hell out of him." He slammed his fist on the table. "My sister's a nurse. She told me that meth can make people do crazy things. I'm just glad Father Murphy's going to be okay. I should have left her as soon as I found out she was fooling around. Maybe none of this would have happened."

"You can't blame yourself for trying to save your marriage. This isn't on you." He gave Brian a moment out of respect before continuing. "Is there any way I could look at the autopsy results? It would help me to compare them to the others and see if there's been some kind of contamination."

"Yeah, sure. Anything to help prevent something like this from happening again." He stood up and went into the other room. After a few minutes, he returned with a folder and handed it to Jack.

Jack looked quickly through the pages it contained. "Do you mind if I make a copy with my phone?"

Brian shrugged. "Go ahead." He stood and got himself another beer.

"Thanks." Jack positioned his phone over the first page and took a photo, doing so until he had all nine pages of the autopsy. Handing Brian his card, he stood. "Again, I'm so sorry for your loss, and I appreciate your talking to me. If you think of anything else, please give me a call."

It was close to four when he left, and he was eager to get home to Taylor and Evan. He felt terrible for Brian. What a series of events—finding out your wife was cheating on you, then having her shoot your priest in front of you, and then kill herself. And to top it off, to find out she was using meth. It wouldn't have been long before he would have noticed the signs. Jack had seen his share of meth use, and it wasn't a pleasant sight.

It couldn't be a coincidence that both Maggie and Shannon had been using drugs and then gone crazy. But the fact that neither of them were known users set alarm bells off. There must be some bad stuff out there—either in street drugs or being used to lace something benign. He needed to tell someone. He knew just the guy. The only problem was that he'd sworn to never talk to him again.

CHAPTER TWENTY

TAYLOR HAD SLEPT ON THE SMALL SOFA IN EVAN'S ROOM LAST night when Jack returned from Boston. Instead of the discussion they'd had offering any resolution, it had only made things worse and she'd been too angry to lie next to him. It was not yet dawn, but she slipped from Evan's room and went to the kitchen to make herself a cup of coffee. As she sat sipping it in the dark, she replayed their argument in her mind.

"I spoke to Sybil, and she *is* sick. I need to do this for her," Jack had told Taylor.

"Do what exactly? What's the plan?" she'd asked.

"I'm not sure yet. Sybil said she'd call me after she picked up Dakota's passport at the bank."

She'd shaken her head, pacing. "I don't like it. I don't trust Dakota."

He said, "But I spoke with Sybil and I trust *her*. You remember how she testified on my behalf during Dakota's trial when she tried to blame me for what she'd done. Sybil is the reason I survived that ordeal, and I can't turn my back on her now."

"I understand that, Jack. But why did Dakota call you if she doesn't have some other agenda? You haven't spoken to her in two years but you're the only person in the entire world who can help her? She's up to something. You can't trust her."

He'd given Taylor a long look. "I know that. I *don't* trust her. But you have to trust me. I'm playing it like I do because I want to know what she's really up to. You know the saying, Keep your enemies—"

She put a hand up. "Do not quote *The Godfather* to me. This is serious. No good can come from your having any contact with her."

He'd tried to pull her to him then, but she pushed him away. "Taylor, you can't really be worried that I have feelings for her."

She was so outraged, she couldn't speak at first. "Is that what you think? That I'm jealous of her? Of course I don't think you have feelings for her. If you did . . . I mean . . . after everything. I'm worried about you. Us. Our family. She's a dangerous psychopath. But the fact that you could think for even one second that this is about insecurity . . . it's really sad. I thought we'd come further than that." She'd turned and stomped out of the room, and he hadn't gone after her.

Suddenly feeling exhausted, Taylor went into the living room and lay down the sofa. Maybe she'd just rest for a little while longer. The next thing she knew, the sun coming through the window woke her up. She heard Jack's and Evan's voices in the kitchen. Glancing at the clock, she was surprised to see that it was close to eight. She rose from the couch and walked into the kitchen, where Jack was making pancakes.

He turned to her as she walked in. "Morning. Hungry?"

She shook her head and took a seat next to Evan at the table.

"Mama!" He reached out a sticky hand to touch her cheek.

"Good morning, sunshine," she said to Evan, then looked up at Jack. "Thanks for letting me sleep."

"No prob. I was awfully lonely last night." He glanced at her quickly then came to the table with the rest of the pancakes.

She didn't respond.

"I'm sorry," he said. "I was an ass. I promise you, I'm not going to do anything without talking to you first. Please, let's not let this tear us apart."

She felt her resolve weaken, but she wasn't going to let him off that easily. "What I want you to say is that you won't do anything without *clearing* it with me first. But promise me you won't do anything more than talk to her so we can figure out the best way to proceed together."

He nodded. "Of course. I promise. I love you."

"I love you too."

Jack leaned over and kissed her and Taylor gave his arm a tight squeeze. She meant what she said last night about being worried rather than jealous. But she couldn't deny that the visceral reaction she had to hearing Dakota's name *was* jealousy. Dakota had stolen Jack from her all those years ago and even though Taylor knew he would never betray her again, especially with Dakota, all the old wounds had burst open. But he was right about one thing, they couldn't let Dakota rip them apart again. And taking opposite sides on this issue would definitely do that.

"I also asked Jeremy to come to dinner with Georgia tonight," she said. "Can you set up the fire pit on the front porch? I want to have cocktails and appetizers out there."

"Sure thing," he said. "But first, let me get Evan outside. You want to do the swings, buddy?"

Evan nodded and Jack scooped him up and took him to the backyard, leaving Taylor with a quiet moment to plan for the evening. She was looking forward to seeing Georgia. After their interview yesterday, she'd picked up a copy of her latest book, *Infidelity: Are Your Genes to Blame?*, but had been too busy, and too upset about Dakota, to crack it open. Regardless, she knew the conversation tonight would be lively and interesting.

Taylor pulled out a pad and made a list of what still needed to get done—florist, grocery store, and bakery. If she left now, she should finish by noon. She dropped the pad when she heard a scream from outside and ran to the window.

Evan was crying and kicking at Jack, who was doing his best to calm him down.

She flung the door open and tore outside. "What's wrong?"

Jack gave her a perplexed look. "I have no idea. All of a sudden, he just started screaming *out, out* and then when I tried to lift him, he started yelling *no* and hitting me. Have you noticed he's been a little off lately?"

Taylor held her arms out to Evan and he flung himself toward her, burying his head in her shoulder and crying inconsolably. "What's wrong, baby?"

"Sleep."

She frowned. He'd been awfully tired lately. "Okay, sweetie, let's go lie down for a bit."

When they got inside, she put him on their bed and was about to leave when he pulled her hand. "No. Stay. Mama stay."

There went the rest of her morning, but she didn't have the heart to leave him. "Okay." She wrapped her arms around him, and he pressed against her, his chest still heaving up and down from his sobs. After a few minutes, he calmed down, and soon she could tell from his even breathing that he'd fallen asleep. She was afraid to move and disturb him, so Taylor closed her eyes. A trip to the pediatrician was warranted—something wasn't right. She had a leaden feeling in her stomach and tried to dismiss the dread that suddenly overcame her. She didn't know what she would do if something was seriously wrong. Praying silently, she told herself she was overreacting. He was just tired. Kids got tired. Maybe he'd been wearing himself out at daycare.

After his breaths turned to soft snores, she extricated herself from under Evan's arm and snuck back to the kitchen, where Jack was working on his laptop while Beau chewed a bone on the floor.

"He asleep?"

She nodded. "He's been having a lot of tantrums lately. It's so unlike him."

Jack tilted his head. "Could be a stage. Maybe the terrible twos are here early?"

"Yeah, but I don't know. He's so irritable and tired all time. I think I'm going to try to work from home or adjust my schedule to go in when you're here, so he's not in daycare."

He gave her an apologetic look. "I'm sorry, babe. I didn't know . . . you said he liked it there. I'm traveling most of next week. I'm hoping I'll have enough for the story at that point—I definitely will if it turns out this meth is the connection."

"It's okay. I'll figure it out. I'll take him to the pediatrician first thing Monday morning."

Jack nodded. "Can't hurt." He stood up. "Listen, why don't you let me go do your errands? That way if he wakes up, you're here. I have a feeling he needs Mommy more than Daddy today."

"That would be great. I can get a head start on getting things ready here while you're out. Let me give you my list."

A few minutes later, Jack was out the door, and Taylor made herself a cup of tea. She turned the television on while she straightened up, but soon stopped, sponge still in her hand, when she heard a breaking news announcement. She threw down the sponge and grabbed the television remote, turning up the volume.

"What we're about to show you is very graphic and disturbing, and not recommended for young audiences." The screen flashed a grainy cell-phone video that showed Pastor Montgomery Pearson, a megachurch preacher whose television show attracted over five million viewers every Sunday; he was so popular, he often held Saturday services. He was speaking fast, his words becoming almost jumbled.

"The time is at hand. Spiritual battles are everywhere. Your fight isn't against flesh and blood but against the spiritual forces in dark places." He pointed to a man in the crowd and screamed: "Like him! He looks like a man, but that's a demon masquerading as a man." His wife, who always sat at the piano, ran over to him, whispered in his ear, and looked past the camera, nodding to someone unseen. The pastor grabbed her by the shoulders and yelled, "You're a Jezebel trying to trick me! To the grave with you!" With speed that didn't seem possible, he grabbed a drumstick from a set of drums behind him and stabbed her in the eye with it. The crowd erupted in screams, and she howled in agony as she fell backward off the stage.

Seconds later, security guards grabbed the pastor and pulled him away. Before they could stop him, he freed himself and leapt from the thirty-foot stage and crashed to the floor below.

The video stopped and the anchor was back. "Pastor Pearson and his wife were taken to University of Pittsburgh Medical Center, where their conditions are unknown. We'll keep you updated as the story progresses."

Taylor felt like all the air had been sucked out of her. What the hell had she just seen? She sank down into a kitchen chair, reeling. This was just insane. His children were in that audience. How were they ever going to get over what they'd just witnessed? His followers would be devastated. She thought back to a conversation she'd had with Jeremy when they'd first met about how Damon Crosse liked to make the church, in all its forms, look bad. If Damon Crosse weren't dead, she would have sworn it was somehow his doing . . . but that was impossible. Though he did have successors they weren't aware of . . .

Suddenly she felt exposed, nervous. She thought about what Jack had witnessed the other night so close to their house. It felt like there was nowhere safe. She went to the bedroom to peek in at Evan, who was still sound asleep. She hoped he was going to be in a better mood tonight.

When Jack came home, Taylor practically ran to him. "Did you hear the news about Montgomery Pearson?"

He frowned. "No. What?"

"He went crazy, ranting on air." She took a deep breath. "He put a drumstick through his wife's eye, then threw himself off the stage. The whole thing caught was on video. He looked insane."

Jack pulled out his phone and searched for the video, his mouth dropping open and his face turning white as he watched. He shook his head. "What the hell? How could he . . . This is unbelievable! You think he was on meth, too?"

Taylor shrugged. "I don't know. I don't know what to think. Could have been . . . but it just seems unlikely. His reputation has been spotless for over twenty years."

"I'm gonna go make a few calls. You okay or do you need help right now?"

"You go. I'm going to get the food ready. I just want to stay busy and try to get that image out of my mind."

○ ○ ○

A few hours later, Taylor looked in again on Evan, who was still asleep, and the familiar clench in her stomach returned. Why was he so tired? Monday couldn't get here fast enough—she really needed to talk to the pediatrician. She was about to leave the bedroom when he called out a "Mama."

She went over and sat on the edge of the bed. "Hi, sweetie. You hungry?"

He nodded. "Hungy. Want cookie."

She laughed. "After dinner. Come on, let's get up." She changed him and he followed her to the kitchen.

Beau ran up and licked his face and Evan giggled. "Doggy." He sat on the floor and Beau continued to kiss him.

"Okay, that's enough. He doesn't need a bath." She gently scolded Beau and picked Evan up to put him in his highchair, but he started fussing and pointing to the table.

"Okay, don't cry." She pulled out the booster seat and attached it to a chair. He climbed up, happier.

After Evan finished eating, Taylor put on his favorite movie, *Elmo in Grouchland*, in the playroom off the kitchen. He sat with his blankie and stuffed dinosaur, absorbed, while she put the appetizers in the oven.

An hour later, Georgia was the first to arrive, right on time. She looked elegant in a pair of tailored black slacks with a beautiful embroidered sky-blue top. True to her word, she had brought wine—a bottle of red and a bottle of white.

Beau ambled over and greeted her, his tail thumping back and forth as she petted his head. "What a beautiful golden," she said to Taylor after greeting her and handing her the bottles. "I lost mine last year. He was the love of my life."

"I'm sorry. How old was he?"

"Fourteen. I was lucky to have him for so long. But it doesn't make it any easier."

Taylor agreed, "It sure doesn't." She shuddered, thinking about losing Beau. She didn't know exactly how old he was; when she'd found him on the street, the vet had estimated that he was around two. That meant he was close to six now, and they'd already been through so much together.

"Shall we go out on the deck?" Taylor suggested, and Georgia followed her outside, where Jack and Evan sat on a love seat, reading a board book.

Jack quickly rose to greet them. "So nice to meet you. Taylor has been raving about you. I'm so glad you could join us tonight. What can I get you to drink? Wine, soda, scotch?"

Georgia smiled. "I'd love a scotch."

"You got it."

Before they could sit, Jeremy arrived, then Jack brought out the drinks. After introductions were made, and everyone made a fuss over Evan, Georgia tilted her head, looking at Jeremy.

"Have we met before?"

He shook his head. "I don't think so."

"You look so familiar, and I don't usually forget a face. You haven't done any lecturing at UConn Stamford, have you?"

"No, but my lab is in Stamford, so maybe you've seen me in passing."

She waved her hand and smiled. "Well, it's nice to meet you now." They stayed outside for the next hour, chatting and nibbling on apps. Taylor went inside, where she put the roast and the side dishes on the table and called everyone in. As they sat down to dinner, Evan was already asleep again—Jack had taken him to his room a little while ago and came out a few minutes later, saying he hadn't put up a fuss when he'd settled him into bed.

Georgia cleared her throat. "So, Jack, Taylor told me you're working on a story about a series of murder-suicides. I hadn't realized there was a pattern, but with that news of Pastor Pearson this morning"—she blew out a breath—"I don't know what to make of it."

Jack said, "I can't believe the news played footage that

graphic. I'm still reeling from it. How could anyone, but especially a pastor, do that?"

"Do you have any theories?" Georgia asked.

"I still need more information, but between us, I've been able to find out two of the perpetrators had methamphetamine in their systems."

She nodded. "Well, that could explain a lot. Methamphetamine causes changes to the brain and floods it with dopamine, a feel-good chemical. But sometimes the rapid change can cause meth-induced psychosis—hallucinations and delusions. That would all fit with what I saw on that video."

"Both the families Jack interviewed were shocked about the drug abuse," Taylor said. "Wouldn't it be surprising for it to go unnoticed?"

"It would be very unusual for someone using meth not to attract any notice for it," Georgia said. "You've all seen pictures of addicts. Is it possible they were drugged against their wills? Or that a batch of meds was tainted?"

"I've been wondering the same thing," Jack said. "I'm trying to find something that ties them all together but so far nothing."

Georgia nodded. "Although, even if a supply of meds was tampered with, the likelihood is slim that it would trigger a psychotic episode in everyone who took it."

"Maybe, or maybe not," Jeremy said. "What if someone deliberately altered the drug so it would affect the brain in a specific way . . . putting, say, ecstasy in the mix, which damages the serotonin receptors? That combined with the meth could ramp up the violence."

"Interesting," Georgia said. "But this wouldn't be a common drug pusher. That would have to be the work of a sophisticated scientist with a lab."

"Someone with a good knowledge of chemistry could concoct something like that," Jeremy said.

"You mean like *Breaking Bad*?" Georgia asked.

Taylor looked at her in surprise. "You watched *Breaking Bad*?"

Georgia chuckled. "I had to know what all the fuss was about."

"Something like that," Jeremy said. "It doesn't preclude it being a plan on a larger scale, I'm just saying it doesn't have to be."

Jack put a hand up. "Let's not get ahead of ourselves. All we know right now is that two women with meth in their systems had psychotic breaks in which they committed murder-suicides. We have no idea what happened with Pastor Pearson. It's way too soon to be jumping to these kinds of conclusions."

"I have to agree with Jack," Georgia said. "Even though I'm not a big believer in coincidences, it could be nothing more than that. If you aren't careful, you can focus on the wrong thing and miss the real connections." She took a sip of wine, then continued. "When you're driving, have you ever looked at the traffic light and been so focused on it that you almost run into the car a few feet in front of you?"

Taylor nodded vigorously. "Yes! I'm embarrassed to say that I've done that more than once."

"If you find out that any more of these people had the drug in their system, then I'd say it's more than a coincidence," Jeremy said.

"Agreed. I've already started asking around to see if anyone knows anything about a tainted drug supply," Jack said.

They ate quietly for a few minutes, before Taylor turned to Georgia and smiled. "Georgia is an author and I've just gotten her latest book, which is on infidelity. It sounds intriguing. She hypothesizes that cheating may be more linked to our genetic makeup than we realize."

Jack looked skeptical. "Um, that's a pretty interesting assertion. I think we'd all like to hear more."

"Well, men have tended to wander more than women, as a result of their evolutionary instinct to produce more offspring—

that's always been chalked up to genetics," Georgia began. "But now studies have shown that women with certain variations in the vasopressin receptor gene are more prone to infidelity and extra pair bonding."

"What's vasopressin?" Jack asked.

"A hormone that affects sexual bonding and trust," she answered.

"Are you saying we have no control over our behaviors?" Taylor asked.

Georgia shook her head. "Not at all. Less than 50 percent of women with one of the five variants were found in the study to be promiscuous. Of course, there are other factors, but it *is* statistically significant, which could mean that it makes it harder for certain women to withstand the temptation to bond with other males."

"Maybe a genetic screening should be mandatory before marriage," Jack joked.

"I'd like to read this book," Jeremy said. "It sounds fascinating. I've already started reading your book on ethics and the brain. I bought it when Taylor told me you'd be coming tonight."

Georgia smiled. "I'm honored."

The rest of the evening passed enjoyably, and the party broke up close to nine. Evan hadn't roused at all. Taylor put a hand on his head again to check for a fever, but he didn't feel warm. Later, as she drifted off to sleep, the image of the woman from her dream filled her mind again and made her shiver.

Stop being silly. Everything is fine, she chastised herself. But what if wasn't? She knew better than anyone that bad things could happen and often did. Despite her wanting to believe that everything would be okay, she couldn't shake the idea that something terrible was waiting.

CHAPTER TWENTY-ONE

JACK WAS STILL PUZZLING OVER HIS CONVERSATION WITH Sybil. He replayed it in his mind, trying to pinpoint what it was that had felt off-kilter. She'd been in such a hurry to get him off the phone, which was unlike her, telling him she'd get back in touch when she'd gone to the bank. If she was so eager to have Dakota come back, wouldn't she have expressed a bit more urgency? He decided to wait until hearing from Sybil again before texting Dakota. So far, he'd heard nothing.

He was eager to see the autopsy reports, which he'd submitted data request forms for before the weekend. But he knew getting the information could take weeks, if not months, for the individual states to process. Luckily, he had a buddy on the police force in Virginia who had agreed to look into another murder-suicide that fit the profile Jack was investigating. His friend told him that the coroner had listed the cause of death not as suicide, but drug-induced psychosis, and the drug was, of course, methamphetamine.

This was no coincidence. It was time to pull out the big guns. He stared at his phone for a long time, then scrolled through his contacts until he reached "S." The last time he'd seen Scotty, he'd almost punched him—it had taken three friends to hold him back. That was the night he saw his brother-in-law making out with a woman who wasn't Jack's sister Maria. The idiot hadn't even had the brains to take her somewhere discreet but had brought her to the bar where they all used to hang out. Scotty had tried to give Jack some lame excuse, but he wasn't buying it. He later admitted to Maria that the affair had been going on for the better part of a year, and she kicked him out. He moved in with the other woman for a few months, but then apparently came to his senses and begged Maria to take him back. She said no at first, but he wouldn't give up, and six months later, he was back in the house. A few months after that, Maria was pregnant again.

That baby was now over a year old, and although Maria had forgiven him, Jack still hadn't. Jack made sure he visited Maria and the kids at their house outside D.C. only when Scotty, who worked for the FBI, wasn't around. Both she and Taylor had tried to get Jack to move past it, but he just couldn't.

He exhaled and hit Scotty's name on his phone screen.

A familiar voice answered on the third ring. "Jack? Is it really you?"

"Yeah. I know I've been scarce, but I guess it's time to mend fences, as they say."

There was silence on the line. "Jack, this is me. Don't give me that bullshit."

Before he'd cheated on Maria, Scotty had been Jack's best friend. They'd played football together in high school and had stayed close through college. During their senior year, when Scotty had become interested in Maria, Jack had been kind of pissed at first. But he soon warmed to the idea of his best friend with his sister, warning Scotty that if he ever hurt her, he'd regret it. A year later, Jack had been best man in their wedding. When he cheated, Scotty hadn't just broken Maria's heart—he'd broken Jack's, too.

He cleared his throat. "The truth is I need your help."

"What is it? Everything okay with Taylor and Evan?"

"Yeah, it's nothing to do with them. It's a story I'm working on."

"Okay, I'm listening."

"Have you been seeing the news reports about these bizarre murder-suicides?"

"You mean like that preacher who killed his wife?"

"Exactly. That one is the eighteenth case. The perps are all upstanding citizens with no criminal records, no history of violence or mental illness, all flipping out and killing on the spur of the moment."

"Okay, so where are you going with this?"

"What if I told you that I've already confirmed that three of them were found with methamphetamine in their systems and that no one in their family or close circle believes they ever used drugs?"

A loud exhale came over the line. "I guess I'd tell you that people have secrets. There's nothing surprising about that."

"Say that's true. Say they *were* using. Don't you think it's strange that they all had psychotic breaks within this short window of time? Maybe they were lying and we're looking at some bad meth on the streets. But what if they weren't users, and they were somehow poisoned, perhaps intentionally?"

Scotty whistled. "Okay, Jack. That's some paranoid shit. Maria told me everything you and Taylor have been through, but that's a stretch. You know better than to jump to this kind of conclusion."

Jack bristled. This had clearly been a bad idea. "Okay, fine. I should never have called you. Forget it."

"Hold on. I'll admit, the thing with that televangelist was cuckoo. But you know, these guys aren't saints, even if they act like it. Even so, I'll bite: What makes you think they were drugged?"

"I've seen meth users—you can tell. Maybe if this were coke or oxy, I'd be inclined to think they'd pulled the wool over their friends' and family's eyes. But I saw recent pictures. They looked healthy and wholesome. And my gut is telling me that there's more to it. I need to see the other autopsy reports and tox screens. If they all had meth in their systems and *no one* around them suspected anything, then I think that's a huge red flag. But either way, if they used willingly, they got some bad stuff, and if they didn't, well, then we're looking at something even scarier."

"Okay. Send me what you have—the names and stories on the other incidents. I'll see what I can dig up."

"Thanks, Scotty."

"Oh, one more thing?"

"What?"

"I'll deliver the report in person. I want to see you, and 'mend the fence,' as you so charmingly put it."

Jack clenched his fist. "You broke the code, man. I told you a long time ago to take good care of my sister."

"I know." Scotty's voice cracked. "I'm sorry for it, you know I am. But are you telling me you never made any mistakes?"

Jack thought about Dakota and was filled with shame. Of course he'd made plenty of his own mistakes. He had no right to judge Scotty or to hold a grudge, but it was hard for him to let it go. This was someone he'd trusted with not only his friendship, but with his family. He wanted to forgive him. He wanted to have his friendship back. But he didn't know how. Maybe this could be a start.

"Fine. Give me a call when you have it and we'll make that happen."

"Good. Take care, Jackie."

Jack stiffened at the endearment. "Slow your roll, man. Let's take it one step at a time. Later." He ended the call. Opening his laptop, he typed *Pastor Montgomery Pearson* in the search engine. He flinched when he saw the thumbnail for the video of the attack. He scrolled down and saw a news alert from a couple of hours ago.

Apparently, the pastor's condition had been downgraded from critical to serious and he was recovering from a nine-hour surgery on his back, which he'd broken in the fall from the stage. His wife hadn't been so lucky. She had died yesterday. Jack assumed Pearson was going to be in the hospital for a while and wondered if an arrest had been made yet. Most likely there would be police stationed outside his door, in any case.

Jack knew that he'd discover more if he could talk to Pearson, the first one not to succeed in ending his life. He found the website for Pearson's church and went to the contact page. He typed a message, explaining who he was and said he thought he might be able to help. Hopefully someone would read it and get the message to the pastor. On a whim, he called the church, too, but was met with a recording saying the mailbox was full. Not surprising—he could only imagine the calls they must be getting. He sighed. He'd try again tomorrow, but it was likely that the only way he was going to get through was to go there in person.

Jack put the phone down and got up. He needed a run. Grabbing his headphones and putting on his running shoes, he headed outside. The sun beat down on him, but the temperature was only in the seventies so it was pleasant. He ran down the hill away from their house and toward the river.

He thought about what Georgia had said about that hormone connected to infidelity. He didn't like thinking that brain chemistry could control the way people behaved. Even though he knew now that he'd been manipulated to fall for Dakota, he couldn't completely forgive himself for betraying Taylor, the only woman he'd ever loved. Jack wasn't willing to accept that humans didn't have free will. If that were true, then what was the point? Because if it *was* true, then it meant they were all just a bunch of robots disguised as flesh and blood.

CHAPTER TWENTY-TWO

IKARIA, GREECE

RENA WAITED FOR THE DOCTOR TO COME OUT OF HER UNCLE'S bedroom, and when he did, she could tell from his expression that the news was bad.

He shut the door behind him and shook his head as he walked toward her. "There's nothing more I can do for him except make him comfortable."

"Is he in pain?" she asked, her chest constricting.

"He says no, but he's having a very hard time getting a breath, which is . . . very uncomfortable to say the least. And when he starts coughing, he can't stop. We could do more for him in the hospital."

"He insists on staying here. He doesn't want to die in a hospital."

He sighed. "I'll call in a prescription for morphine. That will help greatly." He put a hand on her arm. "It won't be long now."

After he left, she pushed the door open and stood at the threshold, watching as her uncle's chest rose and fell in shallow waves, his labored breathing filling the room with a hissing sound. The grayness of his skin made her heart sink. Now that his congestive heart failure had stopped responding to medicine, his time was limited. She sat in a chair next to the bed and took his hand in hers. It was clammy and limp.

"Uncle, can you hear me?"

He didn't open his eyes but she saw them move under his lids. "I don't know how to live in this world without you." Her voice broke, and she wiped the wetness from her cheeks as her tears flowed. "I should have told you sooner. I blamed you for years for taking me from my family, but I forgive you for what you did. I understand that you were only doing what you had to."

He didn't respond, but she thought she felt him give her hand a slight squeeze.

The day her world had come to a crashing end, over twenty years ago, had started off like any other one. Her daughter had left for school, running out the door with a wave and not so much as a backward glance. Had she known that was the last time she'd see her child, she'd have taken her in her arms and never let go. But she had gone about her morning, then met her best friend for lunch. She'd thought it strange when her husband had called her and asked her to pick up his tuxedo for an event that evening—they had plenty of staff for that—but he'd claimed their housekeeper was ill.

In the parking lot of the dry cleaners, she felt something wet on her face before she even opened her car door. The next thing she knew, she woke up alone in a basement. When she began to scream, the door at the top of the stairs opened and a man came down the steps. He looked middle-aged, maybe in his forties, with dark hair and a full beard.

"Who are you? What am I doing here?" she yelled.

"I'm not going to hurt you. I'm trying to help you." He came closer and she recoiled, shielding her face, afraid he was going to hit her. "Here," he said, holding a phone out to her. She took it, surprised to hear her uncle Yiannis's voice come over the line. "My dear. You're safe. You can trust Father Demetrios."

She looked at the man and was more confused than ever. "Father Demetrios? I don't understand."

"He's with the church. Lucky he found out what they were planning to do," Yiannis assured her.

"What *who* was planning?" She couldn't make sense of what was happening.

"He will it explain it all. I will see you soon. He's going to bring you to Greece. To me."

Her heart was racing and she felt as though she could faint. "What are you talking about? I don't understand."

Her uncle continued. "I'm sorry, my dear. There is no other way. Listen to him." The line went dead.

"Theíos Yannis!" she yelled but he was gone. She looked at this Father Demetrios, terror seizing her. "What's going on? Why did you take me? Where am I?"

"You're safe here. But a man was hired to torture you until you told him where the Judas coins are, and then kill you."

How did he know about the coins? She'd been told to never speak of them to strangers. Maybe this was some kind of a trick. She been warned not to trust anyone. Just because her uncle had been on the other end of the line didn't mean he wasn't someone's prisoner, too. She pretended not to know what he was talking about. "What man? What coins?"

His voice was gentle, and he spoke slowly. "The church has people watching over you, protecting you. We have many people making sure these coins are never all brought back together again. We have connections in law enforcement and one of them, posing as a hitman, was contracted to kill you. He got in touch with the church and let us know."

"That's crazy. I don't know anything about any Judas coins," she insisted.

He shook his head. "I know everything. Your uncle brought them to you for safekeeping many years ago, after your parents were killed."

"I don't know what you're talking about."

"I'm on your side. How many times have you watched *Casablanca*?" he asked.

She looked at him in surprise. "Four. You?"

"At least eleven."

That was the code language her parents had included in the letter she'd opened after their deaths. It proved he was one of them.

"Okay, I believe you. But why do you have me down here as a prisoner?"

"You're not a prisoner. I'm saving your life. But you need to leave the country and take the coins. They're not safe anymore and neither are you."

"But the coins have been hidden for years. I've told no one about them. I don't see how anyone could know."

"We don't have time to debate this. There's a powerful and nefarious man named Damon Crosse who has somehow found out you have the coins. His orders were to torture you until you gave up their location."

"So what am I supposed to do?"

"We have to fake your death. You have to take the coins with you to Greece and hide them. Your uncle is leaving Patmos and finding a new island where you can both go, one where no one knows you. You'll live with him and protect them."

"Are you insane? I have a family. My daughter's only fourteen. I can't abandon her."

He gave her a long look. "You're going to leave her, either voluntarily or involuntarily. They'll find you if you stay in the country, and next time we won't be able to save you. And if you don't listen to me, you could be putting her life in danger, too."

Her heart was beating wildly, the information far too much to process all at once. She thought back to the note her parents had left with their will in case anything happened to them. It told her about the coins—their power, their legacy, and her duty to uphold the family's sacred trust. She wondered now if the car accident that had killed her parents had really been an accident. She knew only one thing for sure: she couldn't risk her daughter's life—even if it meant leaving her without saying good-bye.

"Isn't there another way? I could hire guards. Anything. There must be some way for me to protect the coins without losing everything. Even if this man did get his hands on me, I'll never give the coins to him. My uncle has told me what will happen if they fall into the wrong hands. I'll die protecting them."

He stared at her for a long moment. "You think that, but you don't know what these people are capable of." He left and came back with another man—big and bald with a jagged scar running down his left cheek. "This is Minos. He's a bodyguard who works for the church."

Minos grabbed her hand, and before she realized what he was doing, he'd handcuffed her to the bed frame.

"What are you doing?" she yelled, as she broke out in a cold sweat.

He pulled a lighter from his pocket and clicked it. She backed away from the flame as he pulled a cigarette from his pocket. Then he lit it and took a deep drag before he grabbed her uncuffed hand and held the cigarette against her palm.

She tried to jerk away, screaming in agony as her flesh burned. "Stop it! You're crazy!" Tears blinded her eyes, and she felt like she was going to throw up. "Father, help me!"

Father Demetrios merely looked away.

Just when she thought she'd pass out, Minos moved the cigarette away just long enough for her to be flooded with relief . . . until he brought it back down, this time on her arm. She howled again.

"Where are the coins?" he demanded.

"I'll . . . never tell," she choked out.

He moved the cigarette to her cheek and the searing pain lanced through her face. "Your eye is next."

"Stop." She was panting now, out of breath. "Please, no more."

"That's enough," Demetrios said, his voice shaking.

Minos threw the cigarette to the floor and ground it out with his boot, then walked back upstairs.

"They'll do much worse, and by the time they're finished, they will have destroyed you *and* they'll have the coins." Demetrios moved toward the staircase. "I'll be right back."

She rocked back and forth, moaning in pain, her flesh burning, her soul sick.

Demetrios returned and dressed her wounds. "I'm sorry I had to let him do that. But I needed you to understand that you really don't have a choice. Do you see now? We need to get Crosse to think you're dead."

"How?" she asked, resignation heavy in her voice.

"In about a month, the police will find a body in the Potomac River wearing your jewelry. The decomposition will be advanced enough so the body won't be recognizable, but your husband should be able to ID you from your necklace and bracelet."

She shivered. "You're going to kill someone else?"

"Of course not. We have our connections in the police department. We'll get a body from the morgue."

"Can't I go into some sort of protection program instead?"

"No, I don't work for witness protection and I can't get you that kind of arrangement. Unless we make it seem like you are dead, your daughter and husband will never be safe. I know it feels like I'm asking the impossible here, and I wish there was another way. But this is the only hope for you. They will find you and kill you. The only way you and your family are safe is if they believe you're already dead."

"How do I know they won't still come after my family?"

Demetrios said, "Because they are aware of the dictates of this family trust and know that you've taken a vow not to tell anyone, even your husband. And your daughter is not to be entrusted with the knowledge until she's twenty-one. They are safe as long as you're gone. If you stay, they might kidnap your daughter as leverage to get the coins' location from you."

She couldn't allow her child's life to be in danger. She'd rather die a thousand deaths than let any harm come to her daughter. She took a deep breath and wiped the tears from her cheeks. "Okay," she whispered.

They used makeup to make her look beaten and bruised and took photographs that he would develop and send as proof of her death to the man who had hired him.

She told them that the coins had been hidden at Agape Women's Shelter, a short distance from her home in Chevy Chase, Maryland. The coins were embedded in the tile walls along with similar-looking coins.

"I need to figure out the best way to extract them from there," Demetrios mused.

"If you take the coins, their removal will be noticed," she told him.

"We're going to replace them with fakes. We'll just need

some time, so someone can go look at them and create believable forgeries of them."

She stayed in that basement for three weeks, mourning her family and mentally preparing herself to leave them. When everything was ready, she packed the real coins into a small bag and boarded a private plane to Greece.

That was when Eva had died and Rena had been born.

CHAPTER TWENTY-THREE

LEONARD WAS IN BED READING WHEN HE HEARD THE DOOR chime. He glanced at the clock on the nightstand. Eleven. He heard his wife's footsteps stomping up the stairs, and she burst into the bedroom and strode to the foot of the bed. Her eyes blazed and she pointed a red manicured finger at him.

"I don't know how you can sleep at night," she began.

He looked up from his book. "What do you mean?"

"Your policies. People are dying because of your greed."

He felt his face grow hot. "What the hell are you talking about?"

"I was just at the hospital visiting my mom and saw Sunny, the little girl I told you about. Her life could be saved by a new treatment, but she's going to die because your company says it's too experimental. Her family has been paying huge premiums for months to get the best coverage and still your bean counters turned them down."

He shook his head. "How dare you come in here and lecture

me. You have no idea what goes into that decision making or if that treatment would even work. You want to go out and start being the breadwinner around here? When you stop spending my money, you can criticize me. In the meantime, shut the hell up."

Patrice just stood there, an ugly vein pulsating in her temple. Her mother's illness necessitated daily treatments for two-week windows with three-week breaks in between. Patrice went every day, leaving the children in the care of the nanny, and over the course of the long days at the hospital, she was getting to know the other patients. She'd come home at night and bore him with their stories of crippling debt and marginalized care as they had pled with their insurance companies to pay their bills. Sunny's family in particular had really gotten under her skin. The child was seven, just a little younger than their own daughters, and had been battling a blood cancer for over a year. Her prognosis wasn't good, but that wasn't his problem. Patrice had no right to speak to him like this. He turned off the lamp and plunged the room into darkness. Let her stumble to the bathroom in the pitch black.

"You'll be sorry," she shot back. "Just wait."

The only thing he was sorry about was that she wasn't the one needing treatment.

Leonard's relationship with Patrice hadn't always been adversarial. In the beginning, she had adored him, even called him her soul mate. They'd met when they were both working at Jefferson Health Care. He'd joined the management training program when his plans for law school fell through, and she was the administrative assistant to the president of the company. They started dating and within six months had moved in together. She was hot and fun back then, and Leonard figured her proximity to the top couldn't hurt his career. Her putting in a good word for him had helped him get his first promotion.

After a couple of years, he decided it was time to become a

family man, so he proposed. By then he'd been promoted to vice president and he told Patrice she should quit her job. He wanted the whole package—the stay-at-home wife who would cook and clean and cater to his every need. But what she wanted was to write fiction. In the beginning, he encouraged her—not because he thought she was good at it, but because he was trying to seem like a good husband. He thought she'd realize after a while that she had no talent and give up. But Patrice was tenacious, determined to make it into print. So he paid for her to take some classes, hoping the teacher would be honest about her mediocre ability, but that didn't happen either. She stuck with it for the first few years, and he had to grudgingly admit that her writing improved. But Leonard didn't want a wife who would lock herself away for hours at a time pecking at a keyboard, trying to write the great American novel. He wanted someone who would support *his* dreams, *his* goals. He was rising to the top and he needed a wife to take care of the rest. So he pointed out the slim odds that she'd ever make it and began to pressure her to get pregnant. Once the twins came along, it was easy to get her to put away her fantasies of becoming a published novelist and focus instead on him and the girls.

At first it went well. She enjoyed all the perks that his new position as senior VP of marketing afforded them. It wasn't enough for Leonard, though. He had his eye on the top job and there was nothing that was going to stand in his way. He wasn't above climbing over the backs of his colleagues and if he had to ruin a few careers on the way, so be it. When Leonard finally became CEO five years ago, everything changed. He gave up his gym membership and let his diet go to hell. What was he in training for anyway? He had the wife and the job. He was rich and powerful and could have anyone he wanted. He didn't need to punish himself with exercise and diet anymore.

He didn't bother trying to hide his indiscretions from Patrice;

in fact, it amused him to see her sneaking looks at the texts on his phone. He stopped initiating sex and waited to see how long it would take for her to care. After a few months, she began to reach out to him again and he'd go along unenthusiastically. He loved keeping her off balance. But in recent years, she'd made it clear to him that she no longer cared, and in fact, had no interest in spending time with him, in or out of bed. They went through the motions for the sake of the children, and even though she'd broached the subject of divorce with him, he'd told her that it was off the table. He wasn't going to have his children grow up in a broken home the way he had. She didn't have it so bad after all. He worked his ass off and she had every luxury money could buy. Was it too much to ask that she show him a little respect?

CHAPTER TWENTY-FOUR

FRIEDRICH WOULD HAVE BEEN PLEASED WITH THE PROGRESS his adopted son had made. Coming up with a formula that would change human behavior had been the old man's idea, but the delivery method had been Damon's inspiration. The handful of scientists that had come over from the Institute and worked on his secret project were in the final phase of testing. If Damon had followed the letter of the law, then the formula would still be in the lab being tested on animals. But he had never been bound by laws and so their test was a true test. A field test in a live population. It had been in trials for twenty years now, its earliest subjects Institute students who had no one waiting for them on the outside, no one to notice when they never came back from their training. Some of their subjects' brains had been permanently damaged, meaning they couldn't be placed safely back into society. Now that the large field tests were occurring, Damon could barely contain his excitement. He had alerted Brody Hamilton that it was ready, and in turn, Hamilton had set the wheels in motion for Damon's coup de grace.

It was fascinating how much of human behavior was actually caused by chemicals in the brain. People thought they held the power of choice in their weak wills, but Damon knew better. So much of what drove them was chemical and then, beyond that, the subconscious. There were factors at play of which they had no inkling. His recent training in hypnosis had borne that out. But what he found even more fascinating was the effect that serotonin had on the brain.

His new concoction, which he'd named Ravage, was a cocktail of methamphetamine and ecstasy, combined with an accelerator his scientists had designed, that caused a particularly rabid methamphetamine-associated psychosis. An autopsy would just show the meth and ecstasy and everyone would assume that their dear departed mother, sister, brother, or whomever was a closet drug addict. And in the meantime, their atrocious acts of violence combined with their newly discovered secret habit would make everyone look at them in a new light.

Damon knew that Jack Logan was on the trail, and the exposure in the media would only help his case. That was why he'd made sure that his news conglomerate had given it very scant coverage. It wouldn't be long before these unconnected incidents would draw national attention from all the news sources, not just the ones Damon controlled through UBC. Once word of the autopsy results leaked out, it would look like another national drug crisis. That's when he'd make sure it hit all the news channels, with the spin that the recent focus on opioids as the biggest threat had made lawmakers less vigilant about monitoring the purchase of over-the-counter antihistamines commonly used to cook up meth. The authorities would assume there were tainted street drugs and would put all their attention on trying to find the source. Damon made sure to isolate the exposure to the Eastern Seaboard, so it would be believable that a particular batch had been tainted. They would never figure out the truth.

Just as in war, the best way to destroy troops is to take down their leader. When Pastor Pearson had gone crazy on television, his followers had been shocked, unmoored. They'd felt betrayed—the one preaching to them from the pulpit was in actuality a degenerate who indulged in the pleasures of the flesh. They hadn't thought to show him the same compassion or grace that he'd shown them when they first came to church. No, they had their judgment hats on and crucified him. Many would turn from their faith completely, utterly destroyed, as it called everything they believed into question.

Damon remembered the first lesson his esteemed adoptive father had taught him about the easily manipulated nature of human beings. If you wanted to ruin someone, you didn't go after them directly. You didn't call their convictions into question. You distracted them and made them want something else more than they wanted what was good for them. At its core, it was the same reason the diet industry was a billion-dollar business. Humans were unable to withstand temptation for any length of time. Their bad habits were their undoing, and everyone had an addiction of one type or another.

Another driver of people's behavior was herd mentality, Friedrich said, their lemminglike tendencies to follow the crowd. That was the secret weapon used by advertisers, influencers, and marketers for years. Politicians and world leaders understood it, too. After all, if everyone is doing it, it must be right.

"Mass hysteria is easy to accomplish," Friedrich told him. Every day after school when Damon would go to his house, his real education would commence. The older man taught him psychology, sociology, philosophy, and history, brilliantly explaining how they all intersected. "It need only start with one or two people whispering about something terrible afoot. Look at those foolish Puritans. They had no proof, but they put people to death over mere rumors of witchcraft. It happens over and over. And one need only look at the Communist scare here just a few decades ago. People were convinced that their neighbors or even relatives were a threat to the security of the country."

"Surely not everyone is susceptible to groupthink," Damon had replied, wanting to impress Friedrich with his contrarian pushback.

Friedrich shook his finger at him. "Only the extraordinary rise above and can see things for what they are. Those people are the leaders, the ones who use this human failing to their advantage."

Damon had never forgotten that lesson and had seen the phenomenon over and over in business. Need to sell more flu vaccines? Run a news story about people dying of the flu and everyone will clamor for it. Manufactured too many of a certain toy? Make people believe there's a shortage because it's so popular and see droves of customers in search of it. It was almost too easy. The success of all his commercial enterprises had depended on this knowledge. Now, years after he'd learned the foundation he'd used for so many experiments, it would be just a few more weeks until his plan would be complete. That's when the fun would really start.

CHAPTER TWENTY-FIVE

IKARIA, GREECE

ER NEIGHBOR TOULA HAD OFFERED TO STAY WITH HER uncle so that Rena could get back to her self-defense class. When the couple from Canada had come to the island and started their martial arts studio, she'd thought it would fold within a month. After all, Ikaria was a small and safe island where everyone knew everyone. But it was also a place with limited activities, so soon the classes were filled to overflowing. Rena had started going three years ago and had grown to love it. At first, she wasn't sure if she could continue, her body stiff and aching after class, but she found that it kept her in shape and was a great way to get rid of stress. And she also felt like she could protect herself, which was something precious after what had happened to her all those years ago back in America. Poking someone in the eye, bending back a finger, or kicking them in the groin were all tactics that would stop someone even twice her size. It had given her back her self-confidence.

Toula was in the kitchen when Rena returned.

"How is he?"

She shook her head. "I think he's getting worse. He had a coughing fit that lasted over ten minutes."

Rena sighed. "Thank you for staying. I'll go check on him."

Toula rose. "Of course, any time." She hugged Rena and left.

Rena opened the door to Yiannis's room. His breathing was ragged and his face dotted with perspiration. She went to the outer room and got a damp cloth and mopped his head. He closed his eyes and rested, while she sat and waited. Finally, he opened his eyes again and spoke haltingly. "I'll be gone soon, and you will not live forever. What will happen when you die? There is no one here to take your place guarding the coins. You must go back and find your daughter. She has a son now."

Silence settled heavily on them as she tried to get her mind around what he'd just told her.

"Evangelia. Did you hear me?"

He hadn't called her by her real name in twenty-four years. She swallowed. "I have a grandson?"

"Yes. I'm sorry I did not tell you . . . but you made me promise never to speak of your daughter again."

"What is his name? How old is he?"

"Evan. Almost two."

Evan. Taylor had named her child after her. A crushing heartbreak at all she had missed washed over Rena until she felt like it would break her in half.

"Someone is coming to help you." His voice was weak.

"Uncle, how were you able to arrange all this?"

"God gives us strength when we need it. The priest that was here is organizing everything. He has reached out to the church heads. Someone from the archdiocese, a Father Basil, will help you."

She was alarmed. "Are you sure we can trust him?"

"He is a good man. Above temptation." He waved his hand for her to leave, and his eyes closed. Rising, she leaned over and pulled his blanket up around his chin and kissed his cheek. She wanted to ask him more, but she knew she'd get nothing more out of him tonight.

She went into the small kitchen and sank down into one of the chairs. She'd hardly heard anything her uncle had said after he'd told her she had a grandson. How could he have kept that from her? He had summoned her here all those years ago and convinced her that the only way her daughter would be safe was if she stayed hidden, letting them believe she was dead. Not a single day had passed when she hadn't thought of Taylor, hadn't wondered what she was doing, if she was happy. But over time, she'd tried to contain these thoughts. She said a prayer for her daughter in the morning, and then she went about her day, taking care of her uncle, teaching English to the children at the small island school. As her parents had been born in Greece, Rena was fluent in Greek and it was the logical choice for a career on this small island. She'd made a life for herself here among strangers who became her friends and family. She had learned to love it, and after all this time, they had accepted her as their own.

○ ○ ○

The next morning, Rena knew her uncle was gone even before she went into his room. There was a quiet to the house, a stillness that told her in her heart before her eyes ever saw. In a daze, she planned his funeral, accepted the condolences from all her neighbors, and wondered what she was supposed to do next. She'd given up her life in America because of this sacred trust, and now she was supposed to go back? A moment of doubt passed over her. Maybe his entreaties had been the result of his fever, and she didn't really need to do anything. After all, she'd protected the coins for all these years and nothing bad had happened. The more she thought about it, the more she convinced herself that the safest and wisest course of action was to stay. She was now the only one who knew where they were hidden. If something were to happen to her, the secret would die with her. It was much safer to remain here than to dig them up and take them back to a place where others would be after them.

The house was lonely with her uncle gone, but she understood that it would take time for her to get used to this new normal. She still had her students, her neighbors, her books, and, of course, her faith. Living this simple life had enabled her to spend more time in prayer and contemplation than she would ever have been able to in America. It was almost like being a nun . . . and suddenly the idea of joining a monastery loomed brightly in front of her. That could be the answer to all her prayers. She would have a community, and she could serve God. It might be a chance for her to finally find peace and absolution for what she had done. Then maybe, just maybe, if she found she could trust the abbess, she would even tell her about the coins and take them there for safekeeping, where they could stay forever. She began to feel calm for the first time since her uncle had passed. This was a good idea. A divine idea. She would begin preparations tomorrow.

Warming up a pot of stew that one of the neighbors had brought her, she debated walking down to the village square. Nearly everyone would be there for a coffee and a chat; it was one of things she loved about island living—you never had to be alone if you didn't want to be. In fact, this was the first time in over a week that one neighbor or another hadn't stopped in with food and a kind word. Deciding she wasn't in the mood for talking tonight, she ate her dinner in silence, her mind wandering as she thought about the future.

After washing her dishes, she went to her bedroom and changed. She looked at her uncle's computer, sitting on her desk next to the notebook with instructions on how to use it. He'd made her promise that, after he was gone, she would use it to rejoin the modern world. After staring at it for several minutes, she sighed and stood. Bringing it over to the bed, she opened it and waited for it start. She clicked on the icon for the internet the way he had shown her, her heart beating wildly as she typed in the name that was never far from her mind. There were several pages of results, and she clicked the first one. Her breath caught in her throat when she saw the picture of her daughter that accompanied the article. She devoured the words on the screen and then sat back, staggered.

Now that she'd opened Pandora's box, she clicked through to another article and continued to read, her heart growing heavy with each word. She went back to the search engine and typed in more names, more subjects, all prompted by what she'd just read. Every nerve was on fire as the hours passed and she read and read.

By the time she'd finished, the sun was rising. She closed the computer and looked out the window. She couldn't go to the monastery, as much as she wanted to. No, the time for hiding was over. It was time to go back to America. But how? She had no passport, no credit cards. She was still thinking about it when there was a knock at the door. She walked the few feet to the doorway and looked out. Standing there was a man she'd never seen before.

"May I help you?"

"I'm Father Basil. I believe you're expecting me."

CHAPTER TWENTY-SIX

LEONARD FINISHED LOOKING OVER THE PROFIT AND LOSS statement, then closed the file. It had been another excellent quarter thanks to the new program he'd had implemented for the claims department. He'd hired a bunch of PhDs to come up with an algorithm that was saving them millions. It identified those customers who were least likely to go the extra mile in submitting a second claim and would just pay the bill themselves. He also put a limit on the claim amount, so it wasn't onerous for the policyholder to come up with the money. Those customers who were over sixty-five, those with ethnic-sounding names who might not speak English well, and those in certain zip codes where educational levels were known to be lower. The beauty of the score was that it was confidential and proprietary, so it couldn't come under the scrutiny of the insurance commission. Of course, if there were enough complaints to trigger an audit, the commission might realize that a disproportionate number of claims had been pulled from those categories, so he made sure that they mixed them up and had a second score, which was more randomized and which they used every eleven days so that there was never a month in which the claim denials would attract suspicion. He had also made it difficult for all customers to submit the new claims, requiring they do it via fax. Who felt like schlepping to a fax machine? People were lazy. They weren't going to put themselves out over a few bucks. But those few bucks that the company should have paid, when multiplied by hundreds of thousands of consumers, added up to big profits for them, and a nice fat bonus for Leonard.

That money went into a separate account, one that Patrice had no idea about. Leonard needed his discretionary money to fund his darker urges. Women like Sissy provided him with suitable distraction and pleasure to get through the week, but there were things that even they couldn't do. Every few months he withdrew a big sum of cash and used it to purchase services found only on the dark web. He held off as long as he could in between these sessions, knowing that if he were ever found out, it would be the end of not only his career, but his freedom as well. But the thrill of the risk was half the pleasure. It was just that there was so much scrutiny these days on men. He swore, the hardest thing to be in this day and age was a man. Women complaining that if you looked at them too long you were leering at them, or if you complimented them, God forbid, you were sexually harassing them. It infuriated him and brought out his need to punish. When his frustration had risen so high that he started snapping at even his precious daughters, that's when he knew it was time to let the air out of the tire, so to speak. Now was one of those times.

"Hello," a male voice answered.

"I hear it's going to rain. Are you still selling umbrellas?" Leonard asked.

"Yes. What kind do you want?"

"A brand-new one. Disposable."

"Code?"

Leonard's burner phone beeped with a new text message. He read the number aloud.

"You're confirmed. It will be delivered to the usual location. Time?"

"Eight P.M. Eastern," Leonard answered. He hung up and picked up his office phone. "Get my wife on the line."

When his assistant buzzed, he picked up again.

"I have to go out of town on business overnight. Kiss the girls for me."

"You just found out? I was planning on going out tonight with some friends, and you gave the nanny off for her birthday, remember?"

He rolled his eyes. "Well, now you're staying in. Deal with it."

He hung up. He fantasized for a moment about what he would do to her if he could . . . but she was safe. He wouldn't do anything to hurt the children, and making their mother disappear would definitely scar them. Lucky for Patrice, he was a good father.

CHAPTER TWENTY-SEVEN

IKARIA, GREECE

SHE'D BEEN EXPECTING FATHER BASIL TO BE AN OLDER PRIEST, but Eva opened the door to a man who looked to be in his thirties—trim and fit with dark hair and a short beard.

"Let's go to the kitchen," she said, ushering him in. He followed her and she automatically set out plates and some pastries. "Coffee?"

"No, thank you. Just water, please."

Before he sat down, he walked to the window and closed it. "One cannot be too careful."

Pointing to a chair, she waited for him to sit down, his proximity making her nervous. "Would you show me some identification, please?"

"Of course." He took his passport from his satchel and showed it to her. *Basil Parakos.*

She set a glass of water in front of him and poured herself

a strong cup of Turkish coffee. "My uncle was very sick when he told me you were coming. I wasn't even sure you were real."

He looked back at her, unsmiling. "I'm real."

"What can I do for you?" she asked.

"I've come to take you back to America. Are you ready to return?"

"If I must. My mission is the same as yours—to protect the coins," she answered.

He nodded. "It is not safe for them or you to remain here any longer. It's time to take all the coins to America. I have collected the coins that were hidden at Mount Athos, and I have something for you."

Father Basil pulled a folder from his satchel and opened it, handing her a Greek passport with her real name. "I've already booked your flight. You leave in two days."

She reached out and took it from him, studying it. "How did you get this picture of me?" It was a photo from a few years ago that he must have cropped and scanned.

"Your uncle had it sent to me."

He handed her a piece of paper. "Memorize the number, then destroy the paper. It's your daughter's cell phone. Once you land, get in touch with her. Tell her the truth."

She ran her thumb over the number, imagining for a moment what it would be like to hear Taylor's voice again after all these years. The priest went on.

"Credit cards, extra cash. Everything you need is here. Once you're back in the States, you'll take the coins to a church ceremony. That's how they will be transferred to the archbishop."

"How?" she asked.

"I'm getting to that. But first, I need you to show me where your family coins are. I will hide them here," he said, bringing out two wooden icons from his satchel.

"Why can't you leave the icons with me and let me do it?"

"The coins are not safe for you to handle directly. I've been preparing myself spiritually for weeks now." The priest went on. "I've had false backs adhered to these icons so that you can hide the coins within them. You can take the icons back with you to the States. There's a church in Pittsburgh that was damaged by a fire last year, where you will donate the icons. When the archbishop stops there during his tour in a few weeks to bless the icons, he will take your ten coins and get them to the patriarch in Istanbul. I'm going to do the same with the ten coins that have been on Mount Athos."

"Why not try to do the exchange here?"

"This is the order of the archbishop. I don't question him. The plan is for the patriarch to go to Rome to meet with the pope and leave ten of the coins at the Vatican until the final ten are found and we can reunite all thirty. The Eastern and Western Churches will work together. The coins will be safe there until they can be destroyed and—"

"But they can't be destroyed until the other ten are found," she interrupted him.

He nodded his head patiently. "Yes. When the final ten are regained, the patriarch and the pope will meet to destroy them."

"Do you know where they are?"

"Yes."

She gave him an exasperated look. "Well?"

"Damon Crosse has them."

She froze. How could that be? "Damon Crosse has been dead for almost two years now—my uncle told me."

Father Basil shook his head. "That's what everyone believes, but his suicide was a hoax. His son, Jeremy, used the coins as a bargaining chip to get back onto the premises of the Institute. Jeremy had planned to take the coins back after Crosse was arrested, but Crosse tricked him. Jeremy had no idea that they were not the real coins, but the fakes you placed at Agape House before you brought the real ones to Greece. Then Crosse killed himself . . . or so it seemed. After Crosse's supposed death, the coins were gone. The church sent people to investigate; they talked to the emergency staff, the coroner, the funeral director, but nothing turned up. Last month, the coroner finally admitted he had helped Crosse orchestrate his false suicide. He had a crisis of conscience when he got a terminal cancer diagnosis and reached out to one of our investigators to tell us that Damon is alive—and he's looking for the rest of the coins, too."

"Crosse hasn't found them in all these years. Why can't we leave them where they are?"

"You're not understanding. He's not the only threat. Ten, twenty, a hundred years from now, someone else may find them. The coins call out to one another. They corrupt. They want to find a way to be together. This is the first time in over two hundred years that the church has regained a majority of them."

She'd given up her life, her family, to protect these relics, and this stranger wanted her to just hand them over. What if he wasn't actually trustworthy? What if he'd gotten her uncle to believe his lies?

She sat up straighter. "I'll go back. But I'm doing it my way."

He looked taken aback. "Pardon me?"

"*I* will hide them in the icons. I have a strong spiritual life, and I'm sure that I'll be just fine. I'll see you again at the church ceremony back in the States."

He assessed her for a moment. "You don't trust me?"

"I've been taught to trust no one."

He sighed. "I have served His Eminence for seven years."

She folded her arms. "It doesn't matter. I'm not telling you where they are. I will do as you say and take them to America, and once I can confirm that there is indeed such a service planned at a church in Pittsburgh, I'll get in touch with you."

His face turned red and he opened his mouth to speak but stopped himself, seemingly thinking it over. Eventually, he spoke. "I suppose I understand your concerns." He was quiet for another moment. "There's no way Crosse knows you have them, nor could anyone else for that matter. I suppose you can carry them safely if you put them securely in the icons. I have a receipt for them you need to keep on you. Otherwise, if a customs officer searches your bags and sees them, he might assume you're stealing relics from Greece."

She hadn't thought of that. "Okay, thank you. And just so you know, Father, I won't be bringing them out of hiding until after you've left the island."

"I understand."

After he'd given everything to her, Father Basil left and she breathed a sigh of relief. She didn't think he was on the wrong side, but then again, she'd lived with Warwick Parks all those years and never suspected he would betray her. Of one thing she was certain—now that her beloved uncle was gone, there was no one she could take at face value.

CHAPTER TWENTY-EIGHT

As Taylor drove Evan to the pediatrician's, dire scenarios filled her mind, tying her stomach up in knots. When they arrived, the waiting room was crowded, and she hated to put Evan down, worried that he might leave with something worse than what he came in with as coughs and sneezes filled the air. She held tight to his hand as she went up to the receptionist and gave their name, hoping she could get him into the well room before he saw a toy in the main room that beckoned to him.

She rubbed his back as she waited for the receptionist to run her insurance card, and he laid his head on her shoulder, sucking his thumb. He didn't seem remotely interested in exploring the waiting room, which worried her more now than the possibility of his catching something. She tried to put him down, but he started to cry so she sat, still holding him, praying silently that the doctor would find some benign explanation for his sudden fatigue.

When the nurse called their names, she jumped up and carried Evan into one of the small examining rooms. Dr. Manta's nurse, a young woman in Winnie-the-Pooh scrubs, walked in right after.

"Hi, Taylor, Evan. What brings you in today?"

"Evan's been uncharacteristically tired and very cranky lately. I just want to make sure nothing's brewing."

"Okay." She smiled at Evan. "How are you, sweetie?" She inserted a digital thermometer in his ear and pulled it out a few seconds later when it beeped. "Normal."

He didn't answer and turned his face away from her.

"Any fever before now, throwing up, diarrhea?"

"No. Nothing like that."

"Okay, well, Dr. Manta will be in shortly."

She shut the door and Taylor was shifting Evan to her other hip when the doctor walked in.

"So we're feeling tired lately, are we?" Walking over to the sink, he washed his hands, then stood in front of Taylor and Evan, giving the boy's hair a tousle. "Hey, big guy, can you look at Doc?"

Taylor sat Evan on the table and gave him her keys, which seemed to perk him up a little. The doctor touched Evan's neck and felt his lymph nodes, then listened to his chest and gave him a general once-over. "So you said no fever or stomach upset. How's his appetite been?"

Taylor thought. "About the same. He's going through a bit of a finicky stage, wanting cookies instead of food, but of course, I don't give in."

"Smart boy. Who wouldn't prefer a cookie to a veggie? But he does look a little pale to me. Let's do a quick finger prick to check his hemoglobin. Could be running low on iron."

Taylor braced herself as he took Evan's little hand in his and gave it a brief prick, then squeezed some blood onto a slide.

Immediately Evan's lips puckered, and he began to cry.

"I'm sorry, buddy." Doctor Manta pulled a Spider-Man sticker from his lab coat pocket and handed it to Evan. "This is for being a brave boy."

Evan clutched it in his hand, his mouth still in a pout and big teardrops on his cheeks. It broke Taylor's heart.

"I'll be back in a few minutes." The doctor took the slide and left, and Taylor pulled out an oatmeal cookie from the diaper bag and handed it to Evan. That at least brought a smile to his face. The minutes dragged until the door opened again, and Taylor's heart tightened. She didn't like the look on the doctor's face.

"What's wrong?" Taylor asked

He tilted his head. "Evan's hemoglobin levels are low."

"How low?"

He paused. "I'd normally expect them to be between ten and eleven, and his are at nine."

"What does that mean?"

"He's probably anemic, which just means his iron is low. This could be caused by a number of things. Let's try not to panic. You said he's been finicky. It could just be his diet."

She shook her head. "He eats broccoli and spinach. Also grass-fed beef at least once a week. And he's on a multivitamin." Her stomach lurched and she began to think of all the terrible things that could be wrong with him.

He nodded. "I'd like to run a full blood panel. CBC and iron studies. And I'll do a reticulocyte count to make sure his blood is regenerating normally."

She took a deep breath. "You're scaring me."

"I'm not trying to. I just want to be thorough. You mentioned the fatigue and general lethargy. Let's just make sure everything's okay. It could be any number of things, most of which are very treatable. Try not to think the worst."

But of course Taylor went right to the worst. She felt she was going to throw up or faint or both. "But you're also looking to make sure it's not something like a . . ." She mouthed the words *blood cancer*. "Right?"

"Taylor . . ."

"I need to call Jack." She suddenly felt like she couldn't breathe.

Dr. Manta put a hand on her arm. "Take a deep breath. Evan's been a very healthy little boy. I'm just being cautious. I wouldn't be doing my job if I wasn't. We'll run the tests, and we'll have a much better picture in a couple of days—I'll have them rush the results. Please, let's not worry until we have something to worry about."

Easy for him to say, she thought. She would do nothing but worry until they got the results. Taylor pulled out her cell phone and dialed Jack, but it rang a few times then went to voice mail. She hung up. He'd call her back when he saw the missed call.

"So if it's not his diet causing the low iron, what else could it be, on the not-terrifying scale?"

"Well, loss of blood, of course, but that's not the case here. Lead exposure can be a factor. There are some hereditary diseases in which the bone marrow doesn't produce enough red blood cells. There's one, thalassemia, that's more common in Greeks and could be the explanation."

"It's treatable, though, right?" She knew a little about the disease but never thought to be tested, especially as Malcolm hadn't been Greek.

"Yes, very. Usually with some blood transfusions and sometimes chelation. Again, we're getting ahead of ourselves."

"But at least that's a possibility that's less horrifying than . . ." She wouldn't say the word again.

"Let's get him to the lab so we can take blood, and then I want you to go home and try to think positive. I really think we're going to find a logical explanation. He's not bruising, and everything else looks good. We just have to get those iron levels back up." He gave her a sympathetic look. "It could be that he's not absorbing the iron for some reason, but before we put him through any invasive GI testing, let's look at the blood."

She took a deep breath. Then another. What if that's what the dream meant, that he was sick and there was nothing she could do? Tears sprang to her eyes. The doctor put a hand on hers and gave it a gentle squeeze.

"I know you're worried, but let's try to take this one step at a time. I'll take the blood myself. I've gotten pretty good at it." He smiled at her.

Once they walked down the hallway to the lab, Dr. Manta pushed Evan's sleeve up while Taylor held him.

"Hmm. I can't find a good vein in this arm." He looked more closely. "He hasn't had blood taken anywhere else, has he?"

Taylor shook her head. "Of course not. I only bring him to you."

"Must just be a little scab. Let's try the other arm." He put the tourniquet on Evan's left arm and slid a gloved finger over his elbow. "This will work." He pulled a butterfly needle out and inserted it. Evan flinched, then started to cry again. Taylor watched as his blood filled the tube. Her stomach lurched again and she thought about the answer to be found in that red liquid. She prayed it would bring good news.

○ ○ ○

Evan was quiet on the drive back to the house. They greeted Beau when they walked into the house, then Taylor put Evan down in the playroom. She still hadn't heard from Jack, and she needed to talk to someone. Her hand shook as she pulled her phone from her purse and called her brother.

"Jer, I'm scared," she said as soon as he picked up.

The tone of his voice immediately changed. "What's the matter?"

She filled him in on the doctor's visit.

"All right, now, you need to breathe. It's going to be okay. We'll pray."

"What if it's not? Prayers aren't always answered. You know that. I can't survive if anything happens . . ." She choked back tears and was unable to talk.

"Where's Jack?" Jeremy asked softly.

"Pittsburgh."

"I'm coming over. It's going to be fine. I promise."

Taylor hung up and went in to check on Evan, who was now lying on the floor asleep. She couldn't hold in the tears. Sobs racked her body as she gave in to the terror she felt. If God took Evan from her, then he may as well take her life, too. She was strong. But not that strong. No matter what anyone might try to tell her, she wouldn't survive the loss.

CHAPTER TWENTY-NINE

DAMON WAS LIVID. BACK FROM LONDON, HE'D EXPECTED TO have time with Evan today at UBC. He'd checked the security log through his laptop three times to see if Evan had been checked in yet. Frustrated, he'd stormed down to Karen Printz's office. She was on the phone but hung up as soon as she saw him.

"Mr. Wheeler. Is there something you need?"

"I wanted an update on the Supreme Court story. Are you meeting with Taylor Parks today?"

Karen said, "No, we were supposed to, but her little boy's under the weather. She took him to the doctor this morning for some tests. She wants to keep him home until she knows what's going on, so she'll Zoom into our meeting."

He tried to look concerned. "I'm sorry to hear that. Nothing serious, I hope?"

"I hope not. He's been tired lately, and it turns out his iron levels are depleted. They're trying to determine the cause."

"Ah, well, with any luck it will be resolved quickly." He turned to leave, then stopped. "Do keep me updated on everything. And let me know when you've found a replacement story for that girl who needs the heart."

"Yes, sir. We haven't yet, but Taylor's working on it."

Damon returned to his office and paced its length. He should have remembered what had happened all those years ago to that little girl who had become almost zombielike in her fatigue, though there had been no mother around to notice. He had been reckless with Evan. He shouldn't have taken so much blood in such a short amount of time, but it would work out: when the tests came back normal, the doctor would most likely give him an iron supplement and tell her it was just one of those things. Evan would perk up and Taylor would be so relieved that she'd drop her guard again and return to work and bring Evan back to the center.

Ultimately, though, it hadn't even been necessary. Those damn coins weren't the real ones and he'd wasted Evan's precious blood on them, and now he only had a small vial left. But once Damon had the real coins entrusted to the Papakalos family, Evan's blood would grant them more power. In the meantime, he had other aspects of his plans to focus on.

CHAPTER THIRTY

IKARIA, GREECE

EVA WAITED UNTIL TWO HOURS BEFORE DAWN TO WALK THE quiet streets toward Therma, in her pocket a key to the thermal spas that her uncle had given to her years ago. Looking around to make sure there were no spying eyes, she slipped in through the back and walked toward the cave opening that housed the baths and sauna. It was eerily quiet and pitch-black. She pulled out her flashlight to illuminate the path, and when she reached the sauna, she stepped inside and walked straight to the bench in the back. She squeezed behind it and felt along the floor for the drain covering, which she pried open with a screwdriver, then retrieved a small plastic bag from the drain and pulled out the key. After replacing the cover, she inched along the wall and away from the bench.

A slight whistling sound made her freeze, and she held her breath, all her senses on high alert. Its steady rhythm indicated that what she heard was breathing, and she jumped and moved the flashlight around in front of her to try to find the source.

"Who's there?" she called into the black. There was no response. Heart pounding, she hurried from the cave, stopping at its mouth to shine her light around some more, but there was no one in sight. She chided herself for her overactive imagination.

She ran the two miles back up the hill, grateful that she was in such good shape thanks to her training at the self-defense studio. Looking behind her every few steps until she was satisfied that no one had followed her, Eva finally reached the island's funeral home and went inside to the small area that housed the mausoleums. Even though it was after hours, the door was unlocked. She and her uncle had bought one of the crypts, ostensibly to hold his mother's ashes, but a wooden box containing sand and dust had been the hiding place for the coins for the past twenty-four years. As she pulled it out and fished in the sand for the coins, she felt a chill go through her as she placed each coin in the pockets of her dress. She became warmer and warmer, her body filling with an increasingly intense dread. When the tenth coin was in place, she locked the box and ran from the room.

The coins must be exerting their power on her, she realized, as her mind was flooded with images of murder and blood. She barely made it to the edge of the road before she vomited. It was clear the coins could not stay on her person for long.

She hurried back into the mausoleum and found a small silver can filled with sand and a couple of candles. She took the coins from her pocket and placed them into the can, where the candles began to melt from the heat of the coins, then rushed home, out of breath but forcing her legs to take her as fast they could back to the safety of her house. When she got there, she put the can on the floor and grabbed her Bible, praying fervently until the violent images bombarding her began to slow and eventually recede.

Hiding the coins in the icons Father Basil had left was still the plan, but she didn't want to let them touch her skin again. Her uncle had told her that her familial connection to the coins made her particularly sensitive to their power. When enough time had passed that she felt calm enough to handle it, she grabbed a pair of gloves from the closet and began the painstaking work of carefully adhering the coins into the false backs of the icons. Her hands shook, and perspiration dampened her shirt as she worked, but finally she finished and put the icons in a suitcase she hid in the back of her closet, then took her Bible to bed with her and clutched it to her chest as she slept.

Her dreams that night were dark and disturbing.

CHAPTER THIRTY-ONE

LEONARD WAS GLAD HE'D DUMPED HIS STOCK IN ALL THE MAjor companies producing cold remedies last year. The job losses were in the thousands, and unemployment spiked dramatically. The ten-billion-dollar industry had practically dried up overnight thanks to the blazing success of the miraculous new cold vaccine, which was being shown to be 95 percent effective. And Leonard was grateful that he'd gotten the tip to buy stock in Licentia Labs right before the news of the vaccine broke.

Of course the information hadn't come to him for free. He'd had to agree to cover the full cost of the vaccine in all Jefferson's insurance plans, even the low-cost ones. It may have lost the company some money up front, but in the long run, they'd save millions on all those folks who would have ended up with bronchitis and other complications from the cold.

He now had other things to worry about, though, like the fact that he had at best sixty days, at worst thirty, until the Supreme Court decision was handed down. If Jefferson lost, it would cost them billions. And compromising a Supreme Court justice had been harder than he'd anticipated. Leonard was used to taking people down. One of the reasons that Brody Hamilton now occupied the second-highest office in the land was because Leonard had placed skeletons in the closets of his competitors.

But the justices were a different story. Of the five whose votes he doubted, he'd already taken his shot at two. Paranoia ran deep these days, between the #MeToo movement and the ease with which photos and videos were captured. People were scared shitless of being caught doing something wrong. The good old days of picking up a prostitute on the spur of the moment were gone—at least among savvy, high-profile men. He'd dug into all five of the justices' pasts, but of course, they'd been thoroughly vetted already and he was unable to find anything. Three men. Two women. He always started with the men; women were so much harder to corrupt. Sex, drugs, bribes—no takers so far. Justice Landon, who'd been seated just last year, was a good-looking man of only fifty-five with a wife who had a face for radio. There was no way this guy didn't get a little extra on the side. Leonard decided that a call girl wouldn't do. No, he'd need someone genuine to tempt Justice Landon. Someone like Sissy, who by now would do anything Leonard asked of her.

When he arrived at her apartment to prep her for her mission, she buzzed him in immediately, and he groaned when he saw the out-of-order sign on the elevator. Why did she live in this dump anyway? If he had had plans to keep her around longer, he would have moved her somewhere else, but he didn't see the need for it. He was out of breath after walking up the three flights of stairs and he wiped the sweat from his brow with the back of his hand. It was hard to believe there'd been a time when he ran marathons, he thought wryly.

She opened the door with a broad smile.

"What's the hell's wrong with the elevator this time?"

"Sorry, honey. It just happened this morning. Come in."

He'd met Sissy a few months ago at an upscale and very private gentleman's club. He liked dating strippers, but he picked only the cream of the crop, those who were young and intelligent and were using their talents to put themselves through school. He'd start by acting fatherly and concerned, giving them big tips and asking them about their college courses. He'd groom them for a couple of weeks, until they began to look forward to seeing him. Then he would pretend that he was falling for them and start giving them ridiculously large tips. They thought they had him right where they wanted him, but all the while he was playing *them*. He'd abruptly switch tactics and ignore them, giving his attention to another girl. Then they'd try to win him back and he'd let them eventually. It always culminated in their seducing him, kicking off a new affair. Sissy was completely at his beck and call by now.

Looking at Sissy now in the outfit he'd bought her, a fitted black sequin cocktail dress with a V neckline and plunging back, he knew that Landon wouldn't be able to keep his eyes off her. Tonight was the justice's quarterly boys' night out with his pals from Dartmouth. They always met in New York on a Saturday at the Dead Rabbit, had dinner at Benjamin Steakhouse, and ended the evening with cocktails at Augustine. That's where Sissy would come in, but Leonard wasn't taking any chances. If Landon didn't take the bait, Sissy would drop Rohypnol in his drink and whisk him up to her suite at the Beekman. There, she'd take plenty of sexy selfies of the two of them in compromising positions. And she'd been instructed to make sure that they were very explicit pictures. But just in case that didn't prove to be enough to convince him to vote the right way, Sissy's thirteen-year-old sister, Clara, would also stop by for a photo shoot with him after he'd been roofied. While adultery was one thing, Landon would do anything to avoid being labeled a pedophile and have his life ruined. Clara was happy to do it in exchange for a thousand dollars in crisp one-hundred-dollar bills—the money would come in handy for her oxy habit.

And his plan solved another of his problems. After Sissy had given him all the evidence, he'd tell her he wanted nothing to do with her now that she'd slept with another man. But for now, he just smiled at her. "You look amazing, sweetheart. There's no way he'll be able to look away."

She gave him a grateful smile. "You think?"

"I'm sure."

"I'm a little nervous. I mean, he *is* a Supreme Court justice."

Leonard shook his head. "Pretend you don't know that. No one recognizes them. He'll be flattered that a sexy young woman is paying attention to him. Pretend you don't even recognize his name. Where's Clara?"

"My stepfather's dropping her off soon. We'll catch an eight o'clock train into the city."

"Okay. But remember, no texts or calls. We'll meet on Monday. Make sure nothing goes wrong."

She walked over to him and put her arms around his neck, leaning in close to him. "Don't worry. I've got it all under control. After tonight, he won't be able to blackmail you anymore. He'll have to destroy the pictures of him and your wife."

He kissed her long and hard, savoring this last kiss. "I don't know what I would do without you. It would destroy my girls if they knew their mother had done those vile things with him," he lied.

She shook her head. "It's disgusting. He has no right to be on the Supreme Court."

"Well, after this he won't be."

She bit her lip. "Are you sure I really have to do, you know, everything with him? Can't I just make it look like we did?"

Leonard said, "No. It has to be authentic. We can't have him claiming it's been Photoshopped or faked somehow. I know it's asking a lot, but it's the only way."

"What if he won't do it? If he's not interested in me?"

"Then you drug him with the Rohypnol, have your thirteen-year-old sister get naked next to him, and take lots of pictures." Did he have to spell everything out?

"After this is all behind us, you'll tell your wife that you're leaving, right? We'll be together?"

"Absolutely. All right. I'm going to go now. Remember, I believe in you."

"I love you," she called out as he walked to the door.

He stopped and turned to look at her. "I love you too. So much."

As he walked down the stairs and out the door, he muttered, "Good riddance to bad trash," and got into his BMW. How he loved tying up loose ends.

CHAPTER THIRTY-TWO

JACK WAS RELIEVED THAT THINGS BETWEEN HIM AND TAYLOR were back on an even keel. He'd been keeping her apprised of his every move regarding Dakota. The tension had mostly dissipated between them, and they were focusing on more pressing matters, especially Evan's health. When she told him about Evan's visit to the doctor, he offered to cancel his meetings in Pittsburgh and come straight home, but she insisted it wasn't necessary. Jeremy was with her, and she said they'd have the results by the next afternoon. He knew if he disregarded her wishes and showed up, she'd know that he was just as worried as she was, and that could send her over the edge. Despite knowing better, he did a bit of googling that confirmed that his worst assumptions were legitimate. But he also remembered the admonition he'd heard on one of the ubiquitous medical shows—when you hear hoofbeats, think horses, not zebras. Still, he'd seen his share of zebras. But Evan had to be okay. Life couldn't be that cruel . . . could it?

In Pittsburgh, Jack stopped at the hospital where Pastor Pearson was being treated, but the police weren't letting anyone onto his floor. All he had been able to find out was that the pastor's condition was still listed as serious. Jack had emailed and called the church office—someone must have cleared the phone messages because he was finally able to leave one—but hadn't gotten a response yet. Scotty would have the inside scoop on the toxicology report, since it was now an active criminal case and the pastor had been arrested and was under police guard at the hospital. Jack had thought of speaking to the local police, but Scotty had asked him not to. It was part of a bigger FBI investigation now because of multiple states being affected. Jack also was looking into another incident, one that had happened four days ago—this time Frank Morris, a psychologist who'd gone off the rails.

When Jack visited Kate Morris, the psychologist's wife, at their home, she'd relayed her horror story in a monotone trance, likely under the influence of a prescribed sedative. Her husband, who had practiced for twenty-five years with an impeccable record, had conducted his practice from an office attached to their home. The last appointment he'd had was with a couple he'd been seeing for marriage counseling for six months. She told Jack that last week, as the day had grown late and her husband wasn't yet home, she'd looked out the window and seen that his clients' car was still parked out front. She had gone over and knocked on the office door, but when she got no answer, she'd gotten worried and pushed it open.

The couple's bodies had been on the floor, their heads smashed in, a splintered and bloodied baseball bat next to them. Her husband was sitting in his chair, his clothes stained with blood, talking to someone she couldn't see. She'd started screaming his name, and when he'd looked up at her, he'd seemed crazed and yelled that she had to die too. She'd run into the house, locked the door, and called the police, who'd arrived quickly and been able to contain him. Before anyone could make any sense of it, though, he hanged himself in his jail cell in the middle of the night.

Dr. Morris's wife didn't have the autopsy report yet so Jack couldn't confirm if meth was involved, but the scenario was so similar to the others that he was certain it would be. He was typing up his notes when his phone pinged with a text—Scotty.

> Looked into your cases. Three of them were in states where the cause of death is public record and easily obtained. You were right. Meth-induced psychotic break resulting in murder-suicides in all three. Requested subpoenas for the rest. Should have by end of week. Maria and I will expect you for dinner on Thursday.

That made six confirmed cases of methamphetamine found in the bloodstreams of all the killers, and Scotty's help with records on the rest of them would save Jack a ton of time. He still wanted to re-interview the people he'd already spoken to because he didn't believe these people's loved ones had voluntarily used meth—none of them showed signs of prolonged use, and it was too coincidental to think they'd all just taken up the habit. It had to have been slipped to them somehow, but he had no idea how. He'd have to go back over all his notes, make more phone calls, and see if there were any prescriptions they had in common or over-the-counter remedies—even some kind of vitamin or nutritional supplement they'd all ordered.

He decided to start with the four survivors he'd already interviewed. He could cover most of it on the phone, having already established a rapport with them. There was no sense talking to anyone new until he'd exhausted every possible connection between the cases he'd already started investigating. Then he'd consider in-person visits to the rest if he still hadn't found a common denominator. That meant he could go home tomorrow, see Evan, and be there when the doctor called with the test results.

Who was he kidding? Even without the help from Scotty, Jack would have made a detour back home to New York tomorrow. There was no way he'd let Taylor get the results all alone.

Jack's mind started to swirl with worst-case scenarios about what the tests would reveal, so he left the hotel and began walking to clear his head. Their life had finally been getting back to normal. He'd never thought he could be this happy or even that he deserved to be. Every morning he got to wake up next to the love of his life, the woman that he thought he'd lost forever. Taylor had given him a second chance, and he had vowed to never let anything bad happen to her again. It started raining, but he kept going, his thoughts swirling furiously.

After everything they'd been through, he'd wanted to believe he could erect a wall of protection around them and make sure nothing bad ever got in. But he was wrong. Bad things found him—they always found him. He was soaked now and stopped, ready to turn back, but as he stopped, he looked up and saw he was in front of a church.

He reached for the door, thinking maybe he should go in and say a prayer . . . but his hand froze in midair, and he shook his head. What was the point? Either Evan was going to be okay or he wasn't. Jack's going into that church and talking to the air wouldn't make one damn bit of difference. He turned around and hurried back toward the warmth of the hotel.

CHAPTER THIRTY-THREE

THOUGH SHE AND JEREMY HAD STAYED UP LATE TALKING, with him trying to allay her fears, Taylor didn't feel any less worried the next morning.

She wanted to stay busy, knowing that until she heard back from the doctor, she'd be on pins and needles. She still had some follow-up on her story and a video call with Karen at nine, but afterward, she would suggest that they take Evan to the playground. The weather forecast for the day was clear and sunny, and she thought the fresh air would do them all some good. After making coffee and pouring herself a cup, she put some milk on the stove and mixed in some Irish oats.

"Come here, sweetie. Oatmeal's ready."

Evan stopped what he was doing and ran over, crashing into her legs. "Mmm mmm."

He climbed into his booster seat and she put the bowl in front of him. He dug in, singing and kicking his legs while he ate. Beau sat patiently at his feet, waiting for the inevitable drips of food that would be coming his way.

"Nummy."

"Glad you like it."

"He seems more energetic today," Jeremy said from the doorway.

"Hope we didn't wake you," Taylor answered.

Jeremy shook his head. "I've been up since five. Had to finish up some reports." He walked over to the coffeepot, took a mug from the counter, and filled it. He smiled at Evan. "Hey, buddy. Can you show me your nose?"

Evan stared at him.

"Where's your nose?" Taylor asked.

He pointed proudly.

"That's my big boy."

Jeremy looked at Taylor. "Did you get any sleep?"

She sighed. "A little. I just wish the doctor would call and tell me everything's fine."

Jeremy nodded. "He will. I'm sure of it."

"But you know even better than I do what it could mean."

Jeremy reached over and squeezed Taylor's hand. "You can't go there. Listen, there are many, many reasons for low iron. Your doctor is just being thorough. Evan's not sick. His color's good, his energy is returning. It's going to be okay. Really."

"Are you sure you don't mind keeping an eye on him while I do some work this morning? I know you've probably got a million more important things to do."

Jeremy said, "There is nothing more important than spending time with my favorite nephew."

Taylor smiled at him. "Thank you."

An hour later, Taylor was in the study finalizing her notes on a potential case to replace Cora's. When nine o'clock rolled around, she found Karen's Zoom invite and clicked on the link. After a few seconds, her boss's face appeared on the screen, and the rest of the team soon came into view.

Taylor launched into her update. "We're all set with Georgia Lakos for the age discrimination, and Molly and Clyde Edwards cover both the religious and the pregnancy classification, so the last one we wanted to cover was the disability discrimination. I still think our best case is Cora's. It really pulls at the heartstrings," Taylor said.

"Taylor, Mr. Wheeler made his position clear on that. I thought we had agreed that you would find something else," Karen said.

Taylor sighed. She'd had to try one more time; she felt like she owed Cora and her parents that. "We did, and there is another case that might work."

"Great. We're all ears," Karen said.

"Okay. Lawrence is thirteen, on the autism spectrum, nonverbal. He lost his sight when he was four as a result of a car accident, but his doctor believes he can restore his sight through a corneal transplant."

"Poor kid," Karen said.

"Yes, well, the insurance company denied the procedure on the basis that the therapy required for him to adapt to seeing after being blind for eight years is impossible to administer due to his autism."

"So they're just going to leave him blind?" one of the writers asked.

"Yes. They're saying that Lawrence doesn't have the capacity to participate in the required therapy to transition successfully. From what I've been reading, and from talking to his doctor, seeing is not just in the eyes. The brain has a vital role, as it translates what we see into something we can understand."

"Wow. I think this is good. What do the parents look like? Are they attractive and well-spoken?" Karen asked.

Taylor forced herself not to cringe. She was disappointed to see that Karen could be so superficial. She knew that it was easier to garner sympathy for good-looking people, but Karen's blasé tone angered her. She nodded. "Yep. The father is a professor at Yale, and the mom takes care of her son full time. She says he can understand perfectly, and he communicates with some sort of sign language he came up with. He doesn't have an adaptive technology device, because there isn't one for blind people." She took a breath before continuing. "This could open up a whole new world for this child, but the insurance company won't do it."

Karen nodded. "This looks good. I'll send it along to Mr. Wheeler as well. He emailed this morning and wants all hands on deck for meetings next week to finalize the details of the show. Will you be able to come in?"

"That shouldn't be a problem," Taylor said, then quickly added, "I'll call you this afternoon to confirm." She knew Karen would understand that she meant everything was contingent on Evan being okay.

"Good. Great job, Taylor. This is going to be a wonderful piece. Talk to you later."

Taylor disconnected and went into the playroom to see how Jeremy and Evan were doing. Evan was happily building blocks with his uncle and looking more like his old self. She could almost believe everything was fine, but in the pit of her stomach, she felt something gnawing, something deeply amiss. She didn't know if she could trust her gut instinct anymore. If she did, she'd have to take Evan and hide him away to keep him safe forever, but she knew, even in her worried state, that her fear and paranoia could be more dangerous than any of the other threats looming in her mind.

CHAPTER THIRTY-FOUR

W HEN JACK GOT HOME A LITTLE AFTER TWO, HE WAS SUR-prised not to see Taylor's car in the driveway.

"Where's Mommy?" he asked Beau, whose ears went back at the word *Mommy*.

Jack pulled out his phone and sent her a text.

Came home early. Where are you?

A minute later she answered. At the playground. Be home soon.

He went upstairs and unpacked his things, then went to the kitchen and grabbed a bottle of water from the refrigerator and Georgia's book about infidelity from the table.

"Come on, buddy. Let's go outside."

Beau followed him and took a seat by his feet as Jack sat down on the porch swing and drank in the view and breathed in the warm spring breeze. He looked at Georgia's book and thought about Scotty's infidelity. Taylor was going to be surprised, and happy, when he told her that he had called him, but he would make it clear that Scotty was still on probation as far as he was concerned. There was a part of Jack that was relieved he'd had an excuse to reach out. He hated not seeing his sister and his nieces more often. But there was also that part of him that didn't want to be hurt again. He'd always been a believer in the old *fool me once* adage. But it would be good for Evan to see his cousins more often, and it would make Jack's mother happy to see all her children getting along.

He became absorbed in the book quickly, impressed at how well Georgia had managed to explain the intricacies of brain science in a way that was both interesting and easy to understand. As soon as he finished the second chapter, he pulled out the card she'd left with him the other night and dialed her number. She answered on the first ring.

"Hi, Georgia. It's Jack Logan. I was hoping I could take you up on your offer to brainstorm about my story."

"Absolutely! How's it coming along?"

He told her that meth had been detected in all the cases so far. "I've got a copy of one of the toxicology reports that I could email to you."

"Sure." She gave him her email address.

"Perfect. Thanks." Just as he disconnected, Taylor's car pulled up. He walked down to the driveway, opened the car door, and unlatched a sleeping Evan from his car seat, mouthing a quiet hello to Jeremy who was getting out of the passenger side.

"There goes his afternoon nap," Taylor whispered. "Maybe we can get him in the house without him waking." But as the words left her lips, Evan began to cry and rub his eyes.

"Hey, bub, it's okay. Daddy's got you."

They all went in the house and Evan struggled out of Jack's arms and ran over to Beau.

"Doggy," he said, patting Beau on the head, and the two of them tromped off to the playroom.

"How was the playground?"

"Fine," Taylor answered, sounding distracted.

Jack asked, "No word yet, huh?"

She shook her head. "If I don't hear by four, I'm going to call the office."

As if on cue, her phone rang. She glanced at the screen, looked up at Jack, and swiped. "Hello?"

Jack's heart beat like a jackhammer as he waited, watching her face for an indication of the news.

"Dr. Manta, yes?"

Jack held his breath as he waited.

"Okay. . . . Good. What a relief! Yes, I'll do that. Make the appointment for next week? Okay, thank you."

A huge smile broke out on her face. "The CBC was normal. Blood counts all good. Iron a little low, but not significant. The thalassemia results will take a few more days, but he thinks it was really just a fluke. He wants us to try some iron supplements, but he doesn't think it's anything worrisome."

"I told you!" Jeremy said.

Jack hadn't realized just how terrified he'd been until just now. Walking over to Taylor, he pulled her into a hug and she squeezed him back. When she pulled away, he saw tears in her eyes.

"That was the longest twenty-four hours of my life," she said, shaking her head.

"I know," Jack answered.

They went into the playroom, where Evan was running around chanting a steady stream of nonsense words, Beau chasing behind him.

"He certainly seems to have regained his energy," Jack commented.

Taylor nodded. "Yeah. But I still want to know why his iron is so low."

Jack could see her elation had been short-lived, and until she had a complete answer, her worry wouldn't be completely abated. Not that he blamed her—they did need to know why.

"I'm going with you when we take him back," he told her. "In fact, let's make a list before we go so we make sure we cover everything with the doctor."

Jeremy laughed. "That poor pediatrician won't know what hit him, with the two of you interrogating him."

Taylor gave him a warm smile. "Thank you again for being here. You don't know how much it means to me."

Jeremy hugged her. "Where else would I be? I'll always be there for you."

"By the way, I spoke with Georgia Lakos just a few minutes ago," Jack said.

Taylor looked at him in surprise.

"I'm going to send her one of the tox reports and she promised she'd review it." He turned to Jeremy. "I'd like you to look at it as well."

Jeremy nodded. "Of course."

Evan came up to Taylor, arms outstretched. "Up up up up up." Each word becoming more insistent. She leaned down to pick him up. "That twenty-minute nap in the car didn't quite do the trick."

"How about if I take him upstairs and read him a story? Maybe I can get him to fall asleep," Jeremy suggested.

"That would be great. Thanks," Taylor said.

She and Jack went into the kitchen.

"Did your segment shoot schedule get finalized?" Jack asked.

"Yes, Karen just emailed me. They want to make sure everything's ready to go before the Supreme Court decision comes in.

We'll have it taped and ready to preempt anything scheduled then. I'll finish up with Georgia tomorrow. I've already got the first segment recorded. I don't need to go to Colorado tomorrow. They're going to do the shoot without me."

"That's great. So . . . I called Scotty to look into some of the other deaths."

She looked at him in surprise. "You called *Scotty*?"

"Yeah. I'm going over to their house to meet him on Thursday."

"You're going to need to tell me more. Why the sudden change of heart?"

He filled her in on the meth connection and his suspicions. "I needed some help getting that information, and I figured he owed me one."

She put her hand on his. "Jack. Come on. He and Maria are good now. He messed up, yes, but she forgave him, and you need to forgive him too."

He was grateful that she didn't throw his own mistake back at him. "I know. I know. He's going to show me the tox reports on the other deaths and then we'll come up with a game plan."

"You still believe they were slipped the drugs without their knowledge?"

He nodded. "I do. These people just don't fit the profile of your typical meth users. What I can't figure out is how."

○ ○ ○

That night, they had a quiet dinner with Evan, and later Jack was in his home office going through his notes when his cell phone rang. It was Scotty.

"Hey."

"Well, you stumbled onto quite the hornet's nest. This can't wait. I'm flying to Florida later tonight—three more murder-suicides have been reported there. Meth is indicated in all the tox screens, so now we need to see if the drug mix is all the same. Thought you'd want to know. DEA won't be far behind, I'm sure. But we got the jump on this. I should be thanking you for the lead."

Jack let out a low whistle. "Thanks, man. Keep me posted."

"Will do."

Jack decided to try Maggie Russell's widower again. "Dr. Russell? It's Jack Logan. Do you have a few minutes?"

"Sure. What's up?"

"I'm not convinced that your wife voluntarily took any drugs."

There was silence.

"Dr. Russell?"

Jack heard quiet weeping on the other end of the line.

"Sorry. It's just such a relief to think that maybe she didn't do this on purpose. I've been losing so much sleep over it. What's led you to this conclusion?"

Jack couldn't share Scotty's findings, but he could tell him about the other two cases that had been made public. "She's not the only person involved in these incidents to have been found to have drugs in her system. And the others had no history of drug abuse either. I think someone gave it to her without her knowledge."

"How is that possible?"

"Did she order any new products? Diet pills, vitamins, anything like that?"

"I don't think so. She wasn't much for online purchases."

Jack thought a moment, scanning his earlier notes. "You mentioned she'd just been to the doctor for her physical. Did he do any bloodwork?"

"A full work-up and we each got our booster shots for the cold vaccine. That was it."

Jack stopped writing for minute. Brian Doyle had mentioned his wife getting a physical. He wondered if she'd gotten the vaccine. He'd call Brian and find out. "You and your wife both got the vaccine?"

"Yes, why?"

Jack started to say something, then stopped. Could it be the vaccine? Dread filled his body. He, Taylor, and Evan had all gotten vaccinated a month ago. But millions of people had gotten it. And even Kent Russell had gotten it, and he was fine. *I wonder if it could affect some people differently?* Jack thought. He'd have to talk to Jeremy about it. "Just wanted to make sure my notes were correct," he finally answered.

They spoke for a few more minutes, than Jack disconnected, and he called Mrs. Morris, the psychologist's widow.

After a few pleasantries, he dove in. "When we spoke, you indicated that as far as you knew, your husband had never used drugs. This is turning out to be a common feeling among the families I've interviewed. I'm trying to see if there's a way that maybe your husband was drugged without his knowledge."

"I would certainly find that more believable. But why? Are you saying someone deliberately gave him something to make him go crazy? Maybe an angry ex-patient or something?"

"Not exactly." He took a shot. "Has your husband had a physical lately?"

"Yes. The day before he . . . this happened."

"Do you know if he was on any medication or was given a prescription?" Jack didn't want to come right out and ask her about the vaccine.

"I don't think so. He complained of a sore arm, but that was from the vaccine. That cold one. He didn't get any prescriptions that I know of, though; he was in good health."

"Okay, thank you. I'll let you know if I find anything out."

The cold vaccine was seeming to be a common denominator. Jack looked up the cold vaccine to see who manufactured it—Licentia Labs. The company had been in business only a couple of years, which tracked with the timing of Crosse's so-called death. The vaccine had made the company billions. Maybe a certain lot had been inadvertently contaminated. He'd call Scotty with the update. Then they'd have to figure out who to tell next. They had to be careful. The last thing they needed to do was start a national panic.

CHAPTER THIRTY-FIVE

E VAN WAS RUNNING AROUND THE PLAYROOM, DANCING TO the music Taylor had playing. His color was good, and eyes bright. Even so, Taylor was still unsettled. When she'd pressed the doctor about why Evan's iron levels had dipped in the first place, he had assured her that he wasn't worried, especially as the CBC was normal and the reticulocyte count test showed his blood was regenerating fine. He'd also told them that sometimes it could be an absorption issue but that required some invasive tests by a gastroenterologist. So for now, the plan was to test Evan's levels again in a month. The doctor called in a prescription for iron supplements and told them to watch out for any symptoms of fatigue. So far, so good.

She'd placed a phone call to Darlene Sampson, Cora's mother, last night, just to see how she was doing, and had been saddened to learn that Cora had died last week. She hadn't known what to say, had no comfort to offer this grieving mother. Taylor's own emotions were all the more raw because of what she'd just been through with Evan. She was newly outraged at UBC's decision to keep Cora's parents off the show—their story needed to be heard. She had stewed about it all night and felt a sense of guilt that she hadn't pushed harder to make them run the story. But the reality was that as a producer she had limited power if the network decided to cut something. The only way she could retain true journalistic integrity was to freelance. When this assignment was over, she'd be free of her contract and she'd write her own piece about Cora and see who would pick it up.

She was relieved that the story was almost finished. The last piece was happening today, the production crew flying out to Colorado for the shoot with the parents of Lawrence, the young boy who'd been denied the corneal transplant. Taylor felt good about the shape of all three segments. She'd been surprised but relieved when Karen told her she didn't need to accompany them to the shoot. Taylor was usually on-site since hers was the face the interviewees knew. But they were apparently over budget on the segments so only staff that was strictly necessary would be going. As a freelancer, Taylor was the first to be cut.

She heard the front door open and Jack come in.

"I'm in the kitchen," she called out to him.

He came in and gave her a kiss. "How's he doing?"

She pointed to the playroom. "Happy as a clam."

"Awesome. I just got off the phone with Georgia. She went ahead and looked at the tox report on Shannon Doyle that I sent her. She noticed that they listed MDMA along with the meth."

"What's that?"

"The street name is ecstasy or molly," he said. "According to Georgia, it can cause damage to the serotonin receptors in the prefrontal cortex, which can cause violent behavior. It could explain what we're seeing in these cases."

"Wasn't Jeremy saying there might be a drug combination that would cause violence?" Taylor asked.

Jack's eyes widened. "If I recall correctly, that's exactly what he said."

"That would certainly explain why all of them got violent. It really appears as though someone is doing this on purpose," Taylor added.

Jack shrugged. "We still have to consider that most street drugs these days are cut with many other things. You never really know what you're getting. Someone could have thought they were taking ecstasy and it could have been laced with meth, or LSD, even."

"You said she was having an affair, right? That's why they were in counseling. Ecstasy is a drug of choice for partiers. Maybe her boyfriend gave it to her."

"The only connection for sure is the meth," Jack answered. "I'll have to find out from Scotty if the others also had the MDMA in their systems."

"Jack, would someone be able to tell by comparing the tox screens if they've all had the same exact cocktail of drugs in their system?"

"I'm not a toxicology expert, but I would assume so."

"And do you think there are any factors that make some folks more susceptible to this meth psychosis?" Taylor asked.

"Let's google it." He pulled out his phone and tapped. After a few minutes he showed her the screen. "It says here that a family history of psychotic disorder is a factor and it's thought that a history of trauma could be related. But there's no one definitive factor."

"You're sending Jeremy the reports as well, right?"

"Yeah. I'm going to go change and take a run."

"Okay. Jack?"

He turned. "Yeah?"

"Any update on the Dakota situation?"

"No, I'm still waiting for Sybil to call and let me know she has the passport. It's strange actually, but I'm waiting it out."

She nodded. "Okay."

After Jack left for his run, Taylor went to close the door when she noticed a black sedan was stopped in front of the house. Beau was standing beside her, and he didn't seem agitated—by now, she knew to trust his instincts—but she couldn't see who was in the car, as the windows were tinted, and it made her nervous. It began to pull away slowly, but not before the driver's side window went down, and she got a glimpse of a person in the driver's seat holding a long lens trained at the house. Were they taking a picture? Before she could think, she ran out of the house and toward the car, but the driver floored it, and it sped away.

CHAPTER THIRTY-SIX

ATHENS, GREECE

THE SECURITY LINE IN THE ATHENS AIRPORT WAS MOVING AT a snail's pace. Basil had told Eva to put the icons in her carry-on bag, but she was afraid that the scanner would show them and they'd attract attention, so she had packed them in her checked bag instead. She wouldn't be able to relax until she was safely on the ground in America with the suitcase back in her possession. She waited for the security agent to call her forward and stepped through the scanner without incident.

Breathing a sigh of relief, she retrieved her carry-on and her purse and continued down the hallway to wait to clear Passport Control. She glanced over at one of the numerous military police officers standing ramrod straight, the machine gun strapped over his chest and one hand resting on it. She swallowed and took a deep breath.

The line was longer here, and her mind began to wander.

She couldn't imagine what kind of reaction Taylor would have to the news that Eva was alive or how she was going to be able to explain that she'd allowed her beloved child to grieve her loss all these years. The only thing that gave her hope was that Taylor knew about the coins. Maybe Taylor would be able to forgive her, understanding that she really hadn't had a choice in the matter.

Father Basil had brought Eva up to speed on aspects of Taylor's life she couldn't find online. It broke her heart to learn that Warwick had not only been the one to betray Eva but that he had tried to kill Taylor as well. She shivered again at the thought of the hideous violation he'd participated in, allowing that clinic to inject another man's sperm into her. All these years she had believed that her husband was a good man and that she'd left her daughter with a loving father.

A man behind her pushed forward, and she looked up to see that she was next in line. She had her passport ready and smiled at the man behind the counter when she approached. He gave her a bored look as he held out his hand for her passport and boarding pass, but then took his time examining the passport, looking up at her and back at it several times.

"Your name?" he asked in Greek.

"Eva Parks," she answered in what she hoped sounded like a calm tone.

Scratching his beard, he stared at the passport again, then held it up to the light. Putting it through the scanner one more time, he frowned and picked up the phone. Eva's heart began to race. Father Basil had assured her that the credentials were solid. What was she going to do if they figured out her passport was fake?

Minutes later, two armed military policeman came up from behind and stationed themselves on either side of her.

"Please come with us," the one on her right said.

"What's wrong?" she asked, her heart beating wildly.

The other one turned to her and answered. "Passport Control has a few questions before you can board." He turned to the Passport Control officer and told him to remove her luggage from the plane.

She was led to a side door and ushered down a long hallway with concrete block walls and dim fluorescent lighting. When they reached a steel door, she was led through it and into a small office with a cheap metal desk and two plastic chairs. Over an hour passed slowly as she waited, her shirt damp with perspiration and her heart beating fast. It seemed like the room was getting hotter with every minute and her throat was dry and parched. *When was someone going to come and talk to her?* She looked at her watch. Her flight would be taking off about now, and there was no chance of her getting onto it.

Finally, the door opened and in walked a short man with salt-and-pepper hair and wearing a wrinkled suit and pilled white shirt. A cell phone was clipped to his belt, and she spotted a handgun in a holster on the other side. Another man followed him in carrying her suitcase; he dropped it on the floor and left. The short man turned to the armed guards. "You can go." He shut the door and looked at her. It was just the two of them now. "I know from your passport that your name isn't Eva Parks. Our new scanning system flagged its number. Furthermore, when we cross-referenced your name and birth date we found out something interesting. Guess what?"

She remained silent.

"Eva Parks died in 1995. What is your name and why are you trying to leave Greece using a false passport?"

Her mind raced, but for the moment, she remained silent, looking down at the table.

"Who provided you with this false documentation?"

She continued to stare at the table, trying to figure out how she could get her suitcase out of this room. The coins were the only thing that mattered. She couldn't have given up her life, her daughter, and her freedom to protect the coins only to have them confiscated by the Greek police and made vulnerable to their enemies.

His fist came down hard on the table. "Are you mute? I'm talking to you. Answer my questions!" Perspiration dotted his forehead.

His anger was getting the better of him. She looked up at him and smiled.

His face turned red, and he leaned in close to her, yelling now. "You're in serious trouble. If you don't . . ."

In a flash, Eva reached out and grabbed his hand, surprising him and drawing his attention there. Then with her other hand, she pushed his head with all her might, smashing it into the table. Before he had a chance to recover, she brought up her left elbow, swinging it at the bridge of his nose and knocking him unconscious. She grabbed his phone, pressed his thumb to the screen to unlock it, and punched in Taylor's phone number. She picked up her suitcase and ran from the room. The phone rang four times and just when she thought it would go to voice mail, she heard a voice on the other end, one she hadn't heard in too long.

"Hello?"

"Taylor, don't hang up. This is very important." Eva's breath came in bursts as she sprinted down the long hallway back in the direction from which she came. She reached a door marked "lost baggage" and flung it open. The room was mercifully empty, and she fell against the wall, gasping.

"Who is this?"

"I'm calling from Greece."

"I don't understand. Who is this?"

There was no time to break it to her gently. "Taylor, this is going to shock you and I'm sorry to have to do it this way. I was trying to fly to the States and see you in person, but they've confiscated my passport. It's me . . . Mom."

There was silence on the other end of the phone, then in an angry voice. "This isn't funny. How dare you—"

"Taylor, *avgolémono kai psomí*," she said, using the code words she and Taylor had come up with years ago in response to a school program encouraging parents to give their children a password in cases of someone claiming to be picking them up on behalf of their parents in any situation.

"How . . . can it . . . Mom?"

"I need you to come to Athens. You have to come and get the coins. I'll explain when you get here. I'm at the airport, but I don't know where they'll take me next. They're going to arrest me."

Eva heard footsteps. "Someone's coming. I have to hide the coins. Please, Taylor. I need your help. There are things I need to tell you."

She ended the call and ran to the other end of the room, where she crouched behind a large stack of suitcases. She texted Basil on WhatsApp, like he'd shown her, and told him what was happening, asking him to call Taylor and explain things to her. The door opened and the sound of two men speaking filled the room. Their tones didn't sound urgent, though, and she soon realized they were looking for a piece of luggage someone had come to claim. They began to sort through the bags on the opposite end of the room. It wouldn't be long before they came upon her. She had to get the icons out of her suitcase and find a place to hide them before she was captured again. She scanned the room frantically and spotted a My Little Pony suitcase. She crawled over to it and opened it, finding a mess of little girl's clothing and a large teddy bear. She took the icons from her suitcase and placed them under the clothes, zipped it shut, and squeezed it between two larger suitcases, hoping to keep it somewhat hidden. She would have to hope that Taylor would be able to find a way into this room and retrieve it before anyone came to claim it. She rezipped her own suitcase and stood it next to her.

She heard yelling and the door crashed open. She slid to standing, putting both hands up as four armed guards ran toward her, pointing their automatic weapons at her chest. The officer she'd hit stood in front of her, his nose swollen and bloody. He grabbed her wrist roughly, handcuffing her hands in front of her.

"Where are you taking me?" she asked.

The man narrowed his eyes and pulled her arm, jerking her forward. "You're coming with me. The police have some questions for you. This time I suggest you talk."

CHAPTER THIRTY-SEVEN

DAMON READ THE EMAIL A SECOND TIME AND LEANED IN closer to better examine the grainy picture attached. It couldn't be—Eva Parks was dead. He'd seen the pictures of her corpse, read the autopsy. So why was someone using a passport in her name? The woman in the picture *could* be her, twenty-odd years later. He clicked on the photo to enlarge it. It did actually look like her . . . but how was it possible? He went to his contacts and found a listing under S. He'd promised himself he wouldn't use him for a job for a while. He was off his meds again and had made a mess of things last time. But there was no one else he could trust with this. He hesitated only a few seconds before calling.

"Hello," the voice on the other end said after the first ring.

"I have a job for you. Do you think you can execute it cleanly this time?"

"What is it?"

"I need you to go to Athens. Airport police are detaining a woman claiming to be Eva Parks. She'll be transferred to National

Intelligence Service headquarters by tomorrow night. You've only got twenty-four hours. If you leave now, you can be there first thing in the morning."

There was a sharp intake of breath on the other end. "The same Eva—"

"Yes." Damon cut him off. "Question her. Find out if she knows anything about the coins. Do whatever it takes to get the information. Do you understand?"

"I'm on it."

"Good. Don't let me down this time."

But the man on the other end of the phone had already disconnected.

CHAPTER THIRTY-EIGHT

STILL HOLDING THE PHONE IN HER HAND, TAYLOR BEGAN TO shake, the woman's words reverberating in her mind. She sank into a kitchen chair, trying to make sense of it all. Her mother was alive? The thoughts were bombarding her faster than she could process them, her emotions ricocheting from utter joy to blinding fury.

Her mother had been alive all these years and never contacted her? She couldn't conceive of it. A shiver went through her, and she felt her stomach roil. Running into the bathroom, she made it just in time. After she emptied her stomach, she continued to dry heave until her whole body was wrung out. When she'd finally caught her breath, she splashed cold water on her face and returned to the kitchen.

Her phone beeped with a new text from an unknown number and she swiped it open. A blurry picture came through of a woman in her sixties. Taylor enlarged it on the screen and her breath caught. It looked like her mother, only older. Could it really be her? Tears sprang to her eyes and she was choked with emotion. Then she got angry again.

How dare her mother call her out of the blue and demand that she drop everything and fly to her rescue? But as indignant as she felt on the one hand, she knew that was exactly what she was going to do. How could she not? At the very least, she would get an explanation of what had happened all those years ago. And she'd call Jeremy and ask him to go with her—she knew he'd agree. Taylor walked over to the window and looked out at the water, but the view didn't soothe her. She thought back to the day of her mother's funeral and being so overwhelmed with grief that she could barely stand. How could her mother allow her to go through all that if it was a lie? Losing her and believing that she'd been murdered had forever changed Taylor. No matter what, she would never allow Evan to suffer that way. There was nothing in this world important enough for Eva to have put Taylor through what she had.

One thing was for sure, whether the woman who she'd just spoken to was Eva or not, she'd given up the right to call herself Taylor's mother. Because no real mother could ever do that to her child.

CHAPTER THIRTY-NINE

JACK'S PHONE RANG JUST AS HE PULLED INTO THE GROCERY store parking lot.

"I need you to get home right away!" Taylor's voice was panicked.

"What's the matter? Are you okay?"

"Jack . . . my *mother* just called me."

"What do you mean? Another dream?"

"No. She says she's in Greece. Under arrest. She wants me to go there."

"Taylor, what are you talking about? This is crazy. Your mother can't have called you." What was going on with Taylor? Jack did a U-turn and headed back to the house.

He could hear her breath coming too fast. "Jack . . . she knew the code word. It had to be her . . . I just . . ."

"T, try to calm down. Breathe. I'll be home in ten minutes."

His pulse was racing, and it felt like it was taking forever to get back to the house. What was happening? What if she was having a stroke? Was she hallucinating? Maybe it was that damn vaccine. Delayed reaction perhaps? They'd both had those boosters a few weeks ago. What if she hurt herself? Should he call 911? No. He was the one panicking now. It was surely some sort of a mix-up. He pulled onto their street and tore into the driveway, then bolted toward the house and ran through the open front door, yelling her name.

He found her in the kitchen on the phone, pacing and speaking fast. She looked up and held up a finger. "Okay. See you soon."

"Who was that?"

She took a deep breath. "Jeremy. He said we can use his company's jet."

"Hold on. Are you seriously considering flying to Greece on a wild-goose chase?"

"Jack, listen to me. Look." She held her phone up and showed him the picture she'd been sent. "It's her! See?"

He enlarged the selfie and examined the photo. It was Eva. Older, of course, but undoubtedly her . . . but how? "What the . . . ? I don't get it."

"I have to go. You can see that, can't you?"

He sighed. "I'm going with you."

She put her hand on Jack's arm. "No, you have to stay and take care of Evan. I need to know he's safe here with you. Jeremy and I will be fine."

"Taylor, have you considered that maybe someone just aged an old picture and sent it? This deepfake technology has gotten really advanced. You talked to her for what, five minutes? This doesn't feel right."

"Jack, it was her! I know it. I recognized her voice. Even after all this time. Please, you have to trust me on this. Besides, a Father Basil from the Orthodox Church called me right after she did. He's the one who gave her the passport. He's given me the name of a lawyer to see when we get to Athens."

This all sounded more and more ludicrous. "Look, this could all be one elaborate trick. You don't know that the man who called you is really a priest and even if he is, so what? You can't go flying off to Greece. It's crazy."

She replied, "Listen, Jeremy knows Father Basil. He tried to help Jeremy find the coins after Crosse killed himself, and he's been trying to help my mother get back to the States. Father Basil said that he didn't know the airport had installed the new technology and would be able to see that the passport had been forged."

Jack had a terrible feeling in the bottom of his stomach. "Let me go with you. We can have someone come and stay with Evan."

"No! *You* have to stay with him. And I don't have time to stand here and argue with you. I'm meeting Jeremy at Teterboro in two hours."

The old Jack would have pulled some macho stunt to block her from going but he'd evolved, even though it killed him to stand down. But he could see it was pointless to try to dissuade her. "This is nuts. I really don't want you to go, but I realize I'm not going to be able to stop you. Go get ready. I'll drop you."

She leaned in and kissed him and he put his arms around her. "I love you," she whispered.

He closed his eyes. "I love you more than life itself. Please be careful."

CHAPTER FORTY

TAYLOR LOOKED AT JEREMY, SITTING NEXT TO HER. HE WAS quiet, seemingly lost in thought. He'd called the American consulate in Athens and they were arranging for Taylor to meet with her mother, who was being held at the Athens police station. Eva had apparently refused to talk to the police thus far, but she promised she'd tell them everything if they allowed her a visit with her daughter. Was her mother some sort of spy? It seemed ludicrous, but then again so did the idea that her mother was alive. What had she done to get arrested?

She thought back to the last time she'd seen her mother, when Eva had come in to wake her up for school and asked what she'd like for breakfast. Taylor had mumbled something about not being hungry and wanting to sleep for ten more minutes. When she'd finally dragged herself out of bed and gone downstairs, her mother had handed her a homemade muffin.

"You need to eat. Breakfast is the most—"

"Yeah, I know." She'd heard it a thousand times. "I'll grab something at school. I'm going to be late." And she'd run out the door without so much as a hug or kiss, totally unaware that that would be the last conversation they would ever have.

Anger filled her once again as she remembered the awful days of sorrow and mourning that followed her mother's "death," and she clenched her hands in tight fists, tempted to ask Jeremy to turn the plane around. But she decided she'd listen to what her mother had to say and then she'd tell her how horribly unfair her actions had been. This was her opportunity to say all the things she needed to say, to tell her mother what she'd missed out on, what her void had done to Taylor's life.

"I feel like I could jump out of my skin," she said to Jeremy.

He reached over and squeezed her hand. "I can't imagine what you're feeling right now. It's so strange. But it's a good thing. Your mother could be alive!"

"That's the thing. I should be ecstatic, and there's a part of me that is . . . but I can't reconcile the fact that she let me think she was dead all these years. And why did she call me now? Has she become some sort of criminal? It doesn't make any sense."

"Well, we know it has something to do with the coins. She must have the last ten."

Taylor thought a long moment. "That doesn't make sense. Our family only had ten and Crosse has those. You think she somehow tracked down the last ten?"

"It won't do us any good to speculate. We'll know soon enough. Try to get some rest before we touch down."

She looked at him, astounded. "Rest? Seriously? We could be walking into some sort of trap. What are we even doing? Maybe Jack was right. This is crazy."

Jeremy's tone was measured. "We've done our best to vet the situation. Father Basil vouched for her, and she knew your secret code. I know it's hard, but try to have faith."

"I'll do my best," she said, and closed her eyes.

CHAPTER FORTY-ONE

ATHENS, GREECE

THE DOOR TO THE CELL OPENED AND THE GUARD BARKED AT her. "You have twenty minutes, and we'll be watching."

Eva held her breath as a beautiful young woman walked in, followed by a man she didn't know. She'd been transfixed by the pictures of Taylor she'd found online, but they didn't do her daughter justice. She felt another sharp stab of pain at all she'd missed. "Taylor?"

"Mom?"

She opened her arms and Taylor seemed to hesitate for a moment before falling into them. They hugged tightly and she felt Taylor's shoulders shaking as she cried. After a bit, Taylor pulled back.

"But we buried you. You died." Taylor's voice was quiet. "How can you be alive?"

"How can I explain everything in the short amount of time

we have? It was never up to me. They took me." She stopped and looked at the man, registering his familiar features. "This must be Jeremy." She smiled and held a hand out. "Maya's son."

"You know about me?" Jeremy asked.

"Father Basil told me everything. My poor sister—she would be so happy to see that you ended up on the right side of things. You have her smile, you know." Eva could see that Jeremy was getting choked up.

He reached out and took her hand. "I wish I had known her."

"She was a beautiful soul."

Taylor cleared her throat. "We don't have much time. I need to understand something. Why did you let us think you were dead all these years?"

Eva took a deep breath. "I was taken from the mall that day by a man who worked for the church. He told me that if I didn't do what he said, those who wanted the coins would keep sending people to torture me until I revealed the location of the coins I'd hidden, and he convinced me I'd be putting your life in danger if I didn't let them fake my death."

"Why didn't you let me know you were okay?" Taylor asked in a shaky voice. "And why are the police holding you here?"

Eva could see Taylor was getting angry now. Sighing, she spoke quietly. "My passport had my real name on it, but since I'm legally dead, it set off alarm bells." She rushed on. "Taylor, you have to know . . . I didn't want to leave you. I had to choose to keep you and the coins safe or go against the church's orders, and they'd told me I'd be risking your life and everything I held dear if I didn't leave. But it almost killed me. I've been living on the island of Ikaria all this time with my Uncle Yiannis." She lifted a hand to stroke Taylor's cheek, but her daughter pulled away.

"So that's it. You've been living in Greece for the past twenty-four years, oblivious to everything that's happened to me. Do you have any idea of what your *murder* did to me? It almost ruined me. And now you call me for help? What gives you the right?"

"I know you don't owe me anything, but I needed to warn you. Your son is in danger—as long as the coins exist, we all are."

"In danger from whom?" Taylor asked, her voice shaking.

"Damon Crosse."

Taylor stood up. "Damon Crosse is dead. Did you know he was my father when you ran off and hid in Greece?"

"No. I didn't know that when I was forced to leave. I only recently learned about everything that happened to you after your first husband's death. But listen: you are still not safe. Crosse wants Evan."

"Crosse killed himself," Taylor said.

Eva shook her head. "He only made it look that way."

"What?" Taylor and Jeremy spoke in unison.

"Father Basil found out that Damon Crosse faked his own death because the medical examiner who helped Crosse told him," Eva continued.

Taylor's face had gone completely white. "Damon Crosse is really alive?"

"I'm afraid so."

"Where is he?"

Eva gave her a dismayed look. "No one knows. All we know is that he took tetrodotoxin, a drug that mimics death, to fool the EMTs, and that the ME administered an antidote when Crosse arrived. Then he sent another body to be cremated."

"This is unbelievable! All this time . . . we thought we were safe . . . but he's alive. Where is he hiding? What is he waiting for?" Taylor put a hand up to her mouth. "I need to warn Jack."

Jeremy shot up from the table and clenched his fists. "I can't believe this! Why didn't Basil tell me?"

"It's safer if Crosse believes no one knows he's alive. We don't want him to go even deeper into hiding. If we have any chance of finding him, the fewer who know, the better. Father Basil only told me to convince me to go back to America."

"So . . . Crosse still has the coins," Jeremy said, thinking aloud. "That's why I never found them. Now he has twenty of them."

Eva shook her head. "No, that's just it. He doesn't have twenty."

"What?" Jeremy asked.

"Those weren't the real coins. I took the real ones with me when they faked my death. We replaced the ones in the shower . . . and I've been guarding them all these years."

"So you outwitted him!" Taylor said.

Jeremy frowned. "He must know by now that they're not real. He'll be furious. But that means he only has ten." He looked at Eva. "Where are your coins now?"

Eva looked up subtly at the cameras in the corner of the cell, hoping her daughter and nephew would understand it wasn't safe for her to talk about them. "I don't know. I lost them. You have to find Basil when you get back to America. I don't know how long they'll keep me here."

"We have an appointment with a lawyer in a few hours. Father Basil set it up. We'll do our best to get you released," Taylor said.

The door opened and the guard was back.

Eva grabbed Taylor in a tight hug and whispered in her ear. "They're in the lost baggage room. My Little Pony."

The guard pulled them apart and shoved Eva against the wall.

"Hey, what are you doing?" Taylor yelled.

"No touching," the guard said.

"Go. I'll be okay," Eva said.

"Mom, we'll get you out of here. Stay strong."

As she left the room, Eva was filled by a strong and overwhelming sense that this would truly be the last time she ever saw her daughter.

CHAPTER FORTY-TWO

JACK JUMPED WHEN HIS PHONE BUZZED. "TAYLOR."

"I don't know where to start." She sounded out of breath. "Listen, we're on our way to the lawyer's office. But, Jack, Damon Crosse is alive."

"What?" he asked, stunned. "How?"

"He faked his suicide. You've got to find someplace safe for us until we figure out where he is. He's probably watching our every move."

"Are you sure about this?"

"Remember I told you about the priest who authenticated the news about my mother? Well, he's got the details. I'll text you his phone number. Call him. In the meantime, please figure out where you can take Evan and be safe. We'll meet you there as soon as we're back."

"I'm on it. Keep me posted. Love you."

He sat down at the kitchen table and put his head in his hands. Crosse was alive? Jeremy had seen him taken away by the coroner . . . but if anyone would be capable of pulling off something like that, it would be Crosse. Everything was making sense now. Crosse had to be behind this whole meth-induced madness.

His text tone sounded and he saw that Taylor had sent Father Basil's contact info. He dialed right away.

"Hello." The voice on the other end was somber.

"Father Basil?"

"Yes, who is this?"

"Jack Logan, Taylor's husband."

"I've been expecting your call. Eva is in trouble. It's imperative that your wife get those coins out of the country before they fall into the wrong hands."

"You mean Damon Crosse's hands."

"You've heard, then."

"Do you know where Crosse is?" Jack demanded.

"No, but we'll need to find him somehow and get the ten coins he has. When your wife and Jeremy return, we need to create a plan to bring all the coins together and destroy them."

"Why do we need to bring them all together?" Jack asked, skeptical.

"That's the only way their power can be eradicated."

Jack paused for a moment. "And why should I trust you?"

"I'm as involved in all of this as you are. And I'm a man of the cloth."

Jack laughed bitterly. "Sorry, Father. That doesn't mean much to me." He ended the call without another word, then looked around the room.

"Damon Crosse, where are you?" he shouted aloud. It was beginning to make perfect sense. Crosse was behind all these murder-suicides. Jack would bet his life on it.

Before doing anything else, though, he needed to find a safe place for him and Evan to stay. He was just thinking about who he should call when his phone rang.

"Jack Logan."

"Hi, Jack. I've got Dakota's passport."

He didn't have time to deal with this right now. "Sybil, I'm sorry but a situation has just cropped up that I have to take care of. I'm not going to be able to help after all. I'm sorry."

"Jack, I wouldn't ask if I had any other choice. I'm going back to the hospital tomorrow for another treatment. Can you please just get the passport from me here in the city, and you can find someone else to get it to Dakota? I'm still in the same apartment—you have the address, right?"

He exhaled a pent-up breath. None of this was Sybil's fault. He had a sudden flashback to the horrible day when he'd found Dakota in a blood-filled bathtub. Sybil had been the first to arrive at the hospital and she'd taken care of everything for him. He'd been too shattered to think about what to do with the remains of his unborn child and she had arranged it all for him. Even the memorial later that week where he had said good-bye to the daughter that had never had a chance. How could he turn his back on Sybil now that she needed *him*? He could make the arrangements for the safe house just as easily from the car while he drove the hour into the city. He'd call Dakota first, though, and update her. "Okay. I'll be by early tonight."

"Thank you. I'll leave it with my doorman. I'm really not up to visitors."

"Of course, I understand. Take care, Sybil."

"You too, Jack. I'm sorry things turned out the way they did. We loved you."

After he disconnected, he dialed the number Dakota had left for him.

"Jack. Thank you for calling me back."

He got right to business. "I'm getting your passport from Sybil tonight. I have a friend who's willing to meet you. That's the best I can do."

"I don't trust anyone else to know where I am. Can I have

someone I trust come to you then? Pick it up from you? I just
need a few days to arrange it."

He hesitated. "I don't know where I'm going to be." He
wasn't about to let Dakota know where he was once he secured
a safe house.

"You can meet him somewhere public. Please, Jack."

"I can't guarantee I'll be available then, but I'll hold on to it
for a few days. If I'm able to meet him, I will; otherwise, I may
have to find a place to leave it for him."

"I'll call you as soon as I find someone," she said.

"No. I won't have this phone anymore. I'll call you again in
forty-eight hours."

"Okay. Thanks again."

He ended the call without another word. Just the sound of
her voice brought all his anger and outrage back to the surface.
After he did this last thing for her, he never wanted to hear from
her or about her again.

CHAPTER FORTY-THREE

ATHENS, GREECE

A s soon as Taylor and Jeremy reached the sidewalk, she grabbed his hand. "We have to split up. You go talk to the lawyer, I'll go and get the coins."

"You know where they are?"

"Yes, she whispered in my ear when she hugged me."

"Where are they?"

Taylor looked around nervously. "I don't even want to say it out loud. Just go. I'll meet you back in the lobby of the Grand Hotel in a couple of hours, and we can figure out what to do next."

"I don't like you going off by yourself and my not knowing where you are. Maybe I can postpone our meeting with the attorney and come with you."

She shook her head. "No. You need to talk to him, see if we can get her out and bring her home with us."

He sighed. "Taylor, I don't know how realistic that is. And what if something happens to you while you're retrieving them?"

"I'll be fine. They're in a public place. Don't worry."

He looked at this watch. "I have to be at the lawyer's office in an hour and I think it's about a forty-five-minute drive with traffic. I guess I'd better get going. Be careful. I'll see you back at our meeting place." He gave her a hug and they went in opposite directions.

o   o   o

Taylor grabbed a cab back to the airport. Once there, she scanned the arrivals floor until she found the baggage services area. The lost luggage room her mother was talking about must have been behind that counter, but she couldn't just walk behind it and through the door, obviously. She observed two bored-looking women behind the counter. One was flipping through a magazine while the other was processing a form for a customer. As she approached the counter, she noticed the woman looking at the magazine had a cell phone next to her whose case featured a picture of her and a young girl. Taylor waited until she looked up.

"Pardon me," Taylor said in Greek.

"Yes?"

"My daughter lost her suitcase a few days ago, and we still haven't heard anything. She's so upset. Her favorite stuffed animal was in it, and I can't get her to calm down."

The woman's expression remained stony. She pushed a form in front of her. "Fill this out."

Taylor smiled at her. "I've already done that. I know there are a lot of bags to go through, but I'm sure you understand how hard it is for a mother to see her child upset. I was wondering . . . is there any way I could just look through the luggage on my own?"

The woman said firmly, "No, that's a restricted area. You cannot go in there. If your daughter's bag is there, they'll call you."

"Would you be able to check for me?"

The woman shook her head. "That's not how it works. Besides, we're closing for lunch. You can come back in two hours and check again."

Taylor walked away, her brain working overtime to come up with another idea.

She walked to the other end of the airport, scoping out the employee entrance doors, which were guarded by military police holding Uzis. But spotting a young man at one of the ticket counters, she had an idea. She walked up to his kiosk and gave him a shy smile.

He looked her up and down, then smiled back.

"Hello, miss. Can I help you?"

She leaned in toward him and widened her eyes. "I hope so." She told him the same story about her daughter, adding that they were leaving in a few hours on a ferry to go to one of the islands. "The baggage department is closed for lunch. Is there any way you could escort me to the room and I could see if her bag is there? Maybe I could buy you a drink when I get back tomorrow?"

"I don't know. That's against the rules."

She tilted her head and gave him a long look. "I'm sure you're important enough to break a few rules without getting in trouble. After all, what fun is life if you follow the rules all the time?"

He leaned toward her a bit, then inclined his head toward a door to his left. "Give me ten minutes, then go to that door and it will be open. I'll be waiting."

She walked away and watched from a distance as he put up a

sign indicating the counter was closed and then disappeared behind the door. In exactly ten minutes, she walked over and turned the knob. His hand reached out to take hers and he pulled her toward him. "How about a little something to say thank you?"

She swallowed. "Let's get the suitcase first. Then I'll be happy to show you some appreciation," she said in Greek.

He didn't seem pleased with her response but started down the hall, still holding her hand. "Come on, let's go."

As they walked down the long corridor, turning left, then right, Taylor paid close attention so she would know her way out. When they came to a door marked "Baggage," which he opened with a key card, she sighed. There were hundreds of suitcases in the room. How was she going to find the one hiding the coins?

"What does the suitcase look like?"

She had no idea the color or size, only what her mother had told her. "It's got a picture of a pony on it."

He began moving suitcases and looking while Taylor crossed to the other side of the room. They both continued looking for the next twenty minutes, and then she saw a flash of pink between two large black suitcases. She reached out into where it was wedged and yanked it out. She'd have liked to confirm that the coins were in it, but she needed to get out of there before he got any more ideas about her thanking him. Besides, how many My Little Pony suitcases could there be in a Greek airport?

"I've got it." She walked toward the door and he stood in front of it, blocking her.

"Where's my thank-you?" He tried to grab her waist, but she stepped back out of his reach.

He scowled. "Listen, bitch. I gave you what you wanted, now it's your turn."

She smiled at him, then brought her knee up hard to his groin. He yelled out in surprise, and Taylor reached up to his head, pulling down hard as she raised her knee again to connect with his face.

"Didn't your mother teach you not to call a woman names?" Leaving him stunned and groaning on the ground, Taylor pulled the door open and sprinted down the hallway back the way they'd come, the suitcase securely in her hand.

CHAPTER FORTY-FOUR

ATHENS, GREECE

EVA SAT ON THE EDGE OF THE SOILED MATTRESS, HUGGING herself to try to keep her body from losing heat. She needed to use the toilet, but she was holding off as long as she could, dreading the thought of doing it under the scrutiny of the guards. A guard she didn't recognize opened the door to her cell.

"Someone from National Intelligence Service is here to question you," he barked in Greek, then slammed the door shut.

She hadn't decided yet what to tell the authorities. There was always the truth, but if she told them about the coins, the government would seize them and she knew it would only be a matter of time before they fell into corrupt hands. She hoped Taylor had understood her whispered message and would find the coins and get them out of the country.

She heard the clink of the door opening again and looked up, expecting to see a guard, but it was Jeremy.

"Where's Taylor?" she asked.

He didn't answer. "Where are the coins, Eva?"

Something wasn't right. He was looking at her in a predatory way. She felt a shiver go through her and shook her head. "I told you, I don't know."

He leaned in closer to her and smiled. "I'm going to try to make this easy on you. Tell me and your end will be swift and relatively painless. Or we can do it the fun way, and I'll torture you until you tell me. But make no mistake. You will talk. Everyone does."

She shrank back. "What's wrong with you? Why are you threatening me?"

He took a pouch from his pocket, unzipped it, and pulled out a pair of steel pliers.

"Guard!" she yelled.

Giving her a smug look, the man said, "They're on break. Amazing what some people will do for a few thousand euros."

Suddenly, he was on top of her, knocking Eva to the cold cement floor and pinning her beneath him. She tried to raise her arm to gouge him in the eyes, as she'd learned to do in her class, but she could hardly move. Grabbing her right hand, he squeezed the pliers around her thumb and twisted. White-hot pain filled her and she screamed again.

"Shut up," he hissed. "Where did you hide the coins?" He moved to the next finger and squeezed again, sending waves of pain through her.

She was crying now. "Why are you doing this? I'm your aunt! Where's Taylor?" She heard the click of a switchblade and felt the cold steel at her throat.

"Tell me or you die." He pressed the blade harder against her neck.

"I'll never tell you," she spat at him. "Go to hell."

Before she realized what was happening, he'd stabbed her in the eye. Pain like she'd never felt before engulfed her and she gasped through her sobs. "Stop!"

"Unless you want to be completely blind, tell me where they are."

"I hid them."

He held the blade over her other eye. "Where?"

The pain was so intense she began to black out.

He shook her. "Where are they?"

She thought fast through the searing pain. "Airport bathroom, the third stall in the toilet cistern . . ." There was no way she was shirking her duty now, after everything she'd been through, no matter how much it hurt.

"Was that so hard?" He laughed as he pressed the knife to her neck.

The last thing she felt was the blade sliding across her throat.

CHAPTER FORTY-FIVE

ATHENS, GREECE

NCE SHE WAS SAFELY INSIDE A CAB, TAYLOR OPENED THE suitcase and pushed aside clothes and saw a teddy bear. She pulled it out and squeezed it but didn't feel anything solid. Her eyes went to the two icons in the bottom of the suitcase— maybe that's where they were hidden. She needed to find a more secure place to unpack, though.

But first, she had to see what the lawyer had told Jeremy. The Athens traffic was thick, and the sound of blaring horns filled the air. It was over an hour before she reached the hotel, and when she did, she saw Jeremy waiting for her in the lobby, a questioning expression on his face.

"I think I have them," she said. "But I'm going to run into the ladies' room and make sure they're in here."

She found the lobby restroom and entered the handicapped stall, then put the suitcase down on top of the toilet seat and unzipped it again. Removing the first icon, she ran her hand over the front to see if she could feel anything. She turned it over and held it up to the light, then pulled a pen from her purse and ran it along the brown paper covering the back to discover a thicker layer of cardboard behind it. Working the pen until it made a hole, she turned and turned until she could get a finger in, then ripped out a small piece. She held it up again. She saw the glint of silver. *Aha!* She returned to the lobby with a smile.

"They're in here," she reassured her brother. "How did it go with the lawyer?"

"He's already arranged for a hearing, but it won't be until next week. He said there's no way they'll let her out on bail, since she has no real credentials and could be a security threat. They have to verify her identify. Technically she's an American citizen, but she's been living here illegally all these years. I think we're going to need to bring a lawyer back with us and we're going to need a DNA test to prove who she is and have the death certificate nullified." He pulled in a long breath. "In the meantime, she's going to have to stay put."

Taylor shook her head. "What a mess! We can't just leave her there, but we need to get the . . . suitcase . . . back home. Plus we've got to figure out where Crosse is."

"I think we need to fly back tonight. I'll arrange for everything for wheels up at eight. Do you want to go by the jail and see if they'll let you say good-bye to her?"

She nodded. "Yeah. I'll meet you at the airport. Why don't you take the suitcase?" She handed it to him and enclosed him in a hug. "See you later."

o   o   o

When Taylor arrived at the police station and gave them her name, she was made to wait until an older gentleman in a suit came out to get her.

"I'm Detective Stavros. Please come with me."

"Are you taking me to see my mother?"

He gave her a strange look. "Come with me, please."

She followed him through the door and into a room where two other officers already sat.

"What's going on?" she asked.

The detective took a seat across from her. "There's been an incident."

She felt her blood run cold. "What do you mean?"

"Someone came to question your mother. He had credentials. But . . . ." He stopped, looking at the man across from him.

"But what?" Her palms were damp with sweat and she looked back and forth at the two men. Her voice rose. "Has something happened to my mother?"

He cleared his throat. "I'm afraid she's dead."

She heard screaming and it took her a moment to realize it was coming from her. "No. She can't be dead. How did you let this happen?" She stood. "I want to see her! Take me to her now."

"That's impossible. You can't see her until the crime scene has been processed."

Taylor took a deep breath, willing herself to think clearly. She needed to get the lawyer to come back with her. "Can you tell me what happened exactly?"

The detective sighed. "There was a shift change of the guard. The new guard let in a man claiming to be from National Intelligence. When the guard checked on your mother a few hours later, she was lying in a pool of blood. The man had slit her throat."

The image of her mother bleeding out on the floor flashed in her mind. Taylor felt like she would be sick. "When can I see her? Have her buried properly?"

"You can check back in the morning. I'm sorry, there's nothing else we can do for you today."

She stood up and walked from the room on shaky legs. Once outside, she ran as fast as she could away from the jail until she was out of breath, then hailed a cab for the airport. She fell back against the seat, imagined images of her mother's murder bombarding her mind, unable to process what had just happened. She hugged herself tightly, crying loudly. Soon, she was heaving big sobs, and at the light the driver turned to look back at her.

"*Eísai kalá?*" he asked, a concerned look on his face.

"I'll be okay," she answered in Greek, taking deep breaths and trying to calm herself down. Finally they reached the airport and she paid him and jumped out.

Jeremy was waiting outside by the steps to the plane and Taylor ran to him, throwing herself into his arms, her sobs starting again.

"She's dead!"

He pulled back and looked at her in shock. "What? What do you mean?"

"Someone got into my mother's cell and killed her." She relayed what the police had told her. "We have to go to the lawyer's office and have him help us. They wouldn't let me see her . . . so I don't even know if they're telling me the truth."

All the color drained from Jeremy's face. "It must have been Crosse. He must have found out that she's alive . . . which means he might know we're here."

The only thing Taylor could think about was that they had to go back to the jail. They couldn't leave her mother's body there. "I don't know. But we have to get her."

The noise of a loud engine made them look up and they saw a black Hummer racing toward them.

Jeremy didn't waste a minute. "Get in the plane, now!" he yelled.

They raced up the stairs and just as the hatch was closing, the Hummer came to a stop and two men with machine guns in their hands jumped out and began shooting.

As the door closed, and the plane began taxiing down the runway, Taylor saw that the front of Jeremy's white shirt was turning red.

"You've been shot!"

"Tell the pilot to go faster! We have to get out of here."

"But you're bleeding! And what about my mother?"

He stumbled to a seat and sat down as the plane began to lift. "We can't stay here. It's too late to help her now. They must know we have the coins. We have to go!"

Taylor ran to the bathroom and returned with towels, pressing against what thankfully seemed to be only a shoulder graze, trying to stop the bleeding. It didn't look terrible, but she also didn't know how they were going to fly for ten hours with him in this condition. She got up and asked the flight attendant for the first aid kit. When Taylor walked back, she looked at Jeremy. "This is going to hurt." She took off his shirt and poured the alcohol on the wound. He clenched his fists but remained still. Then she took the towels and put pressure on the shoulder. Within seconds it was red with blood. She put on a second then a third before the blood started to ebb. "Maybe we should land somewhere closer and get you medical attention," she suggested.

He grimaced. "No. We need to get to the States. I'll be okay. It's just surface."

She hoped he was right. But as far as she was concerned, they couldn't get back on the ground fast enough.

She called Jack. "We're in the air. Someone came after us. I think they killed my mother. I don't know, they wouldn't let me see her body—and Jeremy's hurt. Bring a doctor. Did you find a place for us to go? We can't be anywhere near home right now."

"What! . . . never mind, yes, yes. . . . It's all set," Jack, sounding shocked, assured her. "I'm taking care of everything. I'll be waiting at the airport when you land. Be safe. Love you."

CHAPTER FORTY-SIX

Jack had arranged to borrow a Suburban that couldn't be tracked to him. As he waited for Jeremy and Taylor's plane to land at Teterboro, he talked with Dr. Larson, a friend of a friend who had come with him to take a look at Jeremy, as Evan dozed in the back row. But Jack's mind was on his trip to Sybil's apartment. He'd have to update Taylor once they got settled, something he wasn't looking forward to. He didn't even understand why he'd gone to pick it up. There was no way he could risk trying to get it to Dakota from their hiding place, and he worried that he'd actually made things worse now.

Jack was brought back into the moment when he heard the sound of the plane's engine. He turned to the doctor, sitting in the passenger seat. "Be right back."

"I'll set Jeremy up in the back seat so I can attend to him while you drive," Larson answered, opening the passenger-side door.

Jack walked over to the plane as soon as it stopped, and when Taylor reached the ground, he pulled her to him and hugged her tight.

"I'm so sorry about your mother. Are you doing okay?"

She tried to speak but was too choked up. She simply pressed into him and hugged him back until she could compose herself. When she pulled back she looked at him. "I'm numb. It still feels surreal."

He nodded. "I know. Listen, we should get going. Get Jeremy in the back. There's a doctor ready to fix him up. We're going two hours upstate."

o   o   o

As Jack drove, and Evan slept, Taylor held a flashlight for the doctor while he cleaned the wound in Jeremy's shoulder and injected him with antibiotics, then stitched the skin.

"You're lucky. It's a surface wound." He handed him a bottle of pills. "Take two every six hours for the next ten days. Call me if it looks infected."

They dropped Dr. Larson off at a hotel half an hour away and continued on until they reached a small ranch house set a mile off the road down a dirt driveway. Jack helped Jeremy inside, settling him on the sofa, while Taylor took Evan to one of the bedrooms and tucked him into bed. Jack made a pot of coffee and took a seat in the living room across from Jeremy, and Taylor poured herself a cup and joined them.

Jack turned to her. "We need to find Crosse. Prove he's alive so he can be arrested. You and Evan aren't safe until he is. For that matter, neither are you, Jeremy."

"You're right. But how in the world are we going to find him?" Taylor said.

"I have an idea," Jack said. "It's this story. Now that we know he's alive, it makes sense. I've been wondering for a while why someone would want to drug people to cause a psychotic break, and the cold vaccine seems to be the connection. So I looked into who made it, and it's—"

"Licentia Labs," Jeremy cut in. "They've become a huge player, fast. That vaccine made them billions, as you can imagine."

Jack tapped his pencil on his pad. "They were only founded two years ago. And I'll bet Damon Crosse has his hooks in this company."

"Licentia means anarchy in Latin," Jeremy said.

Jack expelled a breath. "That tracks. Sounds just like a name he'd choose."

Taylor looked at Jeremy. "Is it really possible that a stimulant could cause someone to commit murder, or suicide?"

"He's likely mixing it with other things." He shook his head. "I should have known he'd never take his own life." He turned to Jack. "Can I see the toxicology reports from all the recent suicides? It might give me some idea of what kind of poison he's mixing."

Jack nodded. "I have a copy of one, and I'm trying to get others. My brother-in-law who works for the FBI is involved now, too; he's going to email them to me when he can."

"Won't we be easier to locate if we're using email on our phones?" Taylor asked.

"Don't worry," Jack told her. "I've got burners for all of us, and I borrowed a clean computer from a tech friend that can't be traced here."

"That's a relief," Jeremy said. "But we have to figure out where Crosse is. Smoke him out somehow."

"We have to use the coins," Taylor said. "Get a message to Crosse that we have them. Arrange a meeting."

"I think you're right. It's the only way to find him," Jack agreed.

Jeremy looked back and forth between the two of them and shook his head. "Absolutely not. He cannot get his hands on any more of the coins. Remember what happened last time we tried that?"

"This time will be different. We'll be more prepared," Taylor argued. "Maybe Father Basil will have an idea of how to lure him."

"Are you sure we can trust Basil?" Jack asked.

Taylor replied, "I'm not sure we have a choice. And I looked into the Pittsburgh ceremony and what Father Basil told me checks out." She opened the laptop and pulled up an article from her desktop, then turned the screen to face them. "See, it talks about the fire last year and the service to reopen the church, with the icons that are going to be consecrated." She pointed. "The Theotokos and the St. Mary of Bethany are being donated by Father Basil Parakos, those are the ones with the silver pieces hidden. And here's the listing for the donation of the St. John and the Holy Family icons—those are the ones Mom hid the coins she had in."

Jack took a few minutes to read it over, then shrugged. "Looks legit to me."

"So we need to figure out how to let Crosse know we have the coins. Do you think he's even in the country?" Taylor asked.

Jack looked up at the ceiling. "Well, let's go with what we know about him. There's no way he's lounging on a beach somewhere. He dedicated his life to building an institute that indoctrinated and trained pawns he could use to manipulate others. Wherever he is, you can bet he's got some kind of plan to cause more harm. I think he's got an agenda that he's using the contaminated vaccine to carry out. I confirmed with Brian Doyle that his wife did get the vaccine. But what does Crosse hope to gain by making people go nuts?"

"Well," Jeremy said. "Let's look at who they are. Is there anything they all have in common?"

Jack snapped his fingers. "A Baptist Sunday school teacher, a Catholic woman in counseling, a respected psychologist, a well-known preacher. They were all good people, with strong values. Religious. Could he want to discredit their faith?"

Jeremy leaned back in his chair, slowly shaking his head. "Not big enough. I mean, yes, maybe the added bonus was that it would besmirch their reputations and make people see religion as hypocritical, but I think it's a test run for something bigger."

Taylor shook her head. "We're jumping to an awful lot of conclusions here. We need to verify first that they all received the cold vaccine. And even then, it could be a coincidence. I mean, a majority of the nation has been vaccinated. We both got it and so did Evan."

Jeremy looked surprised. "I didn't," he said. "I should have told you not to. It's always good to wait until something's been out a few years before you jump on the bandwagon."

"Great," Taylor said. "Too late now."

Jack tried to change the subject. "So if this is Crosse's doing, what do you think his next steps are?" He looked at Jeremy.

"There's a lot of possibilities. One thing I'm fairly certain of is that whatever he's planning is going to happen soon. He can't afford for anyone to figure out that what's been going on recently has been caused by the vaccine or they'll pull it. If the Institute were still around, the testing would have occurred inside those walls." Jeremy took a sip of his drink. "Actually, he may well have begun the testing there years ago."

"So you're thinking he's on the brink of a major rollout but wanted to make sure it worked first?" Taylor asked.

Jeremy nodded. "That would be my guess. But, of course, we could be on the wrong track." He looked at Jack. "It's still possible that this is nothing more than a scientific error." He stroked his chin. "But now that we know he's alive, I'm more inclined to believe he's running Licentia."

Jack's phone rang and he excused himself. "Logan."

Scotty didn't bother with any pleasantries. "All three of these guys got the cold vaccine right before they went crazy."

"That makes six cases now. Are you going to alert the FDA? Have them check out the vaccine?"

"Hey, not so fast, partner. We have to be careful here. We don't have anything definitive yet and if something about this leaks out, we could do more harm than good. Cause a public panic. The vaccine could be totally fine. All we know is that it's a common denominator, nothing more. Plus, we'd have a huge lawsuit on our hands from the pharma company. It would ruin their reputation. This is going take some time. But we will be getting a subpoena to look into Licentia."

Jack sighed. "Good." He filled Scotty in on their current circumstances. "I'm going to dump this phone for now, but I'll text you from my new burner. Stay in contact. I'll let you know if I find out anything new. Thanks again, man."

"Sure thing."

He returned to the kitchen. "Three more cases where they'd had the cold vaccine right before they went crazy."

Taylor's voice was shaky. "We need to find out exactly what's going on and if there's an issue with the vaccine. We can't sit around and wait until it warps our minds!"

Jeremy's eyes met Jack's. Taylor noticed and said, "Look, guys, I'm not being paranoid. People are going crazy! Regular people. If that vaccine has something to do with it, then we're not immune."

Jeremy put a hand up. "You're right. I'm sorry. It's been weeks since you both got it, though, and as you pointed out, millions of other people have gotten it, too. These episodes have all been a few days after."

Jack nodded. "I'll verify that that's true in all these cases. In the meantime, there's really not a whole lot we can do about it, so there's no point in worrying." He gave Taylor what he hoped was a reassuring smile, but inside he was just as worried as she was. The thought that either of them might suddenly lose their minds and commit murder wasn't just terrifying. It was a distinct possibility.

○ ○ ○

When they turned in for the night, Jack seized his opportunity to talk to Taylor about what had been nagging at him.

"So I have an update on the situation with Dakota's passport."

She gave him a stony look, saying nothing.

"Sybil called me and begged me to pick it up from her before she goes back into the hospital. I told her I couldn't possibly take the passport to Dakota, but she asked me to hold it and have Dakota find someone to get it from me. I went to New York before coming to get you. I have it."

She shook her head. "That makes no sense, Jack. Why can't whoever Dakota is going to have get it from you have gotten it from her aunt? If she trusts someone enough to retrieve it from you, there was no reason to involve you in the first place. This whole thing is sketchy."

"I know, but I couldn't say no to Sybil. She's sick, maybe not totally rational, maybe Dakota knew she'd only give it to me. I'm not thinking straight with everything that's going on." His rationale sounded lame even to his ears. "I called Dakota and told her she'd have to find someone to get it from me, and she's working on it. I told her I'd call her back in two days."

Taylor shook her head, her face red. "So what then? You're going to tell her where we are?"

"Of course not. I'll drop it somewhere. Find a safe meeting place."

Taylor snapped the lamp off and got in bed, her back turned to him. He slid in next to her but she moved to the edge of the bed. It was going to be a long night.

CHAPTER FORTY-SEVEN

EONARD TREATED HIS HOUSEHOLD STAFF EXTREMELY WELL, and in return they kept him informed about everything that went on in the home. Just the other day, he'd learned, the girls had asked if they could skip school because it was such a pretty day and they wanted to spend it outside. Patrice, the pushover that she was, had relented and allowed them to stay home. He'd been furious when he found out. Laziness was not to be rewarded. He decided that the only way to know what she was up to all the time was to install surveillance cameras, which he'd handled the very next day. Now he could keep an eye on her even while he was at work. He opened the app on his cell phone and he watched her, curious to see what she was doing in his library.

Patrice walked in, looking around, poking at books on the bookcase. What was she looking for? She turned to one wall and ran her hand over the sills and around each window. Next, she crouched and pulled up a corner of the Oriental rug. The mic picked up her audible sigh. She turned around, staring at the

Jefferson desk. She went over to it and lifted the top. She dropped to her knees and when she stood again he saw that she was holding the small brown envelope he'd taped in one of the corners. Taking it with her, she left the room.

He couldn't see her again until she reached their bedroom suite and that camera picked her up. She'd figured out that the envelope held the key to the silver box on his dresser. He laughed as she opened it and pulled out the pictures one by one. He relished the look of shock and disgust on her face as she saw Sissy doing things to him that Patrice no longer did. Served her right for being nosy. Did she really think he was stupid enough to leave incriminating evidence where she could find it? She was looking for his blackmail ledger, the one he'd stupidly told her about when he'd first gotten his promotion. The one that showed what he'd paid to whom for services rendered, with the details he needed if they ever tried to cross him. But that file was out of her reach in a safe in his closet.

One thing was certain, though: she was trying to take him down. She'd shown her hand today, a grave mistake. She was now officially the enemy.

CHAPTER FORTY-EIGHT

THE NEXT MORNING, TAYLOR WAS STILL HALF ASLEEP AND started to respond to Jack's kiss before she remembered their conversation from the night before and pushed him away. "I'm still upset with you."

He stroked her arm. "T, come on. What would you do if Jeremy was sick and you had to help him? This isn't about Dakota. It's about Sybil. She's family. If it weren't for her, I might not be here right now."

Taylor softened. "I'm sorry. I know your heart's in the right place. It's just so unnerving that she reaches out to you now that we know Crosse is alive. Dakota used to work for him. How do you know this isn't another of his plans?"

"Because she's in hiding from Crosse herself. He tried to have her killed. Besides, I know Sybil would never lie to me." He leaned up on one elbow. "Don't get me wrong, I'm not letting my guard down. But I couldn't live with myself if Sybil died all alone and I could have prevented it."

Taylor got up from the bed. "We're going to have to agree to disagree."

They got dressed and joined Jeremy in the kitchen, where he was already drinking a cup of coffee.

"Morning, guys. As much as I hate to admit it, you're right about Crosse. I had an idea for a way we can get to him. First thing he does every day is read the *New York Times* cover to cover. We can place an ad in their classifieds, something like: 'Rare coins dating back to AD 30. Seeking proper owner. Set of ten from an original thirty. Guaranteed authentic.' We still have time to get it to run this Sunday."

"And then what?" Jack asked.

"Set up an email address he can write to and take it from there. When he gets in touch, we set a meeting, and we lay a trap for him," Jeremy said.

"I think you've watched one too many cop shows. Damon Crosse is much too smart to walk into a trap."

"What do you suggest then?" Jeremy asked him.

Taylor answered instead. "What if we make him think it's someone from the church who has the coins? It might be more believable. Maybe Scotty could help, get the FBI to set it up."

"I don't know," Jack said. "Crosse hates to do his own dirty work. What if he sends someone in his place?"

"He'll come. There's no way he would trust anyone besides himself with the coins," Jeremy assured them. "Besides, after being duped on the last ten, he'll want to make sure that these are the real thing."

"So who would we pretend to be?" Jack asked.

"What about Father Basil?" Taylor suggested. "I can call him and tell him that's the plan. Crosse knows that the coins have the potential to corrupt even the most devout. He'll be inclined to believe that has happened to Father Basil, seeing as Damon hates the church so much. We ask for five million dollars. That way we also find out if he's got access to money; maybe there's a way to connect him to Licentia," Taylor said.

Jack nodded. "I think we're on the right track."

"We have to make it foolproof," Jeremy said. "If he ends up actually getting the coins from us . . ."

"He'd still only have twenty. That wouldn't be the end of the world. Right?" Jack asked.

Jeremy sighed. "Well, no, but that doesn't mean he won't get more power if he doubles the quantity he has. There's a lot we don't know about the coins. No one has ever held more than ten at a time—they've always been divided up. If someone had twenty, that could open more portals for evil. And they could make it easier for that person to find the remaining ten."

"How?" Jack asked.

"There's a theory that if you have a majority of the thirty, those will have the energy to lead you to the others."

Jack gave him a skeptical look.

Jeremy shrugged. "Look, I know you don't buy into all this spiritual stuff, but what I know is that there are angels and demons in a constant battle for the souls walking among us. Those coins allow the holder to either keep a door closed on those demons or open a door and let more of them walk freely as well. When someone does something horrific, something truly unfathomable to most of us, you can bet one or more of these demons is whispering in their ear."

Taylor watched Jack's face for a reaction, but his expression was inscrutable. "Are you saying that people are not responsible for their own actions? That unseen spiritual forces are making them do bad things?" he asked.

"What I'm saying is that we can be influenced for good or evil by the things we invite into our lives," Jeremy said. "Don't forget, I was raised by Damon Crosse and was involved in the occult for many years before I found my way to God. It's very powerful, and trust me, those evil forces are very real."

Taylor looked at Jeremy. "So are you saying there's some sort of correlation between the number of coins one has and the number of demons they can call up to earth?" She believed in God, but this all sounded a bit crazy to her. "I mean they're inanimate objects. I know they have a bad history but—"

Jeremy held his hands out for emphasis. "Have you ever heard of relics healing people? They've been responsible for miracles around the world. These are not just inanimate objects! They are the very coins that were used to betray Christ. To secure his death. Satan *entered* Judas. Do you understand? He took human form in Judas and he touched those coins." He shook his head. "Do you really think your mother would have given up her entire life, given the chance to be with her beloved daughter, if they were just inanimate objects?"

Taylor stood, walked over to Jeremy, and sat next him, taking his hand in hers. "It all just feels so unreal. Finding her after all these years only to lose her all over again. Thank God you're going to be okay. I almost lost you, too." Taylor was still trying to reconcile her mother's reappearance and murder, and she needed to grieve, but they needed to sort this out first. She was preoccupied by one other thing, something she hadn't mentioned to Jack yet. But that would have to wait as well.

"Our plan has to be foolproof," Jeremy said again. "There's too much at stake, and now that Evan is here, you're in even more danger. That's another reason we can never let Damon Crosse get our ten."

A shiver went up Taylor's spine. "I'm going to check on Evan now," she said. She left the two of them and went to the small bedroom where she found Evan asleep on the twin bed, his thumb in his mouth. She sat gingerly on the bed so as not to wake him and stroked his head. Her beautiful little boy. She was filled with a new resolve. No matter what, she would protect him, or die trying.

CHAPTER FORTY-NINE

"H OW'S IT GOING?" JEREMY TOOK A SEAT ACROSS THE TABLE from Jack, wincing as his shoulder hit the edge of the chair.

"You okay?" Jack asked, and Jeremy nodded.

Jack pushed the laptop away from him. "The ad's all set to run tomorrow, but I'm not making any progress tying Crosse directly to Licentia. Do you know of any other alias Crosse might have used or kept his money under?" he asked. "He's got to be accessing his money through some channel."

"No. You can be sure he had it all worked out well before he faked his suicide. Considering he had the means and ability to create false backstories for senators and judges, he had to have made some for himself. I'm sure he's got money in accounts around the world."

Jack stood and stretched. "So you're saying our only hope is if he answers the ad?"

"He'll answer it."

"So in the meantime, we wait." Jack's email pinged. "It's

Scotty. He's got some more tox reports. Why don't you take a look? See if it looks like something Crosse cooked up in his lab."

"Okay." Jeremy took Jack's seat in front of the laptop and immediately engrossed himself in the report.

"I'm going to go take a shower," Jack said, standing, then thought of something and turned to Taylor, who had just entered the room. "Your story airs tonight, right?"

She nodded. "Yes, but it's the last thing on my mind right now."

He hated seeing that worried look in her eyes. He pulled her toward him for a hug. "We're going to find Crosse. I won't let him get anywhere near you or Evan."

She put her head on his shoulder and closed her eyes. "I know you'll do everything in your power, but you can't promise that. You know that as well as I do."

"I'll die protecting you."

She pulled away from him, her expression angry. "Don't say that. You're not dying. No one is dying. I'm not losing you again."

"Sorry. Of course. No one's dying." But if they were going up against Crosse again—if, in fact, they'd never stopped but just had not known it—Jack knew that it was a likely possibility one of them would end up dead.

CHAPTER FIFTY

LEONARD SAT IN A BOOTH IN THE BACK OF THE RESTAURANT, annoyed that Sissy was keeping him waiting. He had told her to meet him here on the Monday following her weekend in New York so he could collect the evidence from her, but she was uncharacteristically late.

He glanced at his Chopard watch. What the hell was taking her so long? He had things to do. He was not a man to keep waiting and he briefly entertained the thought of one more night with her just so he could make her pay. But that wouldn't be wise. No, a clean break was necessary. She'd get a visit from one of his employees warning her to stay away from him or else face public humiliation. He knew that whatever her past, she wouldn't want to find compromising pictures of herself on Snapchat or Instagram. Why were people so stupid? They were careless, so trusting and foolish to think that there wasn't always someone waiting and watching to get the better of them. He'd learned that lesson early enough.

He was about to call Sissy when he heard the chime of the diner door. That had better be her. The sound of clicking heels became louder as she approached his booth. When he looked up, he dropped his cup into the saucer. It rattled loudly, splashing coffee across the table.

"What the hell is this? What are you doing here?"

Patrice smiled at him and slid into the other side of the booth, grabbing his napkin and stopping the flow of liquid before it reached her side. "I think it's time you started treating me with more respect considering I hold your future in my hands." She handed him her cell phone and earphones. "You may want these."

He grabbed them from her and put them in his ears.

Patrice hit the play button, and Leonard's stomach lurched—it was a recording of him and Sissy at her apartment. He watched with growing dread as their entire conversation about framing the Supreme Court justice was replayed in crystal-clear audio.

Sissy had tricked him. How had Patrice found her? "I don't understand . . . How did you . . . get this?" he sputtered.

She yanked the phone toward her and the cord pulled the earphones from his ears.

His wife smiled again. "A better question is: What am I going to do with it?"

CHAPTER FIFTY-ONE

"EXCITED TO SEE YOUR SHOW?" JACK ASKED AS HE CAME OUT OF the bedroom.

Taylor nodded, although she wasn't sure excited was the word she'd use. But she was looking forward to seeing how it would turn out. It would be a distraction at least from the hell they were now in. "Is Evan asleep?"

"Totally out."

He walked over to her and put a hand on her shoulder. "You okay?"

Taylor was still annoyed by Jack's comment about dying to protect her. She wasn't some helpless female in need of a knight in shining armor. She thought about the last time she and Jack had tried to bring down Damon Crosse. Even though it had been only two years ago, it felt like a lifetime. She'd been a different person back then, too trusting, and if Jack hadn't come to her house after her husband had been murdered, she had no doubt that she'd either be dead or a prisoner of Damon Crosse. But she'd grown a lot in two years and didn't need Jack to fight her battles anymore. They could fight them together. And she was proud that she had come through it all stronger than ever. She secretly felt like a superhero. She'd trained hard to learn how to handle a gun with the best of them, but also to defend herself with nothing but her fists and legs. She would never again be unprepared. If Damon Crosse thought he was dealing with the same soft woman he'd encountered back then, he was in for a surprise.

They turned on the television and she took a seat next to Jack on the sofa. She looked over at Jeremy in the armchair and was happy to see that the color had returned to his face. "How's your shoulder?"

"Better."

Their attention was drawn to the screen as a solemn-looking Karen Printz sitting in an armchair delivered an intro to the story from the studio.

Jack squeezed Taylor's hand. "I'm so proud of you."

Karen continued, her tone serious. "As many of you know, Jefferson Health Care is in the midst of a class action suit that reached the Supreme Court. Deliberations are still taking place and we expect a decision any day. Tonight we'll be hearing from three families involved in the suit. As you'll soon see, there are no easy answers, and not everyone is on the same page."

The show cut to commercial.

Taylor looked at Jack, puzzled. "That was a strange cutaway. I wonder what she meant by that last line."

Jack shrugged. "Well, obviously Jefferson's not on the same page."

When the show returned, Karen's narration continued in voice-over. "First we'll meet Molly and Clyde Edwards. Molly is pregnant but the prenatal testing showed the strong possibility of birth defects."

The camera zoomed in on Molly. "I told him there was no way I was aborting my baby. We're Catholic."

Karen's face suddenly filled the screen. "Despite the very real possibility of bringing a child into the world to suffer, Molly's religious beliefs preclude her from preventing a child's pain."

"What the . . ." Taylor sputtered.

Karen continued. "Molly's husband is pleased with the policy."

The camera zoomed in on Molly's husband, Clyde. "We thought the policy was a great deal. Saved us lots of money."

Back to Karen. "How do you feel about terminating the pregnancy?"

Clyde again. "It's so early, not a big deal, and we can try again. Why have a child that's sick?"

The show went to commercial again.

Taylor jumped up from the sofa, incensed. "That's all taken totally out of context. Clyde was mimicking the doctor when he said that. He was furious that the doctor had told them it was no big deal. I can't believe this!"

Jeremy shook his head. "I'm sorry, Taylor. But I can't say I'm surprised."

"They're going to be so upset! I need to call them. I don't want them to think I betrayed them."

"Whoa," Jack said. "Even though we've taken precautions with our tech, you can't reach out to anyone. I understand that you're upset but we have to focus on Crosse right now."

She sighed. "I know you're right. But I feel so terrible."

They watched the rest of the segment in horror and disbelief as Karen pulled the same stunt with every story, taking quotes out of context to make it appear as though Jefferson was only using common medical sense. The last word was from an interview with Georgia. "There's no doubt in my mind their money is wasted trying to save the lives of anyone of advanced age," the scientist said.

"That's not what she said!" Taylor sputtered, rising out of her seat in indignation. "I remember how she put it. She said there was no doubt in her mind that *Jefferson thought* their money is wasted. They cut those two words."

"Won't she and the other interviewees have recourse against UBC for twisting the meaning of their words?" Jeremy asked.

"No, they've all signed releases agreeing to editing. There's nothing they can do. I cannot believe that Karen did this!"

"I'm sorry, babe. This sucks. But how many times have we seen a story spun a certain way and then we get the whole story and see how it's been edited? I'm really sorry, though, that your name is on this."

"When this is over, you better believe I'm going to do something about it." She turned off the television and went into the kitchen, opening the clean laptop and navigating to UBC's website, where she read the comments pouring in.

She called over to Jack and Jeremy. "You won't believe this, but most of the comments are positive. People criticizing the plaintiffs for selfishly wasting resources on lost causes."

What had happened to Karen? She'd always had journalistic integrity. Then Taylor flashed to Karen's face when Crosby Wheeler had come into their meeting. She wasn't just intimidated by him. She was scared, Taylor now realized. She ran back out to the living room.

"Wheeler. It's got to be him. We have to find a connection between him and Crosse."

Jack nodded. "I was thinking the same thing. I have a feeling even a deep search won't reveal much, but I'll try. We can also see if Scotty can find anything out."

Still feeling heartsick, Taylor went into the bedroom and

shut the door. No matter what Jack said, she had to reach out to Georgia. She couldn't have her thinking that Taylor had been any part of this debacle. She dialed her cell, but a man picked up.

"Hello? I'm trying to reach Georgia Lakos?"

"Who's this?"

She was taken aback by the man's abruptness. "Taylor Phillips, a friend of hers. Who's this? Is Georgia there?"

His voice softened. "This is Gus, her son. She told me about you. My mother's in the hospital. She . . ." A sob came over the line. He cleared his throat and went on. "Sorry, she jumped from a four-story window in the middle of class today. The students said she suddenly started talking out of her head and did it before anyone could stop her."

Taylor froze. "Oh no! Is she going to be okay?"

"I don't know. She's in a coma. They don't know if it was a stroke or maybe an aneurysm. I don't know anything else."

Tears sprang to Taylor's eyes.

"If you don't mind my asking . . . Had she had a physical lately?"

"That's what's so perplexing. She'd just gone the day before to get her vaccine shot."

Taylor was now convinced the vaccine was the link to all those murder-suicides. If that was what happened, Georgia must have realized what was happening to her. She probably jumped to save her students. "I'll pray for her. Again, I'm so sorry. I'll call you tomorrow to check on her." She didn't want to say anything just yet, but if the hospital found meth in Georgia's blood work, Taylor would tell him about their theory.

"Thank you."

She ended the call and went out to tell Jack and Jeremy the horrible news.

CHAPTER FIFTY-TWO

DAMON, IN HIS ROLE AS CROSBY WHEELER, WAS PLEASED WITH the way the show had turned out and had made sure that all the comments in favor of Jefferson Health populated first on the UBC website. Karen had known from the outset what the true spin of the story was going to be, having forfeited her journalistic integrity in exchange for Crosby's silence regarding her husband's side hobby. Karen's husband had a predilection for his young interns, many of whom he'd pressured into physical relationships. When Crosby had shown Karen the video of the last young girl, the youngest yet at only seventeen, she begged him to bury it. Her career would be ruined if it came out that not only was she married to a lecherous misogynist, but that she'd known about it and done nothing to stop him. The face of journalistic fairness and justice, Karen was beloved by the American public, and her livelihood depended on it staying that way. So she went along with whatever Crosby asked rather than endure public scandal, though he thought he'd seen her flinch when he ordered her to change this story.

Damon sipped his morning coffee while reading the newspaper. He took a moment to imagine next week's headlines: PRESIDENT GOES ON KILLING SPREE. Of course his people would come up with something far catchier, but he'd keep the paper as a souvenir for years to come.

He looked back to that day's paper and froze when he turned to the classifieds section.

Rare coins dating back to time of Christ. Set of ten from original 30. Guaranteed authentic. Serious inquiries only, email fatherbpottersfield@gmail.com. He read the ad three more times. Who the hell had run it? Could it really be the Judas coins? Which set were they? The ten that had been in Jerusalem, under the church's watch? There was only one way to find out. He went to one of his untraceable email accounts and typed:

Interested in coins. Who was original owner?

If they gave him the right answer, then he'd take it to the next step and meet them. It would make things so much easier if he could get his hands on another ten. It might even help him figure out how to make the set complete. As soon as he hit send, he turned his attention to a bank transaction he needed to complete. Ten million into Brody Hamilton's offshore account and another ten into Leonard Reed's. A final payment of another ten to Leonard Reed after the White House doctor administered the vaccine to the president on live television. The next day, the Ravage would take over and the president would behave like all the others had and then be found to have meth in his system. The country would be in shock, and while they mourned, Brody Hamilton would step in and restore order.

Hamilton's time in the Senate had been well spent, and as president, he'd have no problem getting the bills passed that Damon would feed him. He'd begin by finally making euthanasia legal. He'd start with the easy win—doctor-assisted suicide. But before long, he'd extend the law to doctor-*directed* end-of-life decisions. Those who had outlived their usefulness to society would be put down. The bioethicists would continue to do their job of framing life in terms of utility. And with the rising cost of health care in this country, people would be willing to accept that resources needed to be used wisely. The threat of more increases in health-care costs due to the burden of the old and infirm would be enough to convince most people that it was time to embrace euthanasia as other countries had done. Anything was possible if it was framed properly. After all, what kind of quality of life was there for someone old and sick?

By the time he was finished, individual freedom would be an abstract concept. Hamilton had three years left before the term would expire, and by the time he'd carried through all of Damon's plans, it wouldn't matter if he was reelected or not. Three years was enough time for Damon to destroy America. By then, he and Evan would be living across the Atlantic and Damon would begin his work in Europe.

CHAPTER FIFTY-THREE

Jack returned from the store to find Beau sitting on the front porch. "Hey, buddy. What are you doing out here?" He opened the door and held it for the dog, but he just looked at Jack, not budging. "Hmm. You guarding the place?" Beau gave him a look that seemed to convey an affirmative.

Jeremy was reading Evan a story, and Taylor was sitting at the kitchen table working on the computer. "What's with Beau?"

She looked up and shook her head. "He won't come in. I even tried tempting him with cheese."

"He's a wonder dog," Jack said. "Listen, I hope we're going to have an answer to the ad soon, and we need to figure out where to meet Crosse and who's going. I thought about asking Scotty to back us up, but it's too risky for him. Plus, we can't risk someone in his office tipping off Crosse, since he's got tentacles everywhere."

"So, what, we're going to grab Crosse and take him to the cops?" Taylor asked. "If Scotty doesn't come, it's just you and me." She looked at Jeremy, who was about to protest. "We're the only ones who know how to handle a gun. But we're going to need someone he doesn't recognize to pose as Father Basil. And who knows if he's going to come alone?"

The last thing Jack wanted was to put Taylor in the line of fire, but she was right. She'd spent the past two years at the gun range with him every week and was almost as good a shot as he was. It wasn't wise for him to go alone. "We tell Crosse he has to come alone." He paused. "Maybe I should ask Scotty after all. I'll give him an out."

"Where is he now?"

"On his way back from Florida, or maybe even already back in New York, just gathering all the information he can. He's heading up a task force on this meth outbreak."

Taylor suggested, "Maybe he can get away for a few hours if he tells them you've got info on the story and you insist on seeing him in person."

"Yeah. Maybe. I'll try him now."

He dialed Scotty. "Voice mail," he told Taylor. He hung up and typed a quick text. **Need to talk. Call me.**

"We're going to get him this time," Taylor said. Jack knew she meant Crosse.

Even though Jack was feeling less than confident, he gave her a brave smile. "No doubt. He's going down." But in his bones, he knew that something bad was going to happen. It wasn't just because he knew how evil Damon was. It was something else, something intangible, but nonetheless real. He'd felt it before his father died. He'd felt it when he lost a buddy in Colombia. It was some sort of premonition.

You don't believe in premonitions, he told himself. But the thought made him feel no better.

CHAPTER FIFTY-FOUR

LEONARD LOOKED AT HIS WIFE ACROSS THE TABLE AND FELT A familiar loathing, but this time it was tinged with fear. "How did you get that?"

"What, you think you're the only one who's sneaky? I went to talk to Sissy right after you started seeing her. Made a little side deal of my own. When I showed her the pictures you'd taken of her and told her what you'd done to your other girlfriends, she was more than happy to help. She'll be taken care of financially for a long, long, time."

"What do you want? Money?"

"I want you to settle the Supreme Court case. Pay all those good people the money they deserve and eliminate your death policy."

He laughed. "Oh, is that all? You just want me to lose the company hundreds of millions of dollars, have the board of directors fire me, and then sue me? I don't think so."

"Fine. If you'd rather go to jail, that works too. I'll take this little tape to Justice Landon so he knows how you tried to make him look like a pedophile. Although I have to assume you'd lose your job if you're arrested anyway . . ."

He took a deep breath, scrambling to come up with a solution. "Patrice, we have children. What would it do to them if their father was sent to jail?"

She laughed. "It might teach them not to be sociopathic criminals." She shifted in her seat. "I'd prefer not to put them through that, but I will if I have to. Convince the board that it's in their best interest to settle the case and turn it into a public relations win. Say you didn't realize the devastating effect the new policy exclusions would have on your customers and that you're ready to make amends. They may even believe you have a soul."

He thought some more. "I have to assume that Sissy didn't go through with the plan, since she's in cahoots with you. So all you have is that video, which I can say wasn't real. It was a sexual fantasy, a joke. I can find a way around it."

She leaned forward. "Unlikely, especially since Sissy is willing to testify if necessary. As will her sister. Her very young, thirteen-year-old sister." Then she pulled out a folder and pushed it across to him. "But I think you might have a harder time talking your way out of all these other instances of extortion and money laundering. Settle the case. And sign the divorce papers." She stood. "Thank you in advance for your very generous settlement and full custody agreement."

"How did you get those?"

"You're not the only one who can buy cameras. I had one installed in your closet and got a good look at the combo on that fancy safe. You always think you're the smartest one in the room." She laughed. "Obviously, that's only if it's a very small room."

He sat there, stunned, as she walked away. He'd had no idea she had it in her. He'd find a way to settle the case and spin it to the board. It would cost them, but he'd find a way to make it up. He couldn't let her ruin him, not when he was on the verge of seizing even more power.

In the meantime, he had some thinking to do about Patrice. No way in hell was he handing over all his money and the kids to her. First, he had to find out if anyone else knew what she'd done, see if she'd set up any contingency plans. As much as it would pain him to see the girls grieving, it might be time for him to become a widower.

CHAPTER FIFTY-FIVE

TAYLOR HAD BEEN CHECKING THE EMAIL THEY'D SET UP EVERY five minutes, but the only responses they had received so far were generic-sounding ones with questions about the type of coins and their dollar value. She was beginning to worry that the ad had been a half-baked idea.

A ping sounded and Taylor clicked the email. "Another one." She read it aloud. "*Interested in coins. Who was original owner?*"

"That could be him," Jeremy said.

"What should we write back?" Jack asked.

Jeremy thought for a moment. "How about Betrayer of the Son of Man?"

Jack's forehead wrinkled. "Why not just say Judas?"

"He'll appreciate the biblical reference. Remember this is supposed to be coming from someone in the church," Jeremy answered. "But don't send it right away. We don't want him to know we're waiting by the computer. It might make him suspicious."

"OK," Jack said. "On a different note, now that you've analyzed the tox reports, what do you think?"

"It's definitely more than methamphetamine and ecstasy," Jeremy told him. "Those two in combination can ramp up violent tendencies in a user, but I'm convinced that he's created some sort of accelerant that makes the effect much more potent. A multiplier of sorts. But there's no way for me to confirm this from the reports. It's probably a chemical that the labs can't identify because it's new."

"That sounds pretty bad."

"It was likely a long time in the making," Jeremy said. "He had a lot going on at the Institute. And you know Friedrich worked under Mengele, so who knows what kinds of experiments they did over the years?"

"Even more reason to find Crosse," Taylor answered. "If he's the one behind this, we have a chance to stop it before it goes any further. We have to make him believe our story. In order for someone to have been able to get the coins they have to be pretty high-ranking in the church, right?" Taylor asked.

Jeremy nodded. "Either that or working for someone who is."

"It's always best to stick as close to the truth as possible," Jack interjected. "Even though we're talking about the coins Eva guarded, we know another ten are at a Greek church in Pittsburgh. So let's pretend we're selling those. Who would know about them?"

Taylor hesitated. "I would think they'd keep the information close to the vest, considering the risks. The archbishop who's coming to bless the church likely knows. He's supposed to get those coins to the patriarch."

Jeremy nodded. "I spoke to Father Basil last night. He and the archbishop are the only ones who know."

Taylor's heartbeat quickened. "Was he able to find out anything more about my mother?"

Jeremy gave her a sympathetic look. "Not yet. The lawyer we met with has been trying to get answers but they keep stonewalling him. Father Basil promised to call as soon as he learns anything."

Taylor released a pent-up breath. Until she saw her mother's body with her own eyes, she wouldn't believe she was really dead. She'd been fooled all these years. She wasn't about to be fooled again.

Jack squeezed her hand. "I'm sorry you're going through this."

She inhaled deeply. She couldn't dwell on it right now. Instead, she turned back to Jeremy.

"I've been thinking about it," Taylor said. "What if we have Crosse meet us at a Greek church? We lure him with the coins and then have Scotty cuff him and bring him in."

"Why don't we just have Scotty arrest him as soon as they're in the church? Do we really even need to bring the coins?" Jack asked.

Jeremy shook his head. "There's a lot we don't know about the coins. He may bring his and they may indicate somehow whether more are in the vicinity. It's better to isolate him, make sure he's alone and thinks it's on the level. While he's checking them out his guard will be down."

"I agree," Taylor said. "And he's not going to think he has anything to fear from a priest. You've said yourself that his arrogance is his undoing."

"Nothing is simple where Crosse is concerned. I still think you need to have backup. There's no telling what he might do," Jeremy cautioned.

"If Scotty brings in other agents, we have no way of knowing if they're compromised. It has to just be us," Jack replied.

"I think you're right," Taylor said.

"We'll have to find a church in New York, close to the archdiocese, to meet him," Jack said. "And we need to clear it with the clergy there." He chewed his lip. "Maybe Scotty can just tell them it's some sort of FBI sting."

"The Greek churches are usually locked in the evenings. Maybe Father Basil can find one that we can use late at night," Taylor mused. "Okay for me to answer the email now?"

They both nodded, and she hit send on the response Jeremy had suggested earlier. "We've got to make sure we're really emailing Crosse. It could be anyone answering."

"If it's a random person, when we tell them we want five million for them, they'll be out," Jeremy said.

Seconds later, her email pinged again.

CHAPTER FIFTY-SIX

JACK TRIED SCOTTY AGAIN AND WAS RELIEVED WHEN HE answered.

"Was just gonna call you," his brother-in-law said. "In every single one of those deaths, the victims had received the cold vaccine within a few days of losing their minds. We should have a warrant for Licentia today or tomorrow. I'm also doing some research on them myself to see what I can find out."

"It's got to be Crosse behind it," Jack said. "Have you had a chance to look into Crosby Wheeler, to see if any of his funds have gone into Licentia or vice versa?"

"Not yet. We don't have the authority to go digging around in Wheeler's finances, not without probable cause. He's a big gun with lots of money and lots of lawyers; we have to be careful. Before I set up this meeting to try to get Crosse, tell me more about what you're doing to lure him out of hiding."

"It has to do with these religious relics."

"What?"

Jack gave him a shortened explanation of the thirty pieces of silver. "Between you and me, I have no idea if they are anything more than a piece of history, but apparently men have killed and been killed for them. We're going to ask Crosse for five million dollars."

Scotty whistled. "Seriously? For a bunch of coins?"

"Yep. Listen, you have to keep this part to yourself. I know it sounds nuts, but there are a lot of people looking for them who believe they have powers."

"Okay," Scotty said. "When do you expect to have the meeting?"

"The next day or two. Definitely before Sunday. We're still looking for a meeting place."

"Keep me posted. I'll let you know when we get the green light for the lab."

As they were hanging up, Taylor called to Jack from the other room.

He hurried to the living room. "Did he answer?"

"Yes! And he's willing to pay the five million. He wants to meet tomorrow night. I've got to write back and tell him where," Taylor said.

"I just spoke with Scotty. Let Crosse cool his heels. We'll get back to him soon."

"Father Basil just called me and gave me the address of a church in Astoria. He said he's already cleared it with the priest," Jeremy said.

"Okay, then." Jack's phone rang. "Logan."

It was Scotty again. "Hey, okay, so I just got the word. Apparently Licentia's cold vaccine is scheduled to be given to the president and his family on live television in three days. One of those PR things to get the public on board. It's already been given to Congress, with no ill effects . . . at least not yet. Someone at the lab let us know the shipment's already labeled to go to the White House doctor. We got a sneak and peek warrant and we're going in covert tomorrow night to test the shipment. Quantico is sending chemists and an emergency response team."

"What the hell? Can you imagine if it's contaminated? The president and his whole family going nuts?" Jack said.

"No kidding. It could be a wild goose chase, in which case I'm going to have egg all over my face with my director. That's why it's going to be covert—and obviously, I shouldn't be telling you any of this. If the vaccines are clean, then we'll be out and no one will be any the wiser. We don't need a public panic on our hands."

"The meet with Crosse is tomorrow night. I'll text you the location."

"Damn. I have to be on scene tomorrow night. Can you postpone it a day?"

Jack thought a minute. "I don't know about putting him off another day, and besides, if Crosse is behind this and he finds out the FBI has been to his lab, that may send him running again. I don't trust anyone else. Is there any way you can get someone to stand in for you at Licentia?"

Scotty exhaled on the other end. "Let me figure something out. I'll find a way to be there."

"Thanks, brother." Jack ended the call and turned to Taylor and Jeremy.

"So it looks like tomorrow night is a go."

CHAPTER FIFTY-SEVEN

DAMON HAD BEEN CHECKING HIS EMAIL EVERY TEN MINUTES. He was hopeful that these were the authentic Judas coins. He asked for a picture, and in the one the seller sent they looked real, but so had the fake ones he'd had in his possession for nearly two years without knowing it. If they were the real thing, though, five million was a pittance. He found it incredible that these men of the cloth were so ignorant of their true power. Any member of the clergy should have been warned that the coins were dangerous in the wrong hands, yet they betrayed their own faith for a few dollars. How would they defend themselves on Judgment Day? he wondered. Now he was waiting for a time and a place to be confirmed but after hours had passed with no response, he finally turned in.

The next morning the first thing he did was go to his laptop. His heart began to race.

St. Catherine's Church in Astoria. Come alone. Midnight. Don't be late. Have other interested parties.

So the good father was going to make the trade at a church in his own town. Perhaps the man should change his name to Judas. Damon clicked reply and confirmed the meeting. He went to the safe, counted out the money, and put it in a leather satchel. If this priest brought the real silver pieces, he'd finally have twenty, and they would call out to the other ten. And soon, after a little over two thousand years, they'd be united again—and the destruction would begin.

If people thought things were bad now, they hadn't seen anything yet.

CHAPTER FIFTY-EIGHT

DAMON WAS ABOUT TO LEAVE WHEN HIS PHONE RANG. "YES?" he said impatiently.

"There's a covert operation going down tonight at Licentia. Something about a shipment scheduled for Washington. They've got doctor types coming in from Quantico. A big team. I don't know what they're looking for, but I thought you should know."

How had this happened? "Will you be going?"

"No, sir. I'm not on the team."

After all his careful planning, he couldn't believe it was falling apart at the last minute.

Damn it. The vaccine in that shipment needed to be swapped out before the FBI got there. If they tested it, the whole plan would fall apart. "When?"

"In an hour."

He hung up. If he drove to the lab now, he'd never make it to the church on time and he'd lose his chance at the coins. But if the FBI got their hands on the tainted vaccine, that would be the end of Licentia Labs and his plan to put Hamilton in the Oval Office.

When his car came around, he got in and told the driver where to go.

CHAPTER FIFTY-NINE

Jack and Taylor got to Astoria at eleven and parked around the corner from the church. Scotty had told his boss that he had an urgent family matter to attend to and asked him to assign a different agent to the lab raid. When Scotty arrived at 11:30, dressed in regular clothes, he knocked on the car window. They had debated whether or not to have him wear vestments but decided it would be unlikely that a priest would wear his vestments for a clandestine meeting.

Jack rolled down the window.

"Everyone's ready?" Scotty asked.

"Yes."

Taylor leaned over and handed him the box containing the coins. "Be careful, Scotty. Anything could happen."

He gave her a strange look. "What do you mean?"

"My mother told me there could be some supernatural effects with the coins. And even just holding the suitcase with the icons, I felt something. Just be prepared and pay attention to where he puts them—all of them. We don't want them disappearing again."

"Okay. I'll text when I'm ready for you." Scotty walked toward the church.

Jack and Taylor sat in dead silence, barely breathing. After the door closed behind Scotty, Jack turned to Taylor and took her hand and squeezed it.

His text tone sounded and he pulled out his phone. A message from Jeremy asked how it was going. He typed a quick reply then saw he had a voice mail from yesterday, and he hit play.

Mr. Logan, this is Sister Francis. I remembered the name of the company that made those medallions. Calhoun and Sons. I don't know if they're still in business, but I thought that might help.

"That's something," he said softly.

Taylor questioned, "What's something?"

"That was the nun who worked at the orphanage years ago. She remembered Jonas and his wife adopting a four-year-old boy who had been left with a religious medal."

Taylor's face had gone white. "Jack. Was it a St. Nicholas medal?"

Taken aback, he nodded. "Yeah, how did you know?"

"Because Malcolm had one! Do you think he was the child?"

"I don't know. Possibly."

She was quiet again. "If it was him, there could be family in Maryland. Evan could have cousins, aunts, uncles."

Jack put a hand up. "We'll look into it after we get through all this, but Taylor, we need to be very careful. If it was Malcolm, and that's a big if, we have no idea what his family is like."

"Don't you think Evan has a right to know that side of his family?"

Jack blew out a breath. "What if they don't want to know him?" His voice was kind. "Let's not forget that Malcolm's mother gave him up. They might not be too thrilled to have old wounds opened. And even if that's not the case, you don't owe them anything. They made their choice a long time ago."

"I know. It's probably not even him. But if he does have family, I owe it to Evan to find them. Think of Jeremy and me."

"Okay. Let's agree to back burner this for now. We've got enough going on."

She nodded. "Agreed."

Jack was troubled, though. Yes, Jeremy had turned out to be a blessing, but he wasn't so sure that would turn out to be the case if they did find Malcolm's family. What if they were opening a Pandora's box?

CHAPTER SIXTY

DAMON GOT OUT OF THE LIMO AND WALKED UP THE STONE steps, then stopped at the top, taking a minute to compose himself. It had been a long time since he'd been in a church.

The heavy wooden door creaked as he opened it, and the interior was dark. A few candles were burning in the entryway, and the glow from a portable lantern up near the altar beckoned to him. He was able to make out a figure in the dark.

"You're right on time," the man said, his voice reverberating.

Damon walked toward him down the carpeted aisle, toward the altar, feeling oppressed with all the murals of Christ and saints surrounding him. He was beginning to regret agreeing to meet here. He stopped a few feet from the man, whose features he could now make out a little. He was young, maybe in his thirties, and didn't have a beard, which most priests did. He also looked to be in remarkably good shape.

Damon looked around the church, narrowing his eyes, to make sure that no one was lurking in the shadows.

"Did you bring the money?" the deacon asked him.

"Yes, of course. But I need to see them first."

The man opened a small box, pulling out a velvet sack and placing it on the pew in front of him. Damon picked it up and opened it. Extracting one of the coins, he examined it and felt excitement course through his veins.

"Where's the money?"

Damon looked up at him. "Don't worry. You'll get your money. After I make sure these are real." He moved to one of the pews and laid out all ten coins. He took the vial of Evan's blood he had brought and put a drop on each of them. Before he had even finished, he felt the heat emanating from them, and he watched, fascinated, as blue smoke billowed up from their surfaces, curling and rising until it formed a heptagram.

These were authentic! Damon picked them up and returned them to the pouch.

He walked back toward the priest.

"Here's your money." He pushed the large suitcase toward the man who opened it and looked inside.

The priest smiled. "Good doing business with you."

Damon wasn't about to turn his back on the man. "I'll wait here until you leave."

The man hesitated, began walking toward the exit, then turned back around, a gun aimed at Damon. "FBI. Put the coins down in front of you and you won't get hurt."

The two of them stared at each other a long moment, and Damon watched, amused, as the man slid a phone from his pocket. Before he could press a key, Damon pulled out a handful of coins and began to recite the words Friedrich had taught him so long ago. Within seconds, the man froze, his face contorting in agony, before he dropped the phone and clutched at his chest. His face turned red, and he began to wheeze. "What . . . did you do . . . Can't breathe."

Damon saw the shock in the man's eyes.

He heard heavy footsteps outside. Someone was coming. He had to leave now, no time to wait to make sure the man died. He picked up the satchel with the money and ran up on the altar and through the hidden doorway inside one of the closets. He'd been alerted to the secret exit by Father Basil. Damon never did anything without the proper preparation. He'd come out two streets away with his driver waiting.

Now he only needed the last ten coins. And thanks to the good priest, he knew exactly where they were. They were all so stupid.

Father Basil was the latest in a series of well-intentioned clergy to be corrupted by the coins. When would Logan and Taylor learn to be wiser about who they trusted? He shook his head. Some people never learned.

CHAPTER SIXTY-ONE

Taylor looked at her watch. It was almost half past midnight. What was taking him so long? "Shouldn't Scotty have called us by now?"

"Maybe Crosse was late," Jack said, but Taylor could hear the anxiety in his voice.

She had a bad feeling. "What if something went wrong? Maybe we should drive around the block."

"Give it a few more minutes. We don't want to do anything to scare Crosse off," Jack said.

She tapped her fingers against the dashboard, feeling like a coiled spring ready to explode. "What if Crosse brought guards with him? Maybe we misjudged or underestimated him."

Jack was lost in thought and didn't reply.

Soon it was 12:45. Something was definitely wrong. "Drive around the block. Let's see if Scotty's car is still there," Taylor said.

Jack started the car and drove, finally turning in front of the church, where Scotty's car was still parked. "They must still be inside."

"But I don't see any other cars. Where's Crosse's car? Do you think he didn't show?" Taylor asked.

"I don't know. Maybe. But I think Scotty would have texted us. I'm going in. Scotty could be hurt or tied up."

Before she could stop him, Jack got out of the car and ran up the stairs. Inside, the church was pitch-black. "Scotty?" he called, but no one answered. He heard the sound of ragged breathing. Pulling out a flashlight, he found Scotty lying on the ground in a pool of vomit. He was drenched in sweat and white as a sheet.

"What the hell?" Jack said as he ran to him and helped him up. Scotty's legs buckled twice before Jack was finally able to get him to a standing position.

"Crosse," he managed to croak out. "Those coins . . ."

"Come on, let's get out of here. We need to get you to a hospital." Jack half carried him out and down the steps to the waiting car.

"What happened?" Taylor cried, jumping out of the car and helping Jack get Scotty situated.

"Should we call 911?" she asked.

"No, it'll be faster if we just take him. Mount Sinai in Queens isn't far."

"I don't need to go to the hospital," Scotty whispered.

Jack turned to look at him. "What are you talking about? You can hardly walk."

He shook his head. "It was some kind of supernatural thing. I'm feeling almost normal again now."

"What?" Taylor asked.

When Scotty had explained what had happened, Jack asked, disbelief in his voice, "Are you freaking kidding me? He chanted a spell and you almost had a heart attack?"

"I don't know. The pain in my chest is almost gone. But that's not all. We would have gotten him if he'd come out the front of the church."

Taylor thought for a moment. "Well, he did have a day to check out the site."

Scotty said, "No. There's no other way out of there. I checked it out to make sure all the exits were covered. There's just the side and front door, which both lead out to the courtyard and directly here." Scotty swallowed and took a deep breath.

Jack banged his hand on the steering wheel. "How the hell did he get away then? Did you tell anyone about the meeting?"

Scotty shook his head. "No!"

"Should we go to your office, let them know Crosse is still out there?" Jack asked.

Scotty didn't answer for a minute. "My boss is gonna kill me. I'm going to lose my job."

"Well, we have to do something!" Taylor prodded.

Scotty sighed. "Go." He pulled out a card and handed it to Taylor. "This is the address of my field office." He leaned back against the seat, his breath still coming in short gasps, and closed his eyes.

Jack put the vehicle in drive.

"He has twenty of the coins now," Taylor said in a wooden voice. "And we have no way to find him. The FBI isn't going to be able to do anything. I have to call Jeremy."

He answered on the first ring, and Taylor quickly brought him up to speed.

"He used the coins to make Scotty sick?" Jeremy clarified.

"Yes. And now he's got twenty. We've got to let Father Basil know. It's even more imperative that he guard the last ten."

Jeremy sighed loudly. "I'll call him now. And be careful."

She disconnected and looked out the window as they pulled away, wanting to believe they stood a chance, but her heart was heavy and her hope was gone.

CHAPTER SIXTY-TWO

Jack and Taylor sat quietly while Scotty's boss, Deputy Director Shane, reamed him out.

"Damn it! You lied to me about having a family emergency. If you had told me you were trying to trap Damon Crosse, I would have made sure you had plenty of backup."

"I was worried we would scare him off," Scotty said.

"Yeah? Well, maybe if you'd done it right, Crosse would be sitting here in cuffs instead of being in the wind. I should fire your ass for this. At the very least I'm going to have to suspend you." He shook his head. "What the hell was the meeting about anyway?" Scotty looked down at the floor.

Jack spoke up. "Damon Crosse is collecting ancient relics. We'd gotten our hands on some and pretended to be someone from the church selling them."

Shane gave them an astonished look. "What?"

"It's a long story," Jack said.

He began to speak again when Taylor cut in.

"Were you able to connect Crosse to Licentia Labs?"

"Not yet. We've got teams going through everything there. But since we found that the vaccines scheduled for the president *were* contaminated, it's now a national security and health issue. The National Security branch, CDC, Homeland Security, they're all over it. It'll be the top news story in the morning."

"You're kidding," Scotty said.

His boss shot him a look. "Do I look like I'm kidding?"

"You think it's a terrorist plot?" Jack asked.

"It's an active investigation, so I can't discuss any details." He looked pointedly at Jack and Taylor. "Especially with you. I'd better not see any of what we're talking about in the news. Your journalistic fervor has done enough damage."

Jack didn't bother telling him this was about much more than a story. Besides, he deserved the guy's rancor. He'd thought only about Taylor and Evan when he'd asked Scotty to help them.

They spent the next two hours being interviewed and finally got back on the road after three A.M.

"What are we going to do now?" Taylor said, her voice pleading.

Jack was so beside himself that he couldn't even muster the strength to offer any words of comfort to his wife. She was right—they were totally and completely screwed. Crosse was free, no one knew where he was, and they had just handed him a double dose of power if what Jeremy said about the coins was true.

CHAPTER SIXTY-THREE

TAYLOR COULDN'T FALL ASLEEP, SO SHE CUDDLED UP NEXT TO Evan and watched him through the night. When he woke at six, they went to the kitchen to find Jack already glued to the laptop.

"It's all over the news. People are freaking out," Jack told her.

"The vaccine?"

"Yes. The CDC is putting out a statement and a number to call if anyone has symptoms. The FDA has recalled the vaccine, of course."

That was one bright spot in a very dark landscape. Taylor tried to sound upbeat. "Look what you were able to prevent. If you hadn't been on the story and alerted Scotty to it, our government could have collapsed. Do you realize how huge this is?"

Jack stood up and stretched. "If we hadn't let Crosse get away, I'd be elated." He went on, "I'm sorry. I know how you're trying to make me feel better. We still don't know if this is Crosse or just some kook working at Licentia who laced the vaccine. We have nothing linking him. It could be one big coincidence. But hell yeah, thank God we stopped that batch."

"I can't believe it's a coincidence. The timing of Licentia's existence, the testing, the president getting a contaminated vaccine. It's got Crosse's fingerprints all over it."

Jack nodded. "If his plan had succeeded, Hamilton would have taken over. Crosse would have controlled the Oval."

"It doesn't make me feel good knowing that the man a heartbeat away from the presidency is in Crosse's pocket. This failed, but he'll come up with a new plan. There must be some way to prove Hamilton's direct involvement. Some kind of trail connecting Crosse to the company? I know Crosse is brilliant, but now the FBI is examining everything. He's got to be funneling the money somehow," Taylor said.

"We'll see. I should have gone in with Scotty, been hiding or something."

She walked over and put her arms around him. "It's not your fault, Jack." She could see he wasn't receptive, so she switched tactics. "If we wallow in regret, we're no good. We've got to keep thinking like Crosse, figure out what he might do next."

Jeremy came into the kitchen looking like he hadn't slept either. "I spoke with Father Basil. They're postponing the ceremony until Tuesday due to an unexpected delay in the archbishop's schedule."

"The coins are at the church now, though, right?" Jack asked. "What if they're stolen?"

"Yes, but the priest there has no idea that they're in the icons, and we don't want anyone else knowing. Father Basil still thinks they should stick to the plan," Jeremy said. He turned to Taylor with a somber expression. "I have news about your mother."

She held her breath. "What?"

He shook his head sadly. "She really is deceased. The lawyer is getting her body from the morgue and having it delivered to a local funeral home. They can hold it there until we can tell them what to do."

Jack took Taylor in his arms and she sobbed, letting her grief envelop her, accepting that she'd lost her mother again, this time forever.

"I'm so sorry," Jack said in a soothing voice, hugging her tighter.

After awhile, she composed herself. "We can't even give her a proper burial until this is all behind us. I hate him with every fiber of my being."

Jack simply nodded, unable to come up with any words of comfort.

CHAPTER SIXTY-FOUR

I T WAS TIME TO CALL DAKOTA. HE DIALED HER NUMBER FROM a new burner.

"Jack?"

"Listen, I'll mail your passport to wherever you tell me. I can't do any more than that."

"But I found a guy who can meet you and pick it up. He can come to you."

"Look, Dakota, I've got a lot going on, and I don't trust you. How do I know you're not working for Crosse, and that this isn't a trap? Maybe you made up the whole bit about Crosse trying to kill you."

"Jack, he did try to kill me. Someone helped me get away. That's why I know where he is. I can lead you to him."

His hand tightened on the phone. "What?"

"I'll give you information on how to find him, but only if you take the passport to my contact."

He was torn. She was probably lying. "How do you know where he is?"

She laughed. "You of all people know the power of my charms. The man who helped me escape him told me where he's living and under what identity. You scratch my back and I'll scratch yours."

He groaned inwardly. "Fine. As long I name the meeting place. Nyack Beach State Park. When can your contact be there?"

"Two o'clock. He's already in your area."

"How will I know him?"

She laughed again. "He'll know you."

"I need more than that."

"He'll be wearing an Orioles baseball cap. Can't be too many of those in New York. He'll give you the connection to Crosse."

He glanced at his watch. Almost ten. He'd have to leave around noon to get to the park on time. "OK," he said finally, then hung up.

They were still lying low for now. Tomorrow was the ceremony at the church and Father Basil had promised to call them after the archbishop had left with the coins. They had decided that they would stay at the safe house for another week while they planned their next steps. The only thing they knew for sure was that they weren't going back to their house and that they had to keep moving until they knew where Crosse was.

Taylor came into the kitchen. Jack filled her in.

"I don't like it, Jack."

"Don't worry. I'll be armed, and I'll stay in the open. If this can lead us to Crosse, I have to try."

"I have to go out for a while. I have a three o'clock doctor's appointment," she said.

"Is everything okay?"

"Yeah, just my annual checkup. I'm almost out of Synthroid and they won't refill it without an exam. If we're going to be moving around, I need to get at least a ninety-day supply."

He sighed. Taylor needed her thyroid medicine, he couldn't dispute that. "Can you move the appointment to tomorrow? I don't want you to be alone, but I just set up that meeting."

"No, they book up months in advance." She put a hand on his arm. "I've been thinking, we don't even know if Crosse was really behind what happened in Athens. We know there are others after the coins. Crosse hasn't come after us all this time so I don't think we're in imminent danger."

"Taylor, you can't—"

"I'm not saying we shouldn't be careful but I'm not going to risk my health because I'm scared to go outside. I'll be fine. I'll text Jeremy to see if he can come back to stay with Evan." Jeremy had gone to the lab to take care of some paperwork, but she knew this was his priority.

She quickly sent Jeremy a message and soon her text tone sounded. "Jeremy texted back. He'll come back at one to stay with Evan, and I'll be fine."

"I still really don't like you going out alone right now," Jack said.

"And I don't like you meeting some stranger sent by Dakota." He sighed. "Taylor . . ."

"I'll go straight there and then back here. I'll leave here at one and I'll be back by four."

"I'll go with you. I'll tell Dakota I can't meet this guy."

She shook her head. "No, this could be our only chance to find Crosse."

She was right, but Jack wasn't happy about it. He leaned in and kissed her. "Be careful. Text me when you're on your way back. I love you."

She gave him a serious look, pushing a lock of hair from his forehead. "I love you more."

CHAPTER SIXTY-FIVE

Jack had left and Taylor was getting ready to go to her appointment. She was surprised by a knock at the door. Had Crosse found them? Taylor froze before coming out into the hall, turned around, and took the gun from the top of the closet. Beau padded closely behind her. Sliding along the wall until she reached the door, she looked through the peephole, then heaved a sigh of relief. It was Jeremy. She opened the door and smiled.

"You scared the life out of me! Where's your key?" She put the gun down, taking a deep breath.

"Left it at the lab. Sorry about that!"

Beau ran up to him and began barking aggressively.

"Beau! What's the matter with you? Stop it," she admonished the dog. "You'll wake Evan up." He looked at her then back at Jeremy and growled again.

Jeremy crouched down to pet him, but Beau snapped at his hand, snarling.

Taylor grabbed him by the collar. "What is going on with you?" She looked at Jeremy sheepishly. "Sorry, he's been so weird lately." She took Beau and shut him in the room where Evan was sleeping then returned.

"Evan might wake up from his nap before I return. You know where everything is. He'll probably want a snack."

Jeremy was looking around the room, seeming to only half listen.

"You good?" she asked.

"Huh? Oh yeah. We'll be fine."

She glanced at her watch. Five after. She'd have to hurry or she'd be late. "Okay." She leaned over and kissed Jeremy on the cheek and he seemed to stiffen.

"You'd better get going," he said.

He was acting a little strangely, but she supposed they were all on edge. She put the gun back in the closet and left. As she drove, she kept an eye on the rearview mirror to make sure no one was following her.

CHAPTER SIXTY-SIX

JACK PARKED HIS CAR AND WALKED DOWN TO THE BEGINNING of the trail looking for a man in an Orioles hat. In less than forty-eight hours, they'd lost their shot at Crosse and had been partly responsible for what the Church had spent centuries trying to avoid—putting more of the silver pieces into the hands of a madman.

He checked the time on his phone. The guy should be here by now. A few minutes later, a text came in from an unknown number. On my way, stuck in traffic. Almost an hour passed and he went to text again but saw that his phone battery had died. Shit. He'd forgotten to charge it last night. As he turned to go to his car and plug it in, he caught a glimpse of a man wearing an Orioles cap coming toward him.

"Logan?" the man asked.

"Yeah. I believe you have some information for me?"

"I need to see the passport first."

Jack pulled it from his jacket pocket and held it in front of him.

The man pulled out a piece of paper and handed it to Jack. "I knew it," he blurted out when he saw the name scrawled on the paper. Crosby Wheeler. "I'm going to need proof."

"Turn it over."

Jack did and saw several long sequences of numbers.

"Bank account numbers. Follow the money and you'll connect them."

There was no way he could confirm it now, but what he really wanted to know was that this wasn't a trick. Satisfied that Dakota had kept up her end of the bargain, he held out the passport and handed it to the man.

"I have one more thing for you." Before Jack's brain registered what was happening, he felt a shock and then his knees buckled. The guy had tased him! He reached into his pocket for his gun, but the man hit him again.

Then the man pulled out a needle and, before Jack could react, plunged it into Jack's arm. "Dakota said to thank you for helping her square things with Crosse. And to tell you that you're still a chump." He threw a photo toward a dazed Jack and it landed next to his head. It was a picture of Taylor at home in their hallway—from the angle it was clearly taken from a distance.

"She also wants you to know she's been keeping tabs on you. Said she'll see you soon." As he walked away he added, "Oh, and if I were you, I'd get somewhere safe because shit's about to get real bad." With that, he took off running.

CHAPTER SIXTY-SEVEN

Taylor arrived at the doctor's office right on time and hurried in. The receptionist called her into the examining room a few minutes later, and she caught her breath after changing into a gown. She hadn't told Jack the nature of her visit. She wanted to make sure everything was fine first.

The doctor came in and they exchanged pleasantries. When he was finished with his examination, he smiled at her.

"You were right. You're pregnant. We'll do an ultrasound to see how far along you are. You said you've missed two periods?"

She nodded.

"Okay. I'll be right back."

Taylor had taken a home pregnancy test right before she'd gone to Athens, but she'd wanted to be sure. She couldn't wait to share the news with Jack. After her infertility issues with Malcolm, she had given up on the idea of another child. But lying in the exam room, she began to imagine what a child of theirs would look like. Maybe the baby would have Jack's blue eyes and her dark hair. She hoped he or she would have Jack's dimples and his smile. She found herself smiling from ear to ear as she daydreamed. The doctor returned and she lay back as he rubbed the gel on her stomach then placed the ultrasound wand in it. She heard a sound and realized it was her baby's heartbeat. Elation filled her at the sound and she wished now that Jack was here with her.

"Everything looks great. Strong heartbeat. Looks like you're about nine weeks along. I'll prescribe you some prenatal vitamins and see you back here in a month. I'll also call in a refill for your thyroid medicine as you had your endocrinologist send us the bloodwork you had done three months ago."

"Great. Thank you."

o o o

Taylor tried Jack's cell phone when she got to her car but it went right to voice mail. She made a stop at the pharmacy to pick up the vitamins and her thyroid medication, and when she got back to the safe house a little after four, Jack's car wasn't in the driveway. That was strange, she thought. A niggle of worry nestled in her chest. Flinging the car door open, she sprang out of the driver's seat and hurried to the door.

"Jeremy, I'm back," she called.

He was sitting on the sofa and stood as she entered.

"I was wondering where everybody was."

She frowned. "What do you mean? I told you Jack went to meet someone about Dakota's passport."

He looked at her like she was crazy. "When? I just got here. I was pulled over by the police on the way home, some kind of mix-up. They thought my car was stolen."

Her pulse quickened, and she broke out in a cold sweat. "What? Where's Evan?"

"I don't know. I thought he was with you," he said.

"You? I left him here with you a few hours ago," she yelled, racing to the bedroom where she'd last seen him. The bed was empty. "Evan, Evan!" she was screaming now, looking under the bed and in the closet. She heard Jeremy approach and looked up. "He's gone!"

Jeremy looked confused. "Taylor, what are you talking about?"

"It was you . . . or it looked like you. How is this possible?" She was shaking now.

"What time was this?"

"One."

"I was being detained by the police then."

She pushed past him and ran to the bedroom. She took the gun from the top shelf and came back out, pointing it at him.

"Where's my son?"

"Taylor, please. I told you, I just got here."

She shook her head. "No no no. You were here."

He pulled out a piece of paper and handed it to her. "It's a citation from the police. Look at the time."

She grabbed it from him. He was right. Then who was here before? "He looked just like you. I don't understand."

"Two of us. There must be two of us. Twins."

They looked at each other in shocked silence. As soon as the words left Jeremy's lips, Taylor knew it was true. It had to be. But where had he been all this time and why had Crosse kept him a secret?

Still in shock and hoping she was somehow wrong, she ran into the bathroom, looked in every corner of the small house, continuing to yell for Evan, tears streaming down her face. "Where is he?"

She pulled her cell phone from her purse and dialed Jack. Voice mail.

"Jack, Jack! Where are you? They took Evan. He's gone." She sank to the ground, despair filling her. "He took Evan," she sobbed.

"We'll find him," Jeremy said.

"I have to go. Wait here for Jack."

"Where are you going?"

"To get my son."

"Taylor, wait. You can't just run off alone." He stood in front of her, blocking her.

"I'm sorry," she said as she pushed him hard on his injured shoulder. He fell back in pain and she ran from the house, jumped in her car, and drove as fast as she could.

CHAPTER SIXTY-EIGHT

T TOOK JACK ANOTHER TEN MINUTES BEFORE HE WAS STEADY enough to stand. He limped to the Jeep and floored it. There was no time to get to the safe house—he'd have to go to their house. He plugged in his phone and waited for it to power up as he drove. He tried Taylor's number and cursed as it rang unanswered. He saw a missed call from her over an hour ago and three from Jeremy. He tried her again with no luck and then dialed Jeremy.

"Jack! Thank God! Where've you been?" Jeremy rattled on before Jack could answer. "I don't know how to tell you this, but Evan's gone."

"What do you mean he's gone?"

"Taylor said that someone who looked just like me showed up today. I was on the way when I got pulled over by the police. They claimed I was in a stolen vehicle and wouldn't let me use my phone. When I got to the safe house a few minutes ago, I assumed you had made other arrangements." Jeremy's words came out in a frantic rush.

Jack was flummoxed. "What do you mean someone who looked like you?"

"Someone saying they were me who looked like me. A twin maybe? Or some protégé of Crosse's who's had surgery? I don't know. All I know is that Evan is gone!"

"Where's Taylor?"

Jeremey cleared his throat. "I tried to stop her, but she took off. I don't know where she went, and she's not answering her phone."

Jack's heart beat furiously. His thoughts were all jumbled up. Maybe she'd gone back to their house. "Jeremy, I'm in trouble. I was set up. I've been injected with that . . . stuff."

"What stuff?"

Jack now had arrived home and rushed in. As he ran through the house, panicked, looking for any sign that Taylor had been there, he told Jeremy about his meeting.

"Stay where you are. I'm coming. We need to get you back to my lab and watch you. Put you in isolation. This is bad."

Jack's phone pinged again. All the texts from when his battery was dead were coming in now. "Hold on."

He looked through them and saw one from Taylor.

He's got Evan. I know how to get him back.

Without thinking, he hung up on Jeremy and dialed her. It went right to voice mail. *Taylor, what you have done?*

He collapsed on the floor, holding his head in his hands. Something in the trash can caught his eye and he slid over, pulling it out. It was a pregnancy test. A positive pregnancy test.

Jack stood up and let out another rage-filled scream. Everything was gone. He started throwing things in a suitcase. He was going to find her. He didn't know how, but he was going to find her. His arms started itching and he looked down—bugs were crawling all over him. As he started scratching, the last lucid thought he had was that the drug was kicking in. It would take Jeremy at least another hour and a half to get here, and by then, Jack could be full-blown psycho. He dialed 911.

"Send someone fast. I've been injected against my will with meth and I'm losing it." The bugs were everywhere now, and it was unbearable.

"Get a knife and cut them out," an audible voice said.

His rational mind battled with the drug—he knew it was taking over, and he held on to the thought that at least a part of him knew it wasn't real. He had to hang on to that until someone got there.

But he quickly realized he didn't have time. He needed to knock himself out. Before he could consider whether he had any other options, he ran full tilt into the wall. The last thing he heard before falling to the floor was the wail of sirens.

CHAPTER SIXTY-NINE

AMON AND EVAN WERE IN THE LIMOUSINE HEADED TO TE-terboro Airport. He could only imagine the histrionics that ensued when Taylor realized that she'd been tricked. He'd had Jeremy's phone cloned months ago, and it was easy enough to have his son, Scorpion, intercept the text Taylor had sent to Jeremy and answer it himself. Damon had arranged for Jeremy to be pulled over as well so that his twin brother could go to the house and pretend to be Jeremy. He didn't think she would call the authorities right away—she would call Jack. But Jack would be no help. Dakota had taken care of that. At first, he'd been enraged to discover that Scorpion had been hiding her, but he had to admit that she had her uses. He had been rash when deciding to dispose of her. For now, at least, she was safe. The drug Jack was given would kick in fast; he'd made sure Jack was given an extremely strong dose.

Basil betraying the church had been a surprise, but Damon was used to surprises. After Damon had set up the meeting at the church, he'd received an email from Basil. **The meeting is a setup, but I can help you.** When Damon responded and asked him to explain himself, Basil told him everything. How he'd been working with the archbishop to reunite the coins to destroy them, about his role in trying to bring Eva back from Greece. When Basil had failed to successfully get her out of Athens, he'd been told he was going to be sent to a parish next month, that he was no longer needed as the archbishop's assistant. Damon arranged for a meeting with him and it wasn't long before Damon recognized the same glint of ambition in Basil's eyes that he'd seen in Maya's. Basil had become a zealot, he realized. Damon recalled the meeting.

"The coins have alerted me to the great danger within the church," Basil told him.

Damon nodded. "Do tell."

"There is nothing more evil than evil masquerading as good. They plan to replace me with a fornicator. A priest known to have many women. I have served faithfully all these years. That's why I was entrusted to bring the coins back from Greece. But the coins showed me the truth. Now I know why I was warned not to hold them too long. Because they spill secrets that those in powerful positions don't want anyone else to know."

"You were wise to come to me," Damon said soothingly, aware that the coins had made the priest delusional.

Basil stood and spoke loudly. "Woe to you, scribes and Pharisees, you hypocrites! You clean the outside of the cup and dish, but inside they are full of greed and self-indulgence. Blind Pharisee! First clean the inside of the cup and dish, so that the outside may become clean as well. Woe to you, scribes and Pharisees, you hypocrites! You are like whitewashed tombs, which look beautiful on the outside, but on the inside are full of dead men's bones and every impurity. That's Matthew 23."

"And you wish me to help you with the cleansing?" Damon had asked.

So they'd made their plan and Basil would be bringing the final ten coins to Damon after the ceremony tomorrow. He'd given Basil the fake coins so Basil could switch them out after the ceremony but before the archbishop took them to the patriarch. Basil was, indeed, a good asset. Now Damon would have access to the inner workings of the church through Basil and would be able to learn even more about the power of the coins since the archbishop had ancient books that the church had safeguarded. Before he was moved to his own church, Basil would make a copy of the pages in the book. Basil was foolish to believe that he and Damon were going to work together to cleanse the church. After Damon had gotten all the information he needed from Basil, he would be dispensed with.

Once he had all thirty coins, Damon would need Taylor to complete the generational chain. No one had ever had all thirty before, and while he knew what they could do just on their own, he also remembered Friedrich's teaching about a three-generational bloodline that could bring about the actual end of the world. Since he was Taylor's biological father, she and Evan would complete the chain. But he had time. There were plenty of plans that he could put into place without the three of them, especially as he now had access to an unlimited supply of Evan's blood.

The child was still asleep; Damon had sedated him, and he was nestled in the dog carrier usually reserved for Peritas, who was already safely in England. He couldn't risk even his driver knowing that he had a child with him. He didn't want anyone to be able to tie him to Evan's disappearance; he didn't want to have to lose his Crosby persona because he still wanted to run the network. Television programming was still one of the biggest spheres of influence. Since his plan to take over the presidency had been aborted, he wouldn't need to be in America as much right now. His Crosby identity would serve his purposes for the work he still planned to do there.

He'd made sure to tie up loose ends before leaving. Leonard Reed had been injected with Ravage. Reed's new girlfriend had stuck the needle in his arm while he was snoring post-coitally. Poetic justice really. Damon couldn't risk leaving him alive. He was a loose cannon. And besides, his personal habits were revolting. Damon knew all about his forays into the dark web. He'd never intended to give Reed the chief of staff position. He was only placating him until his usefulness wore off. And it had. He was lucky, Damon had made sure it was a lethal dose. He'd gotten confirmation last night that Reed was dead. Hamilton, on the other hand, was still very useful. He'd proven his loyalty over the years and was patiently waiting in the wings as vice president. Maybe they had made the plan too complicated. There were plenty of other ways to kill a president. Damon's plan to rule the White House was only delayed, not destroyed. In the meantime, he had other things to occupy him. Especially now that he was on the cusp of having all thirty Judas coins.

Once they were at their new home in England, his staff would be told that this was his grandson, which was, of course, true. He would tell them that, sadly, the boy's parents had died and now he was his sole caregiver.

Both he and Evan would have new identities in England. Damon's new name was Darius Bernard and Evan would now be Jude Bernard. It wouldn't take long before Evan forgot his parents and his old life completely and accepted his rightful place as Damon's heir. Together, they were going to rule the world—right up until they destroyed it.

CHAPTER SEVENTY

AYLOR SAT IN THE BACK OF THE CROWDED CHURCH, WAITING for the ceremony to begin. It was difficult to see through the black veil that obscured her face, and the black linen widow's dress clung to her as the perspiration rolled down her back. They would begin the consecration soon, and then it would be time for the icons to be brought to the altar. She had to make sure her timing was just right. An older man stopped at her pew, and she bit back her frustration when he waved his hand for her to move over so he could take the seat next to her. Stepping into the aisle, she indicated that he should go in, and he gave her a sour look but complied. She needed to be on the outside for what was to come.

The smell of incense filled the small church as the priest moved the censer back and forth, chanting in Greek. On the altar stood the archbishop, surrounded by two bishops and two priests, all in their best vestments. From the corner of her eye, Taylor saw Father Basil walking toward the altar, holding the icons. She slid out of the pew and walked down the aisle toward him.

"*Kyrie eleison*," she said, running up and kissing the icon on the top.

"Please, take your seat," he said, looking around, embarrassed. The church grew silent.

"Sorry!" She pretended to fall into him, pushing him off balance, and making him drop the icons. A collective gasp filled the church and she sank to her knees, helping to retrieve the icons.

"What are you doing?" Father Basil yelled. "Be careful."

Before he could react, Taylor grabbed all four icons and pulled the pin from the smoke bomb she'd brought, throwing it behind her. She pulled a mask up from under her veil. Seconds later, the church was filled with white smoke and she ran outside and around the corner to the waiting rental car.

O   O   O

Two hours later, Taylor pulled off the highway to a small motel, paid cash, and went to her room.

After pulling out her new phone, she went to the original email chain about the coins, which she had forwarded to her new email address. She typed.

> I have the last ten. Give me my son back and you can have them.

A minute later, her email pinged with a response. I've been waiting for your email.

ACKNOWLEDGMENTS

By the time the last word is written, there have been so many people whose hard work and dedication have helped to create the finished book. It is always a pleasure to have the opportunity to thank them here. First to my husband, Rick, I so appreciate your unwavering support that makes it possible for me to do what I love every day. I'm grateful to share this journey called life with you.

To my agent, Bernadette Baker-Baughman, you are my touchstone, my calm in the storm, and a friend I can always rely on. I count you as one of my sweetest blessings. As always, deep appreciation to everyone at Victoria Sanders & Associates for your support and friendship.

To Emily Griffin, my amazing editor, your vision and dedication made this book better than it would have ever been without your genius. Thank you for never stopping until the work is truly ready. Huge thanks to the team at HarperCollins: Heather Drucker for your fabulous public relations efforts, Lisa Erickson for terrific marketing, Virginia Stanley and the amazing Library

Marketing team for your enthusiasm and support. Appreciation to Amber Oliver, and to everyone in Sales, Marketing, and Production for your hard work and dedication to excellence.

To Gretchen Stelter, thank you for your help in shaping the early versions of the manuscript and being such a wonderful sounding board. To my friend Dr. Lori Storch Smith, thank you for your medical advice. To my friend, Special Agent Chris Munger, thank you for your help with all things FBI.

To my nephew, Chris Ackers, huge thanks for going over plotlines, sharing ideas, telling me where I needed more action, and helping me to come up with one of my favorite plot twists. Not only are you a brilliant brainstorming partner, your company is always delightful.

To my sister, Valerie, thank you for your steadfast support and always being there when I need you. Words can't adequately convey all you mean to me and how thankful I am for you every day. You've been a champion of Jack and Taylor since their inception, and I so appreciate your valuable input as their story continues.

I'm grateful for the love and support from my extended family and treasure your encouragement and enthusiasm: Stan and Lynn, Mike and Honey, Colin, and all my wonderful nieces and nephews—thank you from the bottom of my heart.

To my readers, thank you so much for your support and encouragement. It's such a pleasure meeting some of you on tour and connecting with you on social media and email.

And to Nick and Theo, you make me proud every day, and being your mother will always be my most cherished and fulfilling role.

ABOUT THE AUTHOR

L.C. Shaw is the pen name of internationally bestselling author Lynne Constantine, who also writes psychological thrillers with her sister as Liv Constantine. Her husband wonders if she is actually a spy, and he never knows which name to call her. She loves to procrastinate by spending time on social media and, when stuck on a plot twist, has been known to run ideas by her silver labrador and golden retriever, who wish she would stop typing and play ball with them. Lynne has a master's degree from Johns Hopkins University and her work has been translated into twenty-eight foreign languages.